GROWING WILD IN THE SHADE

A MAGS MUNROE STORY

JEAN GRAINGER

To Hilda, with love always.

CHAPTER 1

I'm trying to keep a straight face.

Sharon is telling me how she swiped right yesterday on her dating app. She's being very cagey about the details, so she obviously thinks I'm going to laugh. Which I probably am. Still, if online dating helps heal my best friend's broken heart after the awful Danny Boylan broke it by going off with 'Chloe from the chipper', I'm not complaining. It's a big improvement on when she was moping around obsessing about every detail of her ex-husband and Chloe's new life together. That phase of her mourning almost destroyed her and briefly lost her custody of their son, Sean.

The next stage of grief came after she got Sean back. She spent six months trying to be the perfect mother to him. The poor little lad was on a no-sweets-or-treats, organic-food diet, along with wooden sustainable toys and music classes in the library, until both he and she were worn out. Now she has reverted to TV and chicken nuggets for Sean, much to the child's relief, and she's moved on to online dating.

This last phase of her recovery has been great fun so far...for me anyway. The various specimens she winds up meeting have me regularly in paroxysms of laughter. Like the lad who had a picture of himself on the top of Carrauntoohil, Ireland's highest mountain, and it had been clearly Photoshopped because you could just make out that his elbow was leaning on the edge of a bar and he had a cigarette in his hand. All nineteen stone of him came to meet poor old Shar, and she knew he'd never been up the stairs, let alone a mountain, in his life. The only climbing he was interested in was onto the high stool.

Or the fella who said he was French and a chef and turned out to be from Wexford and on the dole, or the one who winked after every sentence, or the one who explained that he was in fact a warlock on the weekends. He'd been particularly fascinating, and I was dying for her to go on a second date with him out of sheer nosiness, but Sharon said one night in the company of a 'carpenter by day, warlock by night' was quite sufficient. He did claim, presumably in an effort to impress, to have cast a spell on a local man, which brought about the man's demise, but he refused to be drawn on who. To my disappointment, he was dressed normally in the photos she showed me. I'd had some kind of Albus Dumbledore in mind.

'So go on, tell us who it is this time.' I smirk in anticipation as Tatiana places two coffees in front of us in the snug of the Samovar. The little room to the front of the public bar, traditionally used by women, was a great place for a chat without the whole parish being privy to it.

Sharon shoots me a warning glance. She doesn't want anyone in Ballycarrick knowing about the online dating; she doesn't want to be thought desperate.

'Online dating is no good for real men,' Tatiana announces in her loud Russian-accented English, proving yet again that keeping a secret in Ballycarrick is impossible. 'I find out by marrying online husband, Benny. No, best way to find man is to night class.' Tatiana always exudes certainty, as if she never once in her life second-guessed herself. It gives all her pronouncements an air of authority they probably don't deserve. She's also absolutely stunning, with the athletic body of a panther, long dark hair and jade-green eyes under straight dark brows. I'm sure she has no end of admirers, but from afar. In the words of my husband, Kieran, 'A fella would want to have

2

his wits about him if he was to venture into that particular Soviet sphere of influence.' Which was something Tatiana's creepy Irish husband, Benny, found out quick enough.

Benny used to own the pub we're sitting in. He picked up Tatiana online, on RussianBrides.com, and brought her over from Vladivostok, but if Leery Benny thought he was getting a gorgeous but docile woman, grateful for his generosity, he was in for a rude awakening. Whatever went on between him and Tatiana, within weeks he'd left for England, and she now runs the pub. Last I heard he was working in Hyde Park as a maintenance man.

'Do you go to a night class, Tatiana?' I ask, interested.

'Yes, the community school. Every Thursday I do accounting, and there I meet lots of nice men.'

'Accountants?' Sharon is also intrigued.

'Not accountants, of course,' Tatiana says, rolling her eyes as if Sharon is a total eejit. 'If they were already this, they would not be doing course in community school.'

'Right.' Shar casts me a glance, and I focus on stirring milk into my coffee.

'But this men who study is going somewhere, you know? Have plans, have future. That's what you want, someone who can work, not lazy, stupid ones who try to find women online. No good.' She walks off, having issued her decree, and Sharon and I relax again.

'Go on, Shar, show me.'

She sighs deeply. 'I don't know, Mags. I'm giving this dating craic one more go, but then I'm hanging up my mouse for a bit. It's hard, you know?'

For all my joking around, I do know. Not personally, obviously, as there was no such thing as online dating before I met Kieran, and we've been married for, as our daughter Ellie says, eleventy billion years.

'You have to kiss a lot of frogs, I suppose,' I say consolingly.

'You're so lucky, Mags, having Kieran. He's so gorgeous.'

Sharon is always going on about how fanciable Kieran is – not in a creepy way, but in a 'you'd want to keep an eye on him' kind of way.

She's scarred after Danny and thinks the world is much more predatory than it really is.

I think of how Kieran made *chilli con carne* last night, using a jar, mind you, and not one hint of a vegetable, and by the time he was finished, the kitchen looked like a particularly gruesome crime scene, with red sauce everywhere. Or how he never once in fifteen years has put the toilet seat down after himself, or how he insists on giving out about English politics and Brexit and what have you, but then watching English soccer and boring the head off me by explaining how Chelsea has messy defending, which is exactly what Coventry City are expecting, and now their back line is going forward or some other such drivel.

'I'm haunted lucky, Shar, no doubt about it,' I say, with a look that she knows. 'Every time I pick up his jocks and socks off the floor to wash them, I realise how lucky I am.'

We both laugh. We've been best friends since junior infants, and we have that lovely open, honest friendship where there's no point in presenting yourself as anything but what you are because the other person knows it all anyway.

Kieran is lovely, by the way. He's a tall hunky Irishman, once dark, now getting grey. And Kate and Ellie think their dad is the bee's knees. Still, it doesn't mean I don't sometimes envy Sharon the excitement of a date. I know Kieran gets admiring looks from women, but we've been together for years and so sometimes a bit of excitement is attractive, do you know what I mean?

'So *tell* me, who is it?'

'Don't laugh,' she warns.

'Of course I won't,' I say, preparing to do just that.

'You will, or you'll have something smart to say.'

'I swear, I'll say nothing. I won't react. I'll be delighted for you and wish you well. Now…tell me who it is before I burst.'

She takes a deep breath, blushes a bit and then says, 'It's Trevor Lynch, and we're going on a date tonight.'

My jaw drops, and I'm way too stunned to laugh. 'Tequila Mockingbird Trevor Lynch? The "Larry Mullen of Ballycarrick" Trevor Lynch?'

Larry Mullen is the drummer with U2, in case you didn't know.

'Keep your voice down,' Sharon commands in a hiss as Tatiana glances with raised eyebrows in our direction.

'But you're going out tonight with *Trevor Lynch*...' I whisper back, incredulous.

'It's just a drink, and nothing might come of it – nothing probably will. But he was on the app, and I was too, and he swiped me, and then, well, then I swiped him.' Sharon colours again, and this in itself is a development, as Sharon isn't one for blushing.

Trevor Lynch is the local rock star. Rumour has it that his band, Tequila Mockingbird, once played support to Coldplay. But it was in Norway and nobody from Ballycarrick can confirm it, so aspersions are cast on the truth of the story. We used to think he looked like Bruce Springsteen when we were younger, and we were all crazy about him, but he was four years ahead of us in school and way too cool for us or Ballycarrick or even Ireland. He left after our last secondary school exam, the Leaving Cert, and went touring all over the world – they were even on *Top of the Pops* once. He came back about ten years ago and became his mother's carer. She had Alzheimer's, the poor woman, and she died two or three years ago. His father was already dead, and Trevor is an only child. Everyone thought he would be gone again once poor old Mrs Lynch was laid to rest, but instead he re-formed Tequila Mockingbird with some local lads, and they've been playing weddings and twenty-first birthday parties ever since.

Sharon is still pink. 'Look, I know when we were young, he was mad about himself, thinking he was God's gift and all that, but when we were texting today, he seemed nice, funny. I always fancied him when we were kids, and now... Well, I know he looks unusual, but time hasn't been that unkind, has it?'

She is right on both fronts. Trevor is still good-looking – just in a weird late-'80s kind of way. He wears snow-washed denim jeans teamed up with a denim jacket and an Iron Maiden T-shirt, and he has a haircut that can only be described as a mullet. He has hoops in both ears and wears boots that inexplicably have spurs on them, so yes, he is a bit…well, a bit unusual. Unlike Sharon, who is gorgeous but not at all 'unusual', unless it counts as unusual in Ballycarrick to always be perfectly turned out in this week's fashion.

'You think I'm mad,' she says accusingly.

'I don't think you're mad.' I try to come up with something supportive to say. 'He came home to look after his mam, and really took good care of her in her last years, so that's in his favour, isn't it? I'd say he's nice. Give it a go.'

Anyway, I reason to myself, what's so bad about a man who looks like he's just walked out of 1989? There are worse ways to look. Shar's ex, Danny, gets a spray tan every week in the beautician's, where he also gets his back and I dread to think what else waxed, and he goes once every two months to a dentist in Galway who got struck off for inappropriate conduct of an undisclosed nature and who has diversified into Botox injections. Danny looks ridiculous.

Kieran, on the other hand, showers and shaves and gets his hair cut by Lydia. There the grooming begins and ends. Lydia, for the record, arrived in town a few months ago. She took over the old hairdresser's, the one that used to have those big beehive dryers, and she put up a sign saying, 'Lydia, Turkish Barber'. Lydia is neither Turkish nor a barber, but the people of Ballycarrick are not big on details and she is doing great business.

I check the time on my phone and drain my coffee, which is delicious to the last drop. Tatiana is importing it from somewhere, and everyone in town is talking about it. 'I've to go, Shar. The neighbourhood watch are coming in this morning.'

We pay and leave. Outside the pub I give my anxious friend a big hug. 'Enjoy your date with the rock star, and don't forget to memorise every detail to tell me later.'

'I'll be sure to.' She turns bright pink again, laughs and runs off to collect Sean from school for his lunch, and I stroll back to the station.

CHAPTER 2

The Garda station is looking very nice these days. It has been newly painted inside and out, there are prints on the walls, and a water cooler was added near the front desk. Better still, the women's changing room, which used to be a converted broom cupboard, has finally been upgraded with a shower and everything. I think after I was shot on duty two years ago, my superiors in the Gardaí – especially Detective Inspector Ronan Brady – have been anxious to give me whatever I want or need for my comfort. Ronan blames himself for what happened to me, but he shouldn't worry so much. I have a nasty scar on my chest and my shoulder still hurts from time to time, but generally I'm all right.

I set out some chairs in a side room for the community neighbourhood watch group meeting, which takes place every Tuesday, put the kettle on and get some milk out of the fridge.

Annette Deasy is the first to arrive, and I notice she's limping. She's dressed eccentrically as usual, today in bright-yellow wide-legged pants and a purple velvet hooded top that has bits of mirror sewn into the cuffs and collar. Her long grey hair is loose and thick and lustrous. She told me once she only washes her face and hair in cold rainwater, and there must be something in it because she hasn't a wrinkle; she could be any age really, even though I know she's nearly sixty.

'Are you in trouble, Annette?' I ask, helping her into the meeting room. She always smells pleasantly of sandalwood.

'Ah, no, not really. Just the arthritis is playing up, and the painkillers aren't working as well as they used to. Dr Mulcair is trying to move me up the queue to see a specialist, but since Covid, everything is at a standstill.' She eases into the seat with a wince and a sigh.

She's right – the pandemic of the last two years means all public services are stretched and waiting times are much longer. We are at the end of it now, hopefully, masks and hand sanitiser and all the rest of it, but what a dose it was. One little bat brought the whole world to a standstill. Mad, isn't it?

'You poor thing. Could you go private?'

'No, I've no insurance. I'll just wait my turn. I'm not complaining. Sure there are plenty as bad if not worse than I am.'

'Well, I think you're being very brave.' I make her a coffee. I like Annette a lot. She lives in an old cottage with a couple of acres just outside the village, and she's one of those refreshingly direct people, a rare enough species in Ireland. She makes you feel you could say anything to her. The usual Irish way is frustrating to outsiders, all bluff and bluster and flowery talk with little substance, and people who often don't say what they really mean. We're used to it, but I've seen more than my fair share of bewildered visitors trying to figure out why someone would have told them one thing when the direct opposite was in fact the case.

Let me give you an example.

A pair of Austrian cyclists arrived into the station last week in a terrible panic. An Irish pair, Julie and Brian Magee, met the Austrians on holiday and invited them to stay in Ballycarrick. Julie, the secretary in the primary school, talks conspiratorially through her teeth and so is impossible to understand, and Brian, her husband, is obsessed with cycling, so much so nobody's seen him in anything but Lycra for years. The poor Austrians turned up as planned, and started ringing the doorbell and knocking, but of the pair of Magees, there was no sign, even though their two cars were outside. Eventually, peering through all the doors and windows, the visitors saw a foot sticking out from behind the couch. They arrived to the station in a panic, thinking maybe one or both of the Magees had a heart attack and was lying there dead.

So I rang and Brian answered. Obviously they were grand.

'Just say we're gone somewhere,' hissed Brian. He had no qualms about leaving the poor Austrians with no accommodation, despite them thinking they were going to spend a week or two with their great friends.

'Tell them yourself,' I said, handing the phone to one of the cyclists. An awkward conversation ensued.

So you get the picture. That's kind of the way we are, all welcoming and chat in the moment, but nobody in Ireland thinks anyone means it, only Austrian cyclists and the like.

I hand Annette the coffee, and she crooks her arthritic fingers slowly around the cup. It's painful to watch, but she's a trooper and doesn't let the pain show in her face.

'I was thinking of advertising for someone to help with the vegetable garden in return for bed and board,' she says. 'Bertie the butcher is always saying he could sell ten times the amount of tomatoes I give him, and potatoes and other veg, and Tatiana and Teresa would love more for the pub and the café, but I'm at the pin of my collar to produce what I'm doing now. If I could grow more, I'd make more money definitely, but the blasted arthritis is slowing me down. I can't even dig up the early potatoes I've had in the ground since February.'

'Well, why don't you put an advert in the community section of the *Western People*? It won't cost you much, and that's where local people will be looking for places to rent.'

Her lovely face creases in a smile. She really does have amazing skin for a woman her age. 'Thanks, Mags, that's a good idea. Ah, look, here come the rest of them now.'

First in is Derry Hartnett. He's the lovely former primary school principal, retired a good few years now, who'd been instructed in no uncertain terms by his wife, Lillian, that he'd better find something to do with himself when he retired, because traipsing around after her all day is not an option. He'd become a community activist and was always the voice of the underdog.

And then there's Oscar O'Leary, a man who'd never put in or out on anyone but has developed what some would say is an unhealthy obsession with religion in recent years. He's very nice but is constantly suggesting vigils and Masses and the like, outside of Father Doyle's timetable. And while people in Ballycarrick are tolerant enough of religion, the days of that level of dogged devotion are gone, but nobody has had the heart to tell poor old Oscar.

Father Doyle used to come to the neighbourhood watch meetings, but he's ducking Oscar these days because Oscar keeps banging on about how there isn't enough being done to bring people back to the Church. Poor old Father Doyle is a nice fella, but he is almost eighty and badly in need of a rest. In the absence of recruits to the clergy, he's stuck baptising and marrying and burying, day in, day out, and he confided to me one morning in weary exhaustion that he needs Oscar's religious fervour like a hole in the head.

As the last two members of the committee filter into the room, my heart sinks. Olive Moran, a tiny bird of a woman who had her house featured in the interior magazine of the *Western People* about ten years ago and has been dining out on it since, and Joanna Burke, the doctor's receptionist, an absolute busybody who has Olive under her thumb, are exchanging theatrically furtive glances. I can tell something is brewing.

At first it all goes smoothly enough. We discuss the community awards night, the plans to petition the council for a pedestrian crossing between the new estate and the primary school, and yet more signs urging people to pick up their dog poop.

There is discussion about lighting for the walkway beside the old castle, and how some members of the committee, Olive and Joanna, needless to mention, think the Gardaí need to sit and wait in the old ruin to catch the underage drinkers who have been congregating there since I was a child. I say the usual, that we patrol regularly, but honestly, you'd swear it was our job to parent the teenagers of the town as well as everything else.

'So if that's everything...' I begin to wrap the meeting up.

Joanna and Olive share a glance once more, and Joanna Burke nods. Joanna knows what side her bread is buttered and won't voice a controversial opinion in a public forum like this one.

'Well, there was one other thing, and I – well, we – thought we might discuss it here...' Olive begins, with another slightly helpless look at Joanna.

'Go ahead,' I say, remaining standing.

'Well, it's just that St Colm's is so marvellous for sports as well as having outstanding exam results...'

Olive is speaking in a particularly irritating, saccharin, wheedling voice, and I'm immediately opposed to whatever it is that she's about to suggest. Isn't that desperate? I'm supposed to be an impartial custodian of the law, the voice of reason, and here I am making my mind up before Olive even says what's on her mind. But she's so annoying, perching her Prada handbag on the table instead of at her feet like a normal person, and saying how the 'powder' in St Moritz is so wonderful for skiing. She's a show-off and a snob, and I can't bear her. There, I've said it.

'It's such a marvellous school, and an asset to the town,' she goes on. 'And it has such a wonderful Catholic ethos. The boys come out as strong in their faith as they are in mind and body.'

Oscar pricks up his ears at that, but Derry is starting to look annoyed. The truth is that St Colm's is a private, elitist boys' school, and teachers like Derry don't approve of private schools when there is a perfectly good co-ed secondary school in the town that's free. Around here, sending your son to St Colm's is as much of a status symbol as owning a skiing chalet in the Swiss Alps. Detective Sergeant Duckie Cassidy had a good old crow at me last year when his son got into St Colm's, while we send Ellie to the Ballycarrick Community School. As if I would be impressed by that. He and Olive are cut from the same cloth. Notions of upperosity.

Olive is still talking in that sugary voice. 'And they really stand a shot at the Connaught Cup next year. They have a wonderful senior team with a professional coach...'

Yes, yes, Olive, we know your son, Raymond, is captain of the school team. I doubt there's a sentient being from here to Dublin who doesn't know of the prowess of Raymond Moran in every single thing in life. She reminds me of my mother-in-law, Nora, who thinks the sun, moon and stars shine out of her kids. Like, I adore my girls. They are smashing and exactly as I'd want them to be, but they are normal kids with all the faults and failings of normal people. I don't understand mothers who talk their kids up to the skies. Kieran told me he used to be disgraced as a young fella when Nora would start blowing about him and his siblings – not that she blows about Kieran any more – and poor old Raymond is probably the same.

'So they really could do with some extra space –'

'But what has all this to do with the neighbourhood watch?' Annette interrupts mildly.

'Well...' Olive looks pointedly at her partner in crime, Joanna, who is suddenly fascinated by the fake woodchip grain on the table. 'There is a suggestion that St Colm's could buy, with the community's support, of course, some more land, and then their sports pitches could be extended and they could put in an open-air swimming pool, which would be a wonderful amenity for the entire community. We would have the use of it out of term time in return for our fundraising –'

'I still don't see what that has to do with the neighbourhood watch,' says Annette. 'And why would a community fundraise for a private business? Surely if the community were to get behind any school, it would be the local free ones that the vast majority of local kids attend? Bad enough the taxpayer already pays the teachers' salaries for the private schools.'

'Hear, hear,' murmurs Derry.

I try to look impartial, but I must say I agree. It's a bit of a bugbear of mine as well. We have some flaws as a country, no doubt about it, but we have a wonderful education system. Free and excellent quality. I've no issue with someone sending their kids to another school, a private one, if that's what they want to do for whatever reason, but I do object to paying for it as a taxpayer when the local schools are good enough for my own kids.

Olive glares at Derry while still speaking in her 'sweet' voice. 'Well, you see, Annette, it's just that if we could get community support for the purchase of the land, a plot just to the east of the school...'

The penny drops, and I realise now what she's getting at. It's not just about the school after all. 'You want to move the Travellers,' I say flatly.

The McGovern Traveller family have been part of the fabric of Ballycarrick for longer back than anyone can remember. Mam says they were definitely around when she was a little girl, and she remembers her mother mentioning them being there when *she* was young, so we're talking years, generations. Then the council back in the '90s decided that allowing the Travellers to line the roads and have their animals graze the long acre, as the grass verges were called, was unseemly; it didn't fit with the image we had of ourselves, and they wanted tourists to just see the pretty bits of the country. So they built halting sites, supposedly for the betterment of Travellers but in reality to hide them away from view. The McGoverns' halting site is at Drumlish, on the far side of the St Colm's sports fields.

'No, well, not move them so much as *relocate* them to a more suitable place, somewhere better for them to be...' She shoots a pleading look at Joanna, who is letting her down badly by studying her fingernails now. Joanna Burke is behind this, undoubtedly, but she's allowing Olive to take the heat, although I imagine it was easy enough to get Olive on board. I can just imagine the Olives of this world being horrified that the precious princes of the wealthy have to pass the halting site to get to their posh school.

'That's Galway County Council land,' I say coldly. 'But more importantly, the McGoverns have been part of this town for over 100 years. They are a well-respected family, and one of them, as you know, is a serving member of the Garda stationed here in this station. So I'd suggest if St Colm's have any queries regarding land acquisition, they should raise them with the council. As Annette says, this is a neighbourhood watch committee, and it has no role in planning applications.'

'Yes, but in all fairness, if the local sergeant and the community group such as ourselves were to support the repurposing of the land, then...' Olive looks like a Pekingese dog, all tiny and barky, and she isn't going to give up.

'Olive.' I hear the disdain in my voice and try to correct it. 'As I said, that is entirely outside the remit of the Gardaí. It is also outside the remit of any individual, or committee. So best allow the school and the council to deal with it, if there *is* anything to be dealt with.' I stand up and open the door.

I'm fuming inside, but I won't let Olive see it. She is only the monkey; Joanna Burke is the organ grinder. Joanna's kids are grown up and gone, and anyway they were girls so didn't even go to St Colm's. But she hates the Travellers, always did. She is always the one behind shutting the shops and pubs on the day of a Traveller funeral so Ballycarrick looks like a ghost town.

Annette rises to her feet, and Derry and Oscar do the same.

Olive opens her mouth to protest but Joanna shoots her a warning glance, and they both pass me out the door with a bare nod. Derry gives me a wink – he was always in favour of getting the Traveller kids to stay in school and worked hard to make it happen – and Oscar gives me a prayer card, which I put in my pocket with a word of thanks. Annette is the last to leave.

'Good woman yourself, Mags,' she murmurs as she passes me. 'That pair needed putting in their place. Might be no harm to warn the McGoverns, though.'

I nod, my faith in the people of this place restored somewhat.

CHAPTER 3

I work at my desk for a couple of hours, then decide to take a stroll through the town. I tell myself it's to make sure everything is as it should be in Ballycarrick, but really it's to walk off my irritation with Olive and Joanna.

I step out through the back door onto the street, enjoying the fresh air. The station is a bit stuffy, and the menopause means my internal thermostat is still on the blink sometimes, although things are so much better since I went on HRT two years ago; honestly, it's life-changing. Before that, I thought I was going mad, with the mood swings, the hot flushes, being awake all night imagining all kinds of things to worry about and all the rest of it, not to mention having no interest whatsoever in my poor lovely husband. But while now it's not all plain sailing, at least the ship isn't sinking any more.

The first person I pass is Maura, Bertie the butcher's wife, who is sweeping the path outside the shop. She's lovely. She helps out with the Meals on Wheels and is very involved with the church.

'Morning, Maura, how are you?' I enquire pleasantly. She is only around my age but has that very settled look that some women adopt: iron-grey hair in a neat set, flat shoes, a knee-length tartan skirt and a beige jumper.

She stops her brushing. 'I'm fine, thank God, Mags, and yourself? Did Marie and Peggy have a nice time dancing in Leitrim?'

'I haven't spoken to Mam yet, but I'm sure they did,' I reply, noting again that nothing happens in Ballycarrick that the whole place doesn't know about.

'Did you hear? Bertie is being awarded the pope's medallion?' The joy beams out of the woman like a beacon.

I arrange my face as best I can. 'I did not know that, Maura. That's a great honour. You must be delighted.'

'Oh, Bertie is making little of it. You know how he is, modest to a fault. But Father Doyle asked Monsignor O'Connell to put him forward for his services to the Church over forty years – he was an altar boy since he was seven – and it was immediately approved once Bertie's contribution was explained to His Holiness.'

I nod and smile. I know from Father Doyle he got worn down over the years by the beatific butcher to nominate him for the medal. I also wonder what His Holiness would make of the information that Bertie Mahony was also the main organiser of a questionable event held outside Ballycarrick under cover of darkness, where several people from all over the county arrived in their cars to get up to all sorts of romantic antics with strangers. No charges were pressed, and so Bertie got off with a warning from me, but he can never catch my eye now when I go in for the lamb chops and mince.

I find myself wondering if Maura has any inkling the kind of man she's married to. Probably not. She's very nice and not a snob, but she's a bit out of touch. She'd been destined for the convent and only decided against her final vows when she met Bertie on a pilgrimage. They have one daughter, Rachel, who once was the bane of Ellie's life. I'm not ashamed that I used my knowledge about Bertie's nocturnal activities to make him stop his awful daughter from bullying mine.

Outside the Samovar, a couple of very drunk, very large Russian builders have just been evicted from the pub and Tatiana is giving them a right earful in their native tongue. I pause for a moment to see if help is needed, but it isn't; Tatiana is more than able for them, and by the time she is finished with them, they look like a pair of bold schoolboys who have been suitably chastened.

I hesitate outside Teresa's Bakery, sniffing the lovely cakey smell, but manage to resist temptation. I wave to Lydia the Turkish Barber, who is standing in her doorway casually playing with a cut-throat razor.

My own hair could do with a job done on the roots, but Gerry, the ladies' hairdresser, has been in Lanzarote for three weeks and the girl he has in for him dyed Sharon a weirdly greenish-yellow blond the last time, so I'll wait for Gerry. I had a dark bob haircut for years, but after the shooting, I went two or three months without a cut. Kieran says he really likes my hair a bit longer, so I've decided to let it grow a bit anyway. I worry I am a bit long in the tooth for long hair, and I might take a notion one of the days and cut it all up again, but actually, having it a bit longer is handy because I can tie it in a ponytail and pop it under my Garda hat. Hat hair doesn't help when you take the hat off in the middle of trying to enforce the law and are left looking vaguely ridiculous with a ring of flattened hair around your head. Of course, whoever designed the Garda uniform was a man, and they all have short hair, so it never occurred to them that hat hair would be an issue. Yet another example of it being a man's world.

Across the street, two youth dressed in neat suits are stopping people in the street. They are members of the Church of Pentecostal Evangelists, a kind of splinter Christian group that have a house on the outskirts of town. Their members are always so neat and tidy and polite, and they don't seem to do any harm, but I don't know why they come here to try to gather converts. It seems pointless, but they come and go from this very ordinary bungalow intermittently throughout the year.

I ran a check on them when they bought the house three years ago, and they seem fine. There's a main house in Dublin, and another in London, I think, but the numbers are tiny. The leader is a former Protestant vicar gone a bit rogue, I believe. But as I say, harmless enough.

Anyway, the people of Ballycarrick have no interest as far as I can see on being brought into the light of Jesus's love or the experiential nature of faith instead of ritual; they are scurrying past at great speed as the evangelists relentlessly try to give out their flyers.

I have a quick chat with Violetta in the flower shop, who's much happier now Mrs Finnegan's Yorkie Poo has passed on – at a suspiciously young age – to doggie heaven and so has stopped doing its business on her doorstep. Then I drop in on Joe Dillon, who runs the menswear store. As usual, Joe enquires tenderly and at great length after my mother. He's looked the exact same way all the years I've known him. Immaculately dressed in a three-piece-suit, matching tie and pocket square, his grey hair combed and tidy, clean shaven. He's a neat man, in every sense, no spare fat but not skinny either and he always smells pleasantly of some fresh smelling cologne. Joe definitely likes Marie a lot, and I've always assumed he plans to ask her out at some stage. Since my dad died when I was seven, she hasn't had anything to do with a man in any romantic sense of the word, and I'd like her to have someone, especially a nice man like Joe Dillon. But in the past three or four years, Joe has never got beyond sharing a weekly lunch with my mother in what was McLoughlin's and is now the Samovar, so perhaps he only looks on her as a friend. I hope that's not too disappointing for Mam.

On the spur of the moment, I decide to drop in on her to see how she is after the Leitrim country-dancing weekend. Mam runs a little boutique in Ballycarrick, and she's held in high regard by everyone who knows her, with good reason. She doesn't gossip, and she doesn't let people go out of her shop in outfits that make them look ridiculous.

It's coming up to the wedding season right now, and so the mother-of-the-bride outfits are in great demand. For some reason, women, who all the rest of their lives wear perfectly normal clothes, seem to be under the impression that dresses and jackets in the most lurid pinks and blues are just the ticket when their child is getting married. They end up looking like something painted by a load of preschoolers. Mam is great at gently coaxing them towards things that look better, and she's a big fan of the sucky-in underwear – you know the kind, made of some kind of greyish-beige elasticated fabric and recycled razorblades?

Anyway, according to her, that hellish fabric covers a multitude of sins, that and a good bra. So she dresses the women of the parish from the skin out and takes pride in the fact that they look lovely on the day their son or daughter gets married. She knows everyone, so she'll make sure the mother of the groom and the mother of the bride look different – always vital too.

'Hi, Mam,' I call as the door pings when I push it. She's behind the till replacing the roll.

'Hello, Mags, love.' She looks up, delighted. I'm fifty years old this year, and I still love that my mam is always thrilled to see me. 'Come here to me. Would you try to get this flippin' thing on the spool? I only brought my reading glasses today, and I'm blind as a bat.'

I fix the till roll as she goes into the back to put the kettle on.

'God bless your eyesight. Have you time for a cup?' she calls through the door. I glance at my watch.

'Yeah, sure. I didn't see you since the weekend – how'd you get on?'

Mam was widowed young and had me and my two sisters to raise alone, as well as looking after the formidable Nana Peg, my father's fearsome mother who terrified us as kids by looking a bit like the child catcher in *Chitty Chitty Bang Bang*. When she wasn't minding all of us, Mam worked all hours in this little shop, making sure we never went without, so I'm glad she's enjoying life a bit these days.

'Great altogether, but I'll tell you what, Mags, you'd want to be on your toes for the Donegal dancers – they're in a whole other league. There's a pair of brothers from Killybegs who everyone wanted, because despite the yellow-orange toupees they had, they are lightning quick on their feet. But they'd only ask up the few that could match them.'

Mam's country dancing is serious business. In case you have a vision of a gang of elderly Irish people line-dancing in Stetsons, it's not that. It's kind of a combination of Irish dancing, ballroom dancing and gymnastics, as far as I can see. I don't know how it works really. I can't dance to save my life. I'd rather have a root canal than darken the door of a dance hall.

I smile. 'And did they ask you and Peggy up?'

Mam gives me a sidelong smirk. 'Well, that'd be telling now, wouldn't it?'

My mother is a brilliant dancer, so I'm sure they did, and she'd have been the envy of the place. Her dream is to compete on one of those shows on the TV where people have to dance every week. She records them all, *Strictly Come Dancing*, *Dancing on Ice*, *Dancing with the Stars*, the whole lot. My girls love to go down and watch with her. She makes them home-made pizza, and they curl up on the couch, commenting on peoples' footwork in the paso doble, and remarking they aren't strong enough in the frame for the American Smooth. I haven't a clue what they're going on about, but they love it.

I, on the other hand, am like a bull in a china shop. Kieran and I danced at our wedding for about five minutes and have never danced together since. He's worse than me, if that's possible.

'So any more news apart from you being the Ginger Rogers of the west of Ireland?' I ask, taking a cup of tea from her.

'Dolores is coming home for a visit,' she says. 'She rang last night when I was only in the door.'

'Oh, that's great.'

'It is, isn't it?'

Neither one of us would say it outright, but the prospect of a visit from my youngest sister doesn't fill either me or my mother with delight. Dolores, or Lori as she is known now, has been living in Montana someplace in a kind of hippy commune with her soulmate, some fella called Hopi. But a few months ago, she emailed and said they'd split up and she was going 'on the road' with a group who were 'hitting up' all the Mind Body Spirit festivals around America, offering ear candling and aura reading and all manner of stuff like that.

Now, don't get me wrong, I love a bit of meditation and I think the powers of arnica for bruises are otherworldly, but Lori is next level. She's all tie-dye and beads, and her hair is down to her waist in dreadlocks. My kids think she's fabulous, of course, and the last time she was here, I came home from work to find her introducing my big plonker of a husband to the wonders of weed. I went mental, nearly murdered Kieran. The sight of the two of them giggling like eejits and eating Coco Pops out of the box in our sitting room was too much for me.

Mam loves her, I know she does, but Dolores is so disruptive whenever she visits. She is always telling Mam that her ornaments and knick-knacks display an 'unhealthy attachment to things and a worrying degree of consumerism'. And she's a vegan, so she is impossible to cook for. She is forever bemoaning the fact that the tofu in SuperValu isn't ethically sourced or that the 'in-your-face attitude to animal slaughter and the theft of infants from their mothers' – that's farming to the uninitiated, by the way – in Ireland is deeply disturbing.

'It could be worse,' I say with a smile. 'It could be Jenny.'

'Ah, Mags, don't say that,' Mam admonishes, but she knows exactly what I mean. My older sister, Jenny, is married to Ahmed Amari, and they live in Dubai. Ahmed is fine, he's nice actually, but he finds us completely unfathomable, and when they visit with their sons, Mohammad, Achmed and Hassan, I have to say the feeling is kind of mutual.

They're strict Muslims and find the fact that the nearest mosque is fifty miles away a huge inconvenience. Much seems to be made of getting there and back when they visit, and Jenny always looks a little uncomfortable, as if it's somehow a bad sign of Ballycarrick that the Muslim population is so tiny. Up until a few years ago, it was zero, and the '100,000 welcomes' were more for the wealthy tourists than anyone fleeing oppression or poverty. But in the last few years, Ireland has opened its borders – a crack, it must be said – and more and more people from all over the world are coming here, and some of them are adventurous enough, or lost enough, to wind up in Ballycarrick. But not in sufficient numbers to warrant a mosque just yet, much to my sister's embarrassment.

Ahmed is well travelled. He works for Emirates airlines, engaging with their foreign clients, and he's perfectly polite. But as I say, we're a different species. I find his culture fascinating, so I used to ask him about it, but again Jenny did her pained expression – honestly, she could have been a muse for one of those medieval martyr portraits – so I stopped. The boys and Ahmed seem uncomfortable that our daughters dress as they do, in shorts and T-shirts or in bikinis at the beach in the summertime, and I've no intention of covering them up, so as I say, lots of confusion and miscommunication. Everyone on both sides breathes a sigh of relief when it's time for them to leave.

'When's Dolores coming?' I ask.

'The fifteenth. She wondered if we could pick her up in Shannon.'

'Of course. We'll both go. Now I better take off, fighting crime on the mean streets of Ballycarrick.' I laugh at my own joke, but Mam looks serious.

'You think you're being funny, Mags, but that lunatic could have killed you two years ago, and then where would we be? You think you're RoboCop or something, but you're flesh and bone like the rest of us. So no more heroics, do you hear me?' Mam looks stern, and I know she's worried. It is almost unheard of for a community guard to be shot in the line of duty, but I managed it, and she's been anxious about me ever since.

'I hear you. No RoboCopping for me.' I wink and dodge her taking a swipe at me.

CHAPTER 4

On Wednesday, I'm in Galway District Court all morning, giving evidence in a couple of cases – driving without insurance, things like that. People hate being pulled on these things; you'd think we were living in a police state to hear them giving out. But it's not about them; it's about the poor person they crash into who gets left having to pay for their own repairs or medical bills because the eejit that did the damage wasn't insured.

Duckie doesn't see or hear me enter the station on my way back from Galway, and at first I don't see him either because I have come in the back door, but I instantly know it's him. That smarmy voice, that double entendre snigger – it can only be one person. My nemesis, Detective Sergeant Donal Cassidy, or 'Duckie' to his enemies, is standing at the public desk.

The man is an insufferable eejit of the highest order, put on this earth as a plague to me personally and women generally. His station is in the next town over, but he likes to stick his oar into mine. He isn't my superior in rank, but nobody has told him that and he goes on like he is. He's been put back in his box more than once, but like those toys kids have – you know, where you whack the little animal on the head and it keeps popping up? –well, Duckie is like that. He's as thick as a ditch, and loud. He knows me as a joyless, cranky feminist, which I'm not at all really, but it suits me that he thinks that because it saves me enduring his dirty jokes.

The guard on the desk is Nicola. She sees me popping my head around the door from the back but doesn't acknowledge me. Taking the hint, I stay where I am, out of sight, listening to what's being said.

'So, Nadia, if you just draft something standard, like a good girl, on headed paper, something saying the McGoverns would be better off in the Tuam road site, blah blah blah, we can get that bit over with. It's not really to do with us, but the council are anxious to get it through. And the local county councillor – do you know him? Andy Maguire? Estate agent?'

Nicola says nothing, but Duckie doesn't notice. Women speaking or not speaking is all the same to him; he can't hear them either way. He's also notorious for hating Travellers, foreigners and anyone not a white middle-class man, and his familiar bleat that 'you can't say anything nowadays without someone getting offended' is still unfortunately to be heard on his regular visits to our station.

'How about you make a list of the things you say that cause offence and stop saying them? That would save everyone a lot of bother maybe?' I'd suggested sweetly only last week, as if going around offending all and sundry every time we open our mouths is a bothersome conundrum we all face, and Duckie went even more red in the face than usual and stormed off. But now, unfortunately, he's back.

He carries on conspiratorially, like 'obviously' he and Nicola are on the same side. 'Andy is president of the golf club, superb golfer actually. We go way back. His wife, Michelle, is Lady Captain, and her indoors is mad for an invite onto the committee – you know the way you ladies love a bit of power, see and be seen and all of that?' There it is, the chortle. 'And I said we'd give them a dig out. Sure you know as well as I do it doesn't make any difference to the knackers anyway, sure aren't they supposed to love travelling? The spin down the road will do them a world of good, and there'll be more room for the horses or donkeys or goats or those damn noisy chickens and whatever it is they'd be keeping or eating or doing unmentionable things to. Anyway, just do the letter up there, love, and I'll be out of your hair.'

I'm not surprised to hear the oily Andy Maguire is behind this move. Andy is a county councillor, elected each time by his grateful public. He's a 'you scratch my back, I'll scratch yours' type of politician. Duckie would love to climb the social ladder, so he's as transparent as glass. Andy Maguire also happens to make a lot of money buying and selling property on behalf of the council. Conflict of interest? Absolutely. But will anyone blow the whistle? Of course not. Andy is connected to everyone. Talking of which, I now remember the new inspector the council sent to the site – even he is somehow connected to Andy; he might be a second cousin or something.

I can't stand this about Ireland, that it's an 'old boys' club' when it comes to this sort of thing. The trouble is, the people who have the power to root out this kind of corruption are the very ones who benefit from it, so they never will. It would drive you daft.

Now Duckie is leaning forwards over the desk, breathing heavily on poor Nicola. 'I noticed you're a while here now, aren't you, Nadia? Maybe it's time for a jump up the ladder, if you know what I mean? A pretty little thing like you can't be kept in the backwaters. I can have a word in a few ears once we get this over the line and –'

I've heard enough. This plonker clearly thought I would be in court all day; he saw me there this morning. So he imagines he can bribe or intimidate my young female guard into endorsing the eviction of the Travellers in my absence.

'Detective Sergeant Cassidy.' My voice cuts across his wheedling.

'Ah, Mags, 'tis yourself.' He at least looks embarrassed. 'You're looking well. The hair is longer with you…and you look…well.'

I think this is where I'm supposed to simper and blush. Eejit. 'I am well. Did you want us to do something?'

'Ah, no, not at all. I was just chatting with the gorgeous Nadia…' He jerks his bald head at Nicola. He'd remind you of a toad for all the world. He used to dye his thinning hair an alarming shade of plum, but that fight has been fought and lost, so now his head is shaved. That can look great on some men, but he's not one. Like, it works for

Dwayne 'The Rock' Johnson but not so much on Duckie 'The Repulsive Eejit' Cassidy. He's got a flat back of the head, and his skin is shiny and white, Lord Voldemort style.

He's quite a bit fatter than he used to be too. Not that I'm anyone to talk, in all fairness, but at least I'm not trying to squeeze into clothes from a decade ago. And it's weird fat for a man. Usually men put weight on their bellies, but his is on his hips and thighs. He's wearing the most ridiculous skinny jeans, which look like someone spray-painted them onto him, and a polo shirt with the collar up. He thinks he's George Clooney.

'Garda *Nicola* Holland,' I correct him.

'Yeah, yeah, Nicola, I said that. Anyway, it can wait...' He goes to leave but I stand in his way.

'Not at all. If we can help, we will?' I'm actually enjoying this. He is such a clown; honestly, you've never met the like, or at least I hope you haven't.

'Detective Sergeant Cassidy was just asking if we could write a letter supporting the council's move to close the halting site at Drumlish,' Nicola says innocently, both of us knowing the score exactly. 'His friend is a golfer and an estate agent? And he's also the local councillor. And if we could, it would help Mrs Cassidy to get into the golf club or something?' She looks perplexed as she hangs him even more.

I wrinkle my brow, joining in, equally bewildered. 'The Gardaí, to write a letter? But why would we be involved? And is the golf club to do with some aspect of the law?' I ask the question as if she's just suggested we take part in a three-ring circus.

'Ah, there's no need really, it wasn't that at all... I was just chatting with Nad...Nicola here and saying... Well, it doesn't matter, it's not anything.' He's actually squirming now and knows his efforts to come in here and bully a young officer into doing something corrupt have completely backfired.

'So do you want a letter from us regarding the halting site?' I press, enjoying watching him squirm.

'No...God, no...nothing like that. She' – he jerks his head at Nicola

– 'got the wrong end of the stick completely. I was just making conversation.'

I could keep on at him but I've things to do, so I let him off the hook. Hopefully he's learned his lesson.

As he slinks out the door, I say loudly to Nicola, 'Anything new, apart from the usual corruption and bribery?'

She grins. 'Someone rang in to say they think there was some activity last night in that house on Pearse Street that's for sale.'

I nod. 'Can you check with the keyholders that all is well there? And just cross-check the remand book, make sure everyone we should see is turning up.'

'No problem, Mags. Cuppa?'

'I'm fine, thanks. My mother just made me one.'

I go into my office and shut the door, and collapse in the chair behind my desk.

I have the usual mountain of paperwork to get through. Also, I should apply for leave for when my sister is home, but on the other hand, I'm really hoping to get a few days away with Kieran on our own and I don't want to use up my annual holiday. I'm thinking of asking Mam to move in to look after the girls, and taking him away to Greece maybe, just the two of us. He was so brilliant while I was recovering from the shooting, and I know we were going through a bit of a rocky patch before it, but all that is forgotten now.

I try not to dwell on the muckraker Gemma O'Flaherty, who decided to pour poison in my husband's ear, trying to make out there was something going on between me and Detective Inspector Ronan Brady. As if. But still, it really upset Kieran and wasn't fair on him.

Kieran took the injury I got more seriously than I did in lots of ways. I was offered counselling and all the rest, but I'm actually fine, and maybe it's Kieran who should have had the therapy. For a long time, he couldn't get past the shooting, and anything more dangerous than me telling people they needed a dog licence made him worry. He even suggested I leave the force, but I've no notion whatsoever of doing that. It was a one-off, 'wrong place, wrong time' thing, but no matter how often I tell him that, I can feel he's constantly worried about me even now.

Like, I know my mam is anxious as well, but somehow that doesn't affect me as much. I mean, all mothers worry about their children; you'd be worried yourself if they didn't.

I'm thinking about all this when my phone rings. It's Kieran.

'Hi, love,' I answer.

'Hiya, how's things?'

Here's an example of what I mean. He never used to do this, ring me at work to check up on me; it's new since the shooting.

'Grand, just in. Just back from court. Hey, I forgot to tell you, I called into Mam a few days ago to see how she got on at the dancing. She had a great time. Dolores rang – she's coming home.'

'Oh, right.' Kieran knows it's too soon to make jokes about the weed incident. I'm not a total prude, but honestly, I'm a sergeant in the Gardaí! It was so reckless of them. Dolores didn't surprise me in the slightest, she's a disaster, but my husband should have known better.

'C'mere,' he says. 'I just had my mother on the phone, and she's planning a family get-together on the last weekend of this month, to watch some bit of that rally before the special election in Nevada or was it California? Anyway, America. So you might put that in your diary, love?'

My heart sinks. Fergus, who is 'very high up in the bank', is married to Kieran's sister, the 'always immaculately dressed' Orla, and this cousin of his is running as a long-shot independent candidate for the House of Representatives to replace some geriatric who has just died. And Nora, my monster-in-law, is nearly giving herself a hernia with the excitement of basking in the reflected glory. To be fair to Fergus, he's told Nora repeatedly that he's never even met this man and that he's not a first cousin or anything, he's the son of his father's cousin or something, but Nora isn't interested in any triviality like that. You'd swear the man was Joe Biden and Fergus was his brother, the way she is going on.

'Ah, Kieran, do we have to?' I groan.

He sighs. 'Ah, you don't if you can't bear it. Don't worry, I'll say you're working that weekend and can't get out of it. I'll go by myself and bring Kate. I know Ellie's allergic to Mam's new-found love of this American politician thing too.'

I hear the disappointment in his voice and feel a pang of sadness for him. Kieran and Ellie have always been so close, but she's having her teenage strops on a regular basis these days and he's taking it all very personally. She used to love going out in the van with him, but now she won't be seen dead in it – it's 'mortifying' apparently. But then Ellie is just fourteen, so every single thing about us is 'mortifying'. It's hard going, I can assure you. Some days she's fine, but other days she's like something possessed and he can't understand where our sweet girl is gone.

I have tried to explain to him that she's not gone anywhere. I read a book about the neurological development of teenagers and how it was a very similar process in the brain to toddlers. So when they're two years old and kicking up all colours of murder in the supermarket, that's an almost identical process to when they're thirteen or fourteen. Except this time, instead of that thing where they can make themselves rigid in shopping trolleys and throw themselves on the ground howling, it's all door-slamming and eye-rolling. Not easy to deal with, certainly, but I try not to take it personally. I feel sorry for him.

'Ah, no, look, it's fine. We'll all go. The four of us. Sure, maybe your mam is right and he'll be the president of America and we'll be well connected then.'

'For what?' Kieran asks, not unreasonably.

'I don't know. If we ever wanted to go to space or anything maybe?' I laugh. 'Or to attend a meeting of the G8, or shake hands with the emperor of Japan.'

'Jays, Mags, we better go so. I don't know how we managed so long without connections in that case.' He laughs, a lovely deep rumbling sound.

'OK, I'll see you later. I better go.'

'No problem, love, take care. What you up to?' He drops it in casually, and to the untrained ear, it could be just a normal enquiry, but I hear the anxiety there. It irritates and disturbs me at the same time. I know he loves me and he's worried and all of that, but I can't live with him terrified every time I go outside the door.

'Just meetings and paperwork.' I lie, knowing he'll have a better day if he thinks I'm in the station. In fact, I'm on my way out again. I've decided I need to talk to Jerome McGovern.

CHAPTER 5

I'm in the middle of listening to a great audiobook, and I drive very slowly to the halting site so I can get to the end of the chapter. It's a book called *My Place* by Sally Morgan, and it's the story of an Aboriginal Australian woman who was raised believing she was Indian. She finds out her true heritage and goes into the bush to try to trace her family, which is fascinating to me. I think as I'm driving along how the so-called problems Travellers cause are the same ones that are blamed on Aboriginal people everywhere – First Nations in Canada and the USA, Maori people in New Zealand, the list goes on. Overdependence on alcohol and drugs, poor educational attainment, feelings of being excluded, making up a higher than should be percentage of the population in prison – you know yourself. Wherever you're from, you can probably name some group that this applies to. Who is judge and jury on these people the world over? Powerful white men. And who can we blame for their destruction in the first place? Yes, you guessed it, more powerful white men, like the sort who send their sons to St Colm's, and the men those sons grow into.

There's no getting away from the fact that money, white skin and being male immediately puts you in a place of privilege in this world.

Maybe this is overly simplistic, but I honestly believe if women had more to do with societal decisions, then things would be kinder, especially to marginalised groups. Women are less about war and conflict, I think, because they love their children. And not that men don't, but women will not send their sons and daughters deliberately into harm's way, and men will, and have done so over and over.

I know some women in politics are the exception to that, but maybe that's because for them to succeed in that world, they have to act like the men they challenge.

Even as I think my thoughts, I can feel the collective eye-rolling of some men. Not all of them, of course, but the Duckies of this world – 'Here we go again, more feminist claptrap.'

But it's not. It's just telling it like it is. I spend at least three days a month in court, and still, although we've had equal opportunities in education in Ireland for a long time now, the judiciary and all its associated professionals are still predominantly men. The gender balance is improving, no doubt about it, but women are fifty percent of the population, so shouldn't they be fifty percent of judges, barristers, doctors, teachers, whatever?

This is why, rightly or wrongly, I see it as a personal triumph that Jerome's daughter Delia has qualified for the Gardaí and is now a full-on member of the Irish police. And I intend to make sure she's not driven out by sexism or discrimination, hence her being stationed in Ballycarrick where I can keep an eye on her. Delia is no shrinking violet; she's well able to stick up for herself. But still, she's a young woman from a marginalised background – it's not going to be easy.

When I reach her family's site, Jerome's HiLux pickup, brand new, thirty grand at least and guaranteed bought for cash, is outside his caravan, so I know he is at home.

I park, pull on a hoodie over my uniform and take off my hat. I haven't been to Drumlish halting site in a social capacity since Dacie's death. I knock at the door of his caravan.

His wife opens the door. 'Sergeant Munroe,' she says warily. Delia's mother can be no more than mid-forties, but she looks older. Her long hair is in a ponytail, and her face is handsome if careworn. She has Delia's vivid blue eyes, and I can see where her daughter gets her looks from. Jerome is a big man, darker and heavyset. The McGoverns all look almost Spanish, with dark hair and eyes and sallow skin.

'Hello, Mrs McGovern, I'm sorry to disturb you. There's nothing wrong. I just wondered if Jerome was around?'

'He's up the yard there, feeding the chickens.' She jerks her head in the direction of the back of the halting site where the family keep their animals. The care of and use of animals is central to the Traveller way of life. Settled people might not understand it or approve, but that is how it is. The McGoverns are regularly inspected by the authorities for animal welfare and have never once been found wanting.

'Thanks. I'll go and find him if that's all right? Or would it be better if I came back later?'

She thinks for a moment, considering it. 'Come in and I'll send someone for him.' She stands back and I step up into the caravan. Unlike Dacie's, it is modern and streamlined, more of a mobile home – what the Americans call trailers – than a caravan you could tow. At one end is a U-shaped seating area with a large flat-screen television and a glass cabinet full of trinkets, in the middle a kitchen, with cooker, washing machine and dishwasher, and to the right are four doors that I assume lead to three bedrooms and a bathroom. Apart from Delia's mother, there is nobody else at home.

'Will you have a cup of tea?' she asks.

'I'd love one if it's not too much trouble.' I smile. To refuse her hospitality would be taken as a slight. 'Milk, no sugar.'

She shows me where to sit, and to my surprise, I find there's a large framed photo of Delia in her uniform on the shelf beside me.

'Delia is a great asset to us, Mrs McGovern,' I say. 'She's such a kind-hearted girl but very sensible too. She's a credit to you.'

A bit of the frostiness melts. We all like to hear nice things about our children; Delia's mother is no different.

'Call me Dora,' she says as she hands me my cup of tea. 'Mrs McGovern was Dacie.'

'Well, I'm Mags,' I say, taking the steaming cup.

She goes to the door and calls a red-haired boy, one of Delia's younger brothers, I suppose, and issues an instruction to him in a mixture of rapidly spoken English and Gammon, the Traveller language, then returns to sit opposite me. 'Jerome will be up now.'

'Your youngest must be twelve now, is he?' I ask, making conversation.

She nods. 'Gerard, he's nearly thirteen. He's with his father and the horses. Stone mad for horses, that boy. I can't keep him at the books at all – he have no interest.'

'Well, there's more than one kind of education, Dora.' I smile. 'My eldest, Ellie, is all about singing and dancing and that sort of stuff and performing, where my youngest is much more into sports. They're all different.'

''Tis hard on your man that he have no son to follow him into the business.' Her words contain no disapproval or admonishment, just sympathy.

I nod. Kieran always says he'll sell the roofing business when the girls are finished college or whatever they do, so he couldn't give a hoot about passing it on, but that wouldn't be the Traveller way.

'But sure, the way things are going, maybe one of your girls will be up on the roofs.' A hint of a smile.

'Well, they don't have their father's work ethic, that's for sure. If I could get them to tidy their bedrooms, it would be a start.' I smile ruefully and hope she sees me as just a woman and a mother like her.

'Ah sure, they're all the same now, only wanting the television and the phones and what have you. 'Tis very different than when we were young.'

I am about to reply, glad that she is melting even further, when her husband appears. His huge bulk fills the van, and Dora gets up to make him a cup of tea without him asking. The roles in Traveller life are traditional, no doubt about that, although Dacie has raised her boys to be respectful of women.

'Thanks, Dora,' he says with a smile as he sits down opposite me. Jerome is at least six foot six, and while his body is running to fat a little now, he was a powerful boxer as a young man and is still very definitely a force to be reckoned with. Only a very foolish person would take him on. Rumour has it that he was the bare-knuckle fighting champion of Ireland for years, a gruesome kind of boxing that takes place between Traveller men in remote areas well away from the Gardaí or anyone else, and huge sums of money are bet on it. For all of that, though, he has never once been in any kind of trouble with the law.

Dora withdraws then; she won't stay for any conversation between me and her husband.

'What can I do for you, Sergeant?' he asks. He isn't wary like his wife, but nor is he friendly.

'Well, nothing really. I'm here in a kind of unofficial capacity.' I feel a pang of self-doubt. Maybe I should stay out of this. It's not my business, and if it gets out that I am meddling in county council affairs, then I will be in trouble. But as if to calm my nerves, my eyes come to rest on another large photograph. This time it is of an old woman, her copper-coloured face wrinkled but her eyes bright and intelligent. How that tiny woman managed to produce this gigantic man sitting opposite me I'll never know, but she did, and I am here for Dacie, for the memory of her.

'I wanted to talk to you, kind of off the record,' I begin. 'But, Jerome, if you use the information I'm about to tell you, I'd much prefer if you kept my name out of it.'

He stares at me for a moment, then nods. 'You have my word.'

I know I can trust him. A Traveller's word is their bond. I take the plunge. 'There's a move afoot for St Colm's Academy to buy more land beside the playing fields to expand their campus. The Department of Education are not going to fund it, so it's up to the local community to raise the money for the school.'

Jerome keeps on staring at me silently.

I deliver the bad news. 'A member of the neighbourhood watch raised the matter at the meeting, and basically this is the site that the school wants to buy from the council.'

I hate to see the darkness that comes over his face. It never ends if you are a Traveller. Nobody wants them, that is the truth, and both I and Jerome know there will be plenty of local support and much enthusiastic fundraising if it leads to the removal of the halting site. Some people, the minority, will be vocal about it, and many more, although they will never openly say it, will tacitly support the idea.

Jerome's huge fists quietly clench and unclench on his knees. Finally he says, 'That new inspector from the county council was out here a few weeks ago. Wouldn't say right out what he was doin', but I got a bad feeling off him. I had a feeling he was thinking about moving us on. I said it to Delia.'

'I wouldn't be surprised if he was involved in it,' I say.

'And where would the council be wanting us to go?' he asks me flatly.

'I heard there are plans afoot to move you out beside the Carmody place on the Tuam road.'

Jerome's face tightens and his jaw twitches. This is even worse than he'd imagined. The Carmody Traveller family are always in trouble, robbing and drugs, in and out of prison. It was the death of Blades Carmody at the hands of a sex trafficker that ended up with Natasha McGovern getting abducted by a Dublin criminal gang, and with me getting shot on a lonely beach in Spiddal. If the McGovern family ends up ghettoised with the Carmodys, their nephews and sons risk getting drawn into a life of crime.

'I assume you won't want to go?' I ask.

'No. We won't.' He is a man of few words.

I nod. 'To be honest, it's nothing to do with me or the guards, but I wanted to give you the heads up on what is being talked about. If your family is at least aware of what's going on, then you can get out there and resist. The first thing I would do if I was you is I'd get a solicitor, because there's people involved in this that stand to make a nice bit of money from the sale of the land to the school.'

He observes me for another long moment, his face unreadable. Then he says, 'Thanks for comin', Sergeant, but we won't be going to no solicitors.'

I look him straight in the eye. 'I think you should.'

He exhales heavily. 'Maybe you do, but I'm a Travellin' man,

Sergeant, and that world of courts and the law are not for us. They'd never take our side, and we'd be foolish to think they would.'

He's absolutely right, of course, but at the same time, if nobody ever challenges the status quo, then it will never change.

'Look,' I say, 'and I'm trusting you not to say where you heard this, and it's up to you obviously, but the councillor that's pushing for this sale is also an estate agent who'll make a nice profit from the deal. His children go to St Colm's, and I'm not sure, but I think he's related to the new inspector somehow. On top of that, a senior member of the Gardaí, not attached to our station, is very well connected to that county councillor so is in favour of the sale as well. If you can show that they are colluding together, and that it's a conflict of interest...'

Jerome stands up. 'I appreciate what you're doin', Sergeant, lookin' out for us, I do. And my mother would too, God be good to her. But how would we ever prove that? And without any proof, nobody will take a tack of notice. And even if we had proof, who would care? We're nothin' to the likes of them, only a bunch of knackers, best got rid of.' He puts his hands in his pockets and looks out the caravan window, towards his huge vegetable garden that feeds the whole family, a labour of love for thirty years.

I follow his eyes to the rows of sprouting carrots, onions, cabbages, potatoes. This is his rightful land, where he keeps his hens, his horses, and grows his family's food. 'Jerome, please don't take this lying down. Someone's got to fight the system. And it has to be you, you know that?'

I am willing him to rise to the challenge, to be worthy of Dacie. 'Your mother would have fought for this family like a tiger, but she's gone, God rest her, and you're the head of the McGoverns now. Think of the future of all the young lads in this family. God help them if you end up next to the Carmodys. And isn't this land worth fighting for?'

'Era, Mags, my fighting days are over now. There was a time...' That darkness crosses his eyes again, and if I didn't know him better, I would think he was close to tears.

His voice is hoarse when he speaks. 'I shouldn't burden you with this, you being who you are, but I trust you, Mags, so I'll tell you a hard truth. Many years ago, I killed a young man stone dead in a bare-knuckle fight. One hit and he dropped. He was my cousin. It was an unlucky punch, a pure accident, and I was forgiven by his family, but I swore never to fight again, and if that makes me look soft to you, then that's the way it is.'

Now I understand. This huge man fears his own strength. I soften my voice. 'There's more than one way to fight for what you want, Jerome. It doesn't have to be fists. Use your words. Your daughter is a very clever, articulate young woman, and she didn't lick it off the floor. She's a credit to you, and there's no reason why you shouldn't be a credit to her. And think about the solicitor too. There's a fella in Galway, Alberto Ramos. He's Spanish but married to an Irishwoman. He's a great advocate for the underdog. He won't turn you away.'

A reluctant smile spreads across his face. 'You're no ordinary shade, Sergeant.'

The Travellers call us the shades, referring to a time when Gardaí were required to wear their hats low over their faces, the peaks casting shadows on their faces.

I return his smile and stand to go. 'Maybe not, and this conversation never happened, but think about what I've said.'

''Twasn't always this way, you know that, don't you?'

I'm not sure what he means, and my face must register that because he carries on.

'My people, we were the tinkers, you know, because we used to mend pots and pans and farm equipment, anything metal, before plastic came, and see what it's done? Fish in the ocean dying from it. My grandfather and his brothers were famous, and when I was a *sooblik*, only five or six years of age, my parents would take us all off for the summer from town to town, all over the country, and the people would be happy to see us coming. I remember one town that'd paint the place up all bright for us. And the women would be welcome too. They'd sing or dance or do the hair of the settled women, or read their tea leaves, and there was friendship there, and respect.'

My heart goes out to this big, kind man. 'My mother remembers you coming here when she was a girl,' I say, 'and how the arrival caused great excitement, seeing the coloured wagons and all the animals.'

His craggy, careworn face is heartbreakingly sad. 'We'd sing too, so many songs, and my father would sit us outside the pub. Children weren't allowed into pubs at that time, but he'd call us in to do a song. We'd be put standing on a barrel, and we'd sing like larks, our own songs, the songs of our people, and everyone would listen.'

'Do you still sing?' I ask.

He nods. 'Sometimes. I was singin' one time after the funeral of a cousin of mine over in England, and this Black man came up to me. He was standin' on the edge of the circle, listenin' to the song, and when it was over, he shook my hand. "We've the same story, brother," he said to me, and he was right. His people, my people, we know hardship. And they let their pain out in their songs, the blues they call it, and we release ours in our songs too. He heard it.'

'People like your mother, God rest her, saw a lot of change, didn't they?'

He nods again. 'They did, and not for the good either. Life now, 'tisn't so hard, I suppose. We've food and heat and roofs. But we're not trusted, and nobody wants to see us comin'. I'd go back to the old days in a heartbeat, when we had nothin' but no door was ever closed to a Travellin' man or woman.'

'Not everyone wants to close their doors even now, Jerome. Your family is well liked and respected by many in this town, and most of them will know deep down it's wrong that you're being asked to leave. If they heard you saying what you've just said to me, it could sway a lot of hearts and minds.'

He shrugs. 'Era, I'm no talker, Mags. The only way I ever changed anyone's mind was with me fists, and like I said to you, those days are long behind me now.'

I don't press the point, but I say, 'Give that lawyer Alberto a ring.'

He smiles politely. He doesn't say yes. But on the other hand, he doesn't say no.

I take my leave, praying I haven't made a bad situation even worse by telling him what I know.

CHAPTER 6

*N*icola and Delia are deep in chat behind the desk when I arrive back at the station.

'Are we all women?' I ask, looking around.

'Michael is out on a call, something about a missing scooter,' Nicola replies. 'And Darren's left already – his brother's getting married tomorrow in Tipperary.' She says this with a quick glance at Delia, who blushes furiously and turns her head away to hide it.

Nicola and I pretend not to notice. We know that Darren asked Delia to go to the wedding with him, and that she refused.

Darren is from Tipperary and a hurler. His local club despaired of his work schedule, as Garda shifts take no cognisance whatsoever of the county championship fixtures, but the other guards here are very good to swap with him when they can, and he's always ready to repay the favour. He's what any Irish mammy would call a lovely lad, and they'd be delighted if their daughters brought him home. He's average height, has reddish-blond hair, is tall enough for the Guards and has a pleasant, open face. I've always liked him.

More to the point, he's been keen on Delia almost since he first set eyes on her, and I suspect – and Nicola suspects – that Delia likes him too. If she weren't a Traveller, it might go somewhere, but unlike him, she's much more realistic about the situation. Being raised in her culture means she doesn't have much time for fantasy. She wouldn't even consider a relationship with a settled young man, knowing the opposition they would face from both their families.

I glance at the clock – 4 p.m. I have a few calls to make before I go home, but I want to take the opportunity to check on our newest recruit. I beckon Delia McGovern to follow me into the office.

'So how are things?' I ask, although I know from the point of view of the town that it's all going well. She's done two weeks in the job, and reports from the others are that she's well able to cope; in fact, she always goes over and above the call of duty. So much so that people in the town are beginning to compliment her. Father Doyle told me the other day that she makes it her business to be outside Mass every morning to stop traffic to allow the older people to cross the road to St Jude's Retirement Home.

And she's fearless too. Last week, two girls were being jeered at by a bunch of men as they came out of the Chinese takeaway, and she went right over to the four or five big builder types and gave them chapter and verse of the law on the Non-Fatal Offences Against the Person Act of 1997. They were inclined to be a bit sneery at first, but she soon had them behaving themselves once they realised she would happily arrest them for harassment.

And only yesterday, she was called with Darren to a domestic dispute, where a teenage son was high as a kite and wrecking his mother's house. In Darren's report, which I read this morning, Delia shines bright as the heroine of the piece. By the time they left, she had the boy securely in a bedroom upstairs, sleeping it off, and a cup of tea made and the place put back together for the poor woman, while Darren reassured the mother that they were on hand if she ever needed them.

Some of her methods are a little unorthodox, like she locked the young fella into his bedroom and gave the key to his mother, but at least he couldn't do any more harm. The mother begged them not to arrest him; he's on probation for brawling, so if he was arrested, he'd be automatically taken into custody. So Delia thought on her feet. Lots of this job is just that.

'Great, Sergeant, thanks. I'm loving being a real guard, not just Reserve,' Delia answers, beaming, and I can tell she means it, that she's delighted to be here. Her uniform is pristine, and her very long blond hair has been trimmed a couple of inches and is tied back in a sober ponytail. She's also much more open and friendly than she used to be when she first arrived as a volunteer Garda Reserve officer. Back then there was an aggressive cut to her jaw brought about by the years of discrimination, real and imagined, that she had endured as a member of the Travelling community. Now she seems more secure in herself.

'Good. Glad to hear it. Take a seat, why don't you?' I'm her superior officer and there are very clear lines of command within the force, but that said, she and I have shared a lot, so I don't like to leave her standing. 'I'm hearing great things about you from the community, so keep it up. I know you're sick of me saying it, but this job isn't about control or enforcing the law inasmuch as it's about relationships and bringing the community along with you. If you build up relationships with people, then it's easier to deal with them when they need you or are in trouble.'

I take personal pride in Delia, and I really want her to succeed. She is the first member of her extended family and one of only a handful of women from the Travelling community to ever join the force. It was her granny, Dacie McGovern, who asked me if Delia could join the Gardaí Reserve, and it's just as well she did, because Delia hadn't been in the Reserve for very long before she saved my life that time I got shot trying to stop the gang of sex traffickers who kidnapped Natasha McGovern.

'How's Natasha doing?' I ask now.

'She's grand. Expecting her first for Christmas, so...' She shrugs. Delia's cousin, Natasha, was with poor Blades Carmody when he was killed. She'd been seeing him behind her parents' back, while all the time she was engaged to a Traveller boy from Longford called Joseph Ward. I knew it had been touch-and-go for a while if the Ward family would have her, as the Blades thing was so public, but Joseph was mad about her, it would seem, and they married last year.

'Good, I hope she's happy.' I genuinely mean it. Natasha is a nice girl, full of life and not beyond giving a bit of guff to the guards now and again when she was younger, but basically decent. She'd had a horrible ordeal.

'Joseph is weak for her, and he bought a brand-new caravan for them, flat-screen telly and en suite and the works, and when he found out the baby was on the way, he bought her an enormous diamond. He went to Antwerp to find it, I think.' Delia sounds impressed but not envious. She seems in no rush at all to be married herself. Most Traveller girls marry young and have lots of children, and I know Delia's failure to comply with that norm is a source of constant consternation to her family.

Still, Delia is her father's pet, and it was his adored mother's wish that her granddaughter be allowed to choose her own career. It was such an enormous leap for them to allow her into the actual guards, but they did it. I've backed her every step of the way, but in truth she did it all herself, first convincing her family to allow it, then studying hard, putting up with the discrimination I know she faced at the Garda College in Templemore and graduating as a fully qualified member of the force.

She was so proud of herself for graduating that she invited me and Kieran to her passing-out ceremony along with her parents. Kieran was a bit allergic to going, but I told him he had to. The truth is, Kieran, like most people in Ireland, would be appalled to be considered racist, and he would never say or even think anything bad about someone based on their nationality or skin colour, but when it comes to the Travellers, he is just that.

He'd say, 'But that's different. They deserve the reputation they have – they bring it on themselves.' And to a certain extent I have to agree, some of them do. There are far more Travellers in prison than there should be and there is a higher instance of violence than in the general population, but how much of that is because they are born disadvantaged? Their life expectancy is fifteen years less than settled people, and their access to education, healthcare and so many things we take for granted is a struggle for them. It's not all the settled community's fault, of course not, but there are issues there, and until they're addressed, this situation won't change. Constant blaming and whataboutism isn't helping. It's complicated. I don't have all the answers, neither do the Travellers actually, but we all have to keep trying. We can't live at such loggerheads forever.

Anyway, Delia invited us to her graduation, and we went. The end. God knows I've gone to enough tortuous social events in the Munroe family, so he owed me. Given a choice between hanging out with my monster-in-law, Nora, or a bunch of Travellers, it's no contest. At least the Travellers will give you a cup of tea without looking you up and down, every pore of their body exuding disapproval.

The day at the college was lovely actually, and seeing the new recruits standing to attention before the Irish flag, hearing the Garda band play the national anthem, well, it's special, you know?

I don't get nationalism usually, not really. I mean, it makes no sense. You happen to be born on that rock and I happen to be born on this one, and somehow then we must feel rivalry, or inferiority or superiority or whatever? Rubbish. But still that combination of flag, anthem and uniforms is moving.

'I know you've been mostly in the station and around the town these last two weeks,' I say, 'so next week I'll assign you to the patrol car and you can do a bit of road traffic work and that sort of thing. Is that all right?'

She nods enthusiastically.

'So Michael and Nicola here, and you and Darren in the car.'

A flash of something crosses her face. I hate sounding like a Reverend Mother, but I feel I kind of have to say something, if only to let her know that I know. To her I must seem about 900 years old, and to be honest, some days I feel it, but I haven't forgotten completely what it is to be young.

'Look, Delia, I know Darren...'

She colours, and I can sense she is squirming.

'I know he asked you to his brother's wedding.'

'Sergeant, there's nothing going on.' She is anxious to point it out to me. 'There's nothing that would get in the way of my duties.'

'I know that.' I smile. 'And if there was something "going on", I don't care. So long as you both do your jobs and keep your personal life outside, it's nothing to do with me.'

'But there really is nothing. He's a lovely lad, and I'm fond of him, and if things were different...'

'I know.' I can see she's struggling with it, and this was always going to be the way. One foot in either camp is a hard place to be. Anyway, that's not my business, so I move on to the main reason I want to talk to her. Her father will tell her about St Colm's and the council tonight, and I don't want it to look to him like her new colleagues have kept her in the dark, reluctant to tell her the truth because of who she is, a Traveller.

So I tell her all about the threat to her family's site, and explain that I've already spoken to Jerome, while adding the caveat that this is not Garda business and she needs to be discreet.

'They wouldn't even try this if my nana was still alive,' she says, her voice infused with grief and bitterness. I suspect she might be right. Dacie McGovern was a formidable matriarch, and nobody ever took her on, not inside nor outside her family. I am desperately hoping that Jerome can step up and exert the same level of command, but Dacie's tiny shoes will be hard to fill.

'You might be right,' I say sadly. 'But your father has great strength of character as well –'

'So we'll be turfed out then? Where will they put us?' Just like her father, she clearly doesn't think that she and her family stand a chance against the authorities and public opinion.

'Not necessarily, but –'

'They will.' Delia is certain. 'That new inspector was there a few weeks ago, giving out about the ponies on the side of the road. Sure they're only grazing and they're tied up, but he was saying that the location of our place wasn't safe with the bypass or something. He's had complaints apparently. It's been fine for years, but my father thought he was driving at moving us on. So the ponies were just the excuse they needed.'

'I told Jerome you should get a lawyer to make your case to the council, and I gave him a name.'

Delia laughs, but there is no humour in it. 'You think the county council would listen to us or any lawyer who worked for us? Ah, Sergeant, you know as well as I do, they would do no such thing.' She is getting upset now. 'No, they'll move us out beside the Carmodys, just the way people want us, hidden away where they can pretend we don't exist.' Her voice cracks, and I know how hard it is for her to get emotional like this. 'Where we are, we can walk into town, but out there, apart from the fact that we can't live alongside the Carmodys – they're trouble, you know they are – how would the older people get to Mass or the kids get to school?'

'I wish I had some answers for you, Delia, and I give you a guarantee that if I'm asked, I will support the McGoverns staying exactly where they are, but the council won't consult us. You know there will be a task force set up and the council will do a feasibility study –'

'Where they know the answer they want, and they'll fix the data to suit it. And then the town will fundraise so St Colm's can buy our land.'

'You don't know that, Delia.'

'With all due respect, Sergeant, I actually do. I'm not saying this to make you feel sorry for me, but last week Darren and I went into Teresa's Bakery, and a woman muttered to the one working there, "A knacker in a uniform is still a knacker." Not everyone in the town is like that, I know, but enough people think like that to be happy to see us go.' She breathes deeply and stands up. 'But thanks for letting me know. I appreciate it. And I'm sure my father appreciates it too.'

I nod slowly. She's right, of course, about the obstacles her family are facing, but it's so sad that they feel there's no point in fighting. Still, I suppose it's up to them.

* * *

DARREN ARRIVES BACK into work a couple of days later, looking somewhat the worse for wear, like he's played two hurling finals back to back. He's supposed to be manning the public desk, which I'm currently working myself because everyone else is out on a call, but first he goes straight to the water cooler.

'So how was your brother's wedding? Did it go well?' I grin, leaning my forearms on the desk.

He nods as he gulps down a plastic cup of water. 'It did,' he says, pouring himself another one. 'Too well. They tried to get married about three times but the pandemic restrictions stopped them, so I think they were so glad just to get it done.'

'Is he the eldest, the first to get married?'

'Yeah, my other brother, Barry, is going with a girl from Maynooth, and my sister, Aine, is engaged to a fella from Cork. They think there's no hope for me at all.'

'Is there nobody that catches your eye? A grand lad like you must have them queuing up for you?'

He laughs, then looks miserable. 'If they were, it's only pointless. Delia is the one girl I'm interested in, and that's a waste of time.'

I normally don't pry into my colleagues' personal lives, but I get a feeling he wants to talk about this. As he joins me behind the counter, I ask, 'Have you told her how you feel?'

'She says it's no good whatever we feel about each other, that her father and mother won't have it, so that's that.'

'Jerome is very traditional, that's true. You don't think if Delia asked him…'

He shakes his head. 'She's not going to do that. She had such a hard job to convince him to allow her to join the Gardaí, and one of his main objections was that she would become settled and turn her back on her family, her culture. She swore to him that she wouldn't, that it was just a job, so she says it would feel like a betrayal of her word if she asked his permission for us to see each other. I know it sounds like something from the last century, but her identity is important to her, being a Traveller and all it entails. She's broken out a bit with her career, but she doesn't want to hurt him any further, and apparently getting involved with me would do that.'

'Romeo and Juliet so?' I give him a sympathetic smile.

'Except hopefully nobody dies at the end.'

I shrug. 'I suppose blood is thicker than water.'

He turns away from me and brushes the back of his hand across his eyes, and I instantly regret my words and try to soften things. 'Still, faint heart never won fair lady and all that. Remember when you were keeping guard over the Drumlish site when Delia's cousin went missing? I think Jerome really liked you for that, and that must count for something.'

He turns back, looking hopeful. 'Do you really think so?'

Once more I regret my words and backtrack, because false hope is often worse than despair. 'Although even if Jerome would allow it, could you live that life?'

'In a caravan, you mean?'

'Not necessarily. Lots of Travellers live in houses now, even if they don't like it, but just supposing you got married and had kids, could your mother be one granny and Dora McGovern the other? Could you go to Traveller weddings and funerals as Delia's husband? Would you expect her to turn her back on her culture to embrace yours? Or vice versa?'

He looks me in the eye. 'I don't know, Sarge, I honestly don't. I just know that I love her, and I think we could survive.'

I admire his courage, and half of me hopes he'll get what he wants. Yet even if Jerome agrees to let him date his daughter, the odds are stacked so high against the pair of them, the other half of me hopes that he'll fail.

CHAPTER 7

A couple of weeks later, while all is still quiet on the Traveller front apart from a complaint from Olive about Jerome's chickens escaping into the sports fields and disturbing the rarefied atmosphere of St Colm's, I bump into Annette and her new lodger.

I really didn't mean to go into Teresa's Bakery for lunch – I meant to pop into the Samovar for a healthy salad – but the smell of baking drifting up Main Street overcame my feeble resistance. Honestly, it's like she puts some kind of drug in the aromas coming from the shop, that combination of sugar and fat that every single diet guru in the world says is a complete disaster.

Part of the problem is, I'm feeling a tiny bit better about my weight. Kieran and I were watching this programme the night before, a slimming thing, and this emaciated female doctor on it – I swear she looked around eighty – was saying we should only eat green vegetables and no sugars, even fruit, no fat except avocados and olives, and no booze. I started berating myself aloud as she spoke, having succumbed to a millionaire's shortbread and a creamy latte with Mam at lunchtime and then having a glass of Rioja with my dinner.

Kieran looked up from checking the football results on his phone and said, 'So we can all look like a cadaver, is it? The state of her, she looks desperate altogether, not a gorgeous curvy woman like you.' He leaned over and slapped my thigh. OK, not the world's most romantic gesture, but it made me smile, and Kate giggled while Ellie was, yes, you guessed it, 'mortified'.

So Teresa's Bakery, here I come, for coffee and an apple turnover. Might as well be hung for a sheep as a yak. I'll go on a diet next week for sure.

While looking around for a seat – it's packed as usual – I spot Annette deep in conversation with another woman and a teenage boy. She smiles and waves me over, pointing to the empty chair beside her. She and her two friends are at a table for four, so there's a place for me.

I get my coffee and turnover at the counter, then join them. Annette is dressed in her usual eccentric way, a long purple cardigan over a multicoloured dress made of felt and her handmade red leather shoes. Her companion is a little younger, late forties, I would say. She reminds me of Meryl Streep, that same kind of face, square with a very defined bone structure. She has short fair hair with grey running through it and has on no make-up or adornments. She wears a navy polo shirt and jeans. She looks physically strong, but she is slim, and though she is sitting down, I can see she is tall. The young man is short, broad and smiley, with thick dark hair. He looks to be in his late teens, and I can tell he has Down's syndrome.

'Hi, Annette,' I say as I sit down. 'Thanks for the seat. I promise I won't stay long, I've only a few minutes.'

'Martha, this is Mags Munroe, the local sergeant. Mags, this is Martha Turner, my new lodger. And this is her lovely son, Phillip. They've been living in Canada, but now they've come home to Ireland.'

'Hi, Martha. Hi, Phillip.' I smile as I take a sip of my coffee.

'Hello.' Her eyes meet mine for a fraction of a second, and I see it, that subconscious flinch. I know some people feel instantly guilty when they meet a guard – I've been told often enough – but that flinch, I don't know, it's not that common.

'Hi, Mags,' says Phillip. 'Can I ride in your police car?' No flinching there.

'I expect you can, one day,' I say. 'But I haven't got it with me right now, I'm afraid.'

'This is my mam,' he says. 'Mam, Mags is going to give me a ride in her police car.'

Again, that tiny recoil.

Annette hasn't noticed anything amiss. 'I was just telling Martha what a nice place Ballycarrick is to live, peaceful.'

'It's that certainly,' I agree, then take a bite of my turnover. I've already decided to find out a bit more about Martha Turner. So much of my job is this kind of thing, keeping an eye on vulnerable people. Not that Annette would think of herself as vulnerable, but she's a disabled woman living alone in a remote cottage, and I want to make sure she's going to be OK with her new lodger, who doesn't seem to like the police. 'What brings you to Ballycarrick, Martha?'

Martha smiles stiffly. 'We were looking in Galway at first, but it was too busy for Phillip, too many cars and people. He's never liked the city, and I'd promised him trees and cows and chickens if we moved to Ireland.' She touches Phillip's hand tenderly, her eyes full of love. 'Then I saw Annette's advert, and when I rang and told her about Phillip, she didn't mind at all.'

'And why would I? He's a wonderful boy,' says Annette.

Phillip grins at her, his mouth full of sugary doughnut. 'I'm wonderful,' he says.

Both women laugh fondly, and Martha says, 'You are, my love. And everyone in Ballycarrick seems so friendly, and it's beautiful, the castle and the river and the sea so close. I love it here already. And Annette's cottage is so cosy.'

'Well, my place isn't a palace' – Annette beams – 'but Phillip says he doesn't mind the small room.'

'Still, Ballycarrick must make quite a change from Canada,' I say. 'What brought you home in the first place?'

She hesitates. 'I suppose...I'm looking for a sense of community. Somewhere Phillip can safely go around by himself, and people will know him and keep an eye on him. Ireland's great for that, you know? That sense of belonging.'

She sounds genuine about wanting a safe community for Phillip's sake, but I still get the impression she's not telling me the full story. Being a guard gives you a nose for stuff like that; they train us in Templemore College what to look for. Lies are usually simple to spot, as your average person is almost always a terrible liar, but telling half the story is something else. 'Do you have family here in Ireland?' Her accent is definitely Irish but not from around here. A trace of Dublin maybe?

Martha shakes her head. 'My parents died when I was in my late teens, a year apart, and I was an only child, so...' She stops.

'You went to Canada?' I ask.

'Yes.'

'For work?'

She doesn't quite meet my eye. 'Yes. I got odd jobs gardening for people. I've always loved growing things, since I was a child.' She smiles, her handsome face lighting up. 'Like, I was so happy when my parents moved out of Henrietta Street tenements to what they saw as the countryside. They hated it, though it was a darn sight better than the rat-infested damp place they left, living on top of the neighbours, and at least we had a bit of a garden to grow things in.'

I was right, a slight trace of working-class Dublin in her accent, but she is mostly kind of neutral, probably as a result of living abroad and having to make herself understood.

'So it's perfect, Mags. Martha's going to help me put up a poly-tunnel and everything,' says Annette happily. 'She's an expert horticulturist, and she says the soil here is so fertile, you could grow anything you wanted. She's already harvested the early potatoes – Tatiana was delighted with them. And she's planted out the runner beans and peas. It's late for sowing, so we bought local seedlings, and we're even thinking of getting a second polytunnel for salad stuff and extra tomatoes. I think we're going to be able to grow more of everything. We might even do so well, we can set up a proper little business.'

She and Martha smile at each other, and I sense something, I don't know, nice and cosy between them. An understanding. They start discussing plans to expand their empire. There is a small boreen behind Annette's place leading to a few more tiny stone-walled fields that she owns but has never used because they are steep and inaccessible. Martha is advocating for putting the second polytunnel up there.

'What's so good about tunnels?' I ask. The word makes me think of smuggling, although why one would have to smuggle tomatoes…

Martha explains that polytunnels prolong the gardening season, like a greenhouse, only bigger and cheaper. Since everything I have ever tried to grow dies instantly, I'll take her word for it.

'It's still a serious investment,' Annette tells me. 'But the supermarket says it's willing to take everything we can grow. There is a huge demand for local organic vegetables around here apparently.'

I'm not that surprised. There used to be a young couple doing the organic stuff, Poppy and Dean, and they made a good living out of it, but they took off for India just before the pandemic hit and were never heard of again, so Annette and Martha will have the entire market to themselves.

'I want chickens,' says Phillip loudly. 'I like chickens.'

Martha smiles at him. 'Free-range hens and vegetable plots don't really mix, my love. The hens peck up everything.'

'I want chickens! Lots of chickens!' He starts to make incredibly realistic clucking sounds, attracting the delighted attention of several small children in the shop and a few amused looks from the adults.

I have an idea, partly to please Phillip and partly as a way of keeping an eye on his mother. 'Phillip, if your mam brings you to the station, I'll give you a ride in the police car and introduce you to a man who has lots of chickens.'

'Oh no, we couldn't possibly take up your time,' says Martha instantly, but Phillip claps his big hands, showering sugar everywhere.

'Thank you, Mags!' he says, and his mother is forced to relent.

'Well, if the sergeant really doesn't mind…'

'Of course not. Come next week. Monday would be perfect.' I take another bite of my turnover. 'So where were you based in Canada?'

'Oh, here and there. I was moving around, you know yourself.'

She's not giving much away, but I'll get to the bottom of it eventually. 'I'll see you on Monday, young man,' I say to Phillip, wiping my hands on my napkin and getting to my feet. 'Don't forget now.'

'See you on Monday, Mags.' He beams.

I leave his mother and Annette deep in conversation about the best soil for carrots and how to stake beans for maximum return.

I keep thinking about Martha as I walk back to the station. She started when she realised I was a guard, and I wonder why. Yet she seems very sincere when she talks about the importance of community. And she and Annette are getting on great, and it's so useful she's a gardener, so maybe there's nothing to worry about.

On the way, I pass by the butcher's. Bertie Mahony is on the doorstep of his shop, accepting the congratulations of Sister Assumpta on his nomination for the papal medal; she is gushing at such an honour being bestowed on such a worthy head. He has the good grace to look embarrassed as I pass. I try not to smile. Bertie has been on his best behaviour since the nocturnal forest 'incident', so it's forgotten from our perspective, but he knows I know and that rankles with him.

As soon as I'm settled back in my office, Sharon texts.

Tonight's the night. Am I mad?

I grin. We are not eighteen, but sometimes she behaves like we are. I suppose it's going back to the whole dating thing again. She and Trevor have been really getting on well, so much so I've hardly seen her. They went away with Sean last weekend. Camping. Sharon and I went camping once years ago, and my only memory of her is in her wellies and a nightie running down a field after the flysheet because it was her brother's tent and he would slaughter us if he knew we took it. We're neither of us outdoorsy that way. Kieran wanted to go glamping last summer, but myself and the girls put our feet down... Is that the collective term for several people putting their foot down? I suppose so. Anyway, this place was an alpaca farm in Leitrim. I mean, after working all year, he wants me to milk alpacas or something? No way. The girls were equally adamant, so we went to Lanzarote and had a lovely sunny time lying by the pool and reading.

Sharon said Trevor was fabulous with Sean. They built a bridge over a river with sticks and cooked sausages over a fire and everything. I'm delighted for her. Danny Boylan would never do anything like that; he's all about see and be seen. Flash car, flash house, but no substance.

Obviously the relationship wasn't going to go to the 'next level', as the euphemism goes, in a tent with an eight-year-old, so this weekend Sean is with Danny. Sharon is cooking dinner, and Trevor is going to stay over.

I text back. *Well, if you don't kill him with food poisoning first, I think it will be grand.*

Sharon is an atrocious cook. Kieran refuses so much as a cup of tea from her after she baked what were supposed to be bread rolls with cheese inside. She'd cut holes to make smiley faces, but the cheese oozed out of the eyes and mouth and they ended up looking like tortured souls begging for release. Another time she demolished her cooker hood by leaving the pressure cooker on too long; the whole thing exploded, and the lid flew off at warp speed.

She texts back. *How dare you!*

Seriously, what are you cooking?

Sharon has a habit of trying incredibly complicated recipes that even the most experienced chef would approach with caution.

She texts at length. *Sean and I went to Trevor's last Wednesday, and he made this amazing thing with fresh and smoked salmon and vegetables and everything, so I can't just get takeaway. I saw a recipe online for home-made gnocchi with burned butter, trout and walnuts. He's pescatarian. Too hard?*

Toast is too hard for poor old Shar, but I don't say that. *Ask Luigi to make it for you, and put it into your own dishes. A salad and some fresh bread from Teresa's, and you'll have no stress.*

But I want to make something myself! Show him what a wonderful homemaker I am.

OK, cornflakes?

Thanks for the vote of confidence. #somefriend!!!

Look, the main event isn't going to be the grub anyway. He's not going to care what he eats.

I'm sick with nerves. Nobody but Danny in years and years.
Stop. You'll be grand.
OK. Breathe. And it's a definite no on the gnocchi?
Definite no.

It's lovely to see Sharon happy. She had a miserable life with Danny, and though she was heartbroken when he left her, it's the best thing that's ever happened to her. I wish it was she who left him, but she never would. Maybe she'd be there still if he hadn't gone off with Chloe from the chipper. Shar will never see it, but that uppity little madam has done her a favour taking Danny off her hands.

Danny and Chloe are living up in the new estate now and they've had a baby, but I saw him last week in Galway with another woman in a café. Leopards and spots and all of that. Eejit. It's a low bar, but '80s-throwback Trevor is definitely a massive improvement so far, and I'm delighted for her.

CHAPTER 8

*I*t's Saturday morning, and Kate and Ellie are fighting over something. I bury my head in the pillow and hope Kieran is still in the bed beside me and will get up and deal with it. I worked late last night. I had to visit a family whose mother was killed by a drunk driver three years ago. The driver is due out of prison this week and intends on returning to the town. He's entitled to, and he's served his time, but it's going to be hard for them to see him walking down the street. I wasn't technically obliged to pay them a visit, but it was the right thing to do.

Trish Cronin, the woman who was knocked down, used to be very active in the school, the parents' association and all of that. I dread those things so honestly do as little as I'll get away with, but Trish was brilliant. She was forever collecting money for new play equipment and things like that. Her husband, Liam, is raising the two boys on his own now, Caelan and Fiachra, and they're like sad little shadows walking to and from school.

The driver of the car, Mike Cantillon, was forever drinking and driving. I don't know how many times we caught him, but he always wriggled out of a custodial sentence. But not that time. His wife,

Sandra, is almost afraid to show her face, and their son, Kevin, is in Fiachra Cronin's class, the poor lad.

To be honest, if it was me, I'd have moved, but people are strange. Now Sandra Cantillon comes out of the house rarely, shops in Rathdown, two towns away, and has no interaction with anyone in Ballycarrick. Mike's off the road for life, and the bus service here is desperate altogether. I can't force them to move, but it would be best for everyone.

I try to go back to sleep.

'You said I could borrow it!' cries Kate.

'The green one, not that one!' Ellie roars back, then a bang, then a scream, then theatrical crying.

No movement from Kieran's side of the bed. I turn my head hopefully, but he is up and gone already. He's a roofer, and the weather on the west coast of Ireland is not for the faint-hearted. There were ferocious winds last night. Undoubtedly someone rang him to say their roof was a casualty of the storm, so he'll be gone to try to fix it.

The door opens and Kate appears, tear-stained and furious.

'Mam, Ellie is being horrible! I asked her if I could borrow her hoodie last night and she said I could, so I did, and by accident – it wasn't even my fault – but Cormac Murphy had a chocolate milkshake, and Jessie O'Leary did the *casadh* in Irish dancing too hard and spun Kelly Hartigan into Cormac, and the milkshake got all over me, and it's her new pink hoodie, and now she says she's going to kill me stone dead.'

I pat the bed wearily, indicating she should sit.

'I heard her say you could borrow the old green one, not the new pink one, so let's call a spade a shovel, will we, Katie?' I keep my voice low.

'But I...' There's mock innocence and indignation on the face of my eleven-year-old.

'Kate,' I warn. She looks like an innocent little flower, but she's well able for a bit of skulduggery, as well I know. 'You knew Ellie would go mad if she caught you in that one – she only got it last week with her birthday money – so here's what's going to happen.'

'But, Mam –' she protests again.

'Listen,' I interrupt. 'Now, you're going to go upstairs and get the fifty euro Nana Nora gave you for doing all the hoovering and dusting for her station, and you're going to give it to Ellie to buy a new hoodie.'

Kate's face is working furiously now, more tears not far away. It's Nora Munroe's station – that's when the priest says Mass in the house, and one home is picked from a townland to be the host – and the place has to be polished and scrubbed to within an inch of its life. Nora lured Kate in with the promise of money, but she got her pound of flesh. The poor child worked for about ten hours.

'Mam, that's not fair...' She's sobbing in earnest now.

'It *is* fair. Because you took her hoodie without permission and got it all dirty. So you have to replace it. But here's what we'll do. We'll compensate Ellie with the fifty quid, and then we'll give the one with the chocolate milkshake all over it to Granny Marie, and as you know, there isn't a stain on earth that stands a chance against her. She'll have it good as new in no time, and you'll have a lovely new hoodie out of it, so not all bad, right?'

Before Kate has time to agree, Ellie bursts into the room bearing the offending garment. In an effort to hide the evidence, Kate had clearly stuffed it in a ball under the bed, and it has gone hard and crusty and smelly into the bargain.

'Did you see what that little maggot did to my new Adidas hoodie? Don't try to defend her this time, Mam! I'm going to kill her.' Ellie in a rage is a fright to behold.

I throw back the duvet and sit up. 'Kate, do what I said,' I instruct, and I take the dirty one from Ellie.

'You're not letting her get away with this now, are –'

'Ellie, Kate is going to give you the fifty euro she got for cleaning Nana Nora's so you can replace it, but we're going to ask Granny Marie to do a cleaning magic job on this one.' I hold it at arm's length; the smell of sour milk is nauseating. 'And Kate gets to keep it.'

'What? It's mine!' Ellie explodes.

'Yes, but she's going to buy it from you for fifty quid, and you got that in the sale for thirty-five, so you're fifteen euro up. And Kate didn't spend an entire day scrubbing the skirting boards in Nana's house for nothing.'

'But, Mam...' she starts again as Kate appears with her precious fifty-euro note, looking miserable.

'This is the only deal on the table,' I say sternly.

'And if I refuse and batter her instead?' Ellie asks, looking murderously at her little sister.

'Then I'll arrest you for assault and you'll go to a juvenile detention centre, where you will learn only the ways of the criminal. You'll come out, but your associations will lead you directly into law-breaking, and as a result, you will be destined to live your life in and out of the revolving door of crime and incarceration, dying young in a gangland gun battle.'

I wink at Kate, who giggles behind her hand as she hands Ellie the fifty euro. 'I'm sorry, Ellie, I shouldn't have taken it.'

'You shouldn't.' But I hear a softening in her voice. 'But also Deirdre shouldn't have great big lumps of children like Kelly Hartigan being spun around in the *casadh* at Irish dancing, causing them to spin off, doing all kinds of carnage.'

She reaches into her jeans pocket and extracts fifteen euro. 'Dad gave me this for cutting the grass,' she says. 'Don't tell him you know, Mam. He was supposed to do it, but he wanted to watch the match and asked me so...' She shrugs and hands Kate the notes. 'The hoodie is still for sale for thirty-five, so I'll replace it and keep the fifteen-euro change, and Granny Marie will make that one good as new.'

I love my kids. I know everyone does, but mine really are great.

'Thanks, Ellie, and we'll be like twins with the same hoodies.' Kate is thrilled with the outcome.

'You must always check if I'm going to wear it, and if I am, then you can't.' Ellie lays down the law. Fair enough, I suppose.

Kate hides her disappointment well. I remember when they were little and they insisted on being dressed the same. Kate would still love to do it, but Ellie at fourteen has a very sensitive 'morto meter', as Kieran calls it, and would rather eat her own arm than do it now. The list of things that Ellie finds mortifying in our family is growing by the day. Currently it includes our car, his van, him and me, Kate, our house, my taste in music, Kieran's taste in music, words I use and, oh, about a million other things.

* * *

KIERAN RINGS after lunch to say he's on his way home because the winds are getting too strong to be on the roof of the farmer's barn outside of town. I love that about him; he never takes chances with safety. He'd rather lose money than risk himself or his crew being hurt. So many construction industry injuries and even deaths are due to people taking stupid chances and risks to save a few quid.

He then plunges me into gloom by reminding me about his mother's 'rally party' later that afternoon, the family get-together where she's going to make us all watch this American politician's last debate before the special election they're holding in whatever state he's from.

I'd forgotten completely but pretend I've remembered. I don't bother to pretend to be looking forward to it, though; he'd think I'd lost my mind if I did.

'Sure, hooray. I'll start getting the girls ready.'

They're listening to music in the living room. I call to them to get showered and dressed because we're going to Nana and Granda's to watch a rally for an American politician who is rumoured to be somehow distantly related to us all by marriage.

'Nana Nora's obsessed with this fella, Mam,' Ellie says crossly, heading for the stairs. 'Like totally obsessed. It's totally...'

'Mortifying,' I mouth to Kate with a wink.

Kate giggles with her hand pressed over her mouth. Ellie would go mad if she knew we were laughing at her.

Ellie's scowling face appears over the upstairs banister. 'And Uncle Fergus tries to tell her that he hardly knows him and he's only a distant cousin even if they do have the same surname, but she's not having a bar of it and is telling everyone we're related to a very high-ranking politician in America. She's mortifying, that's what she is.' Her face disappears again.

'I know, love, but Nana Nora is very excited about it for some reason,' I call up the stairs after her.

Her bedroom door slams.

'Nana Nora is bonkers, though, Mam,' whispers Kate.

I have to smile. Normally I wouldn't allow the girls to be rude about people, but Kieran's mother is the last word in annoying. They'll be fine up there today because all of the cousins will be there too, so they'll have a great time. 'Tis myself and Kieran who will suffer, listening to her going on and on about this American who wouldn't recognise her in a line-up.

At least this new obsession is giving us a break from Nora's other favourite topic, the dead and almost dead of the parish and environs. Loves a good cancer story, my monster-in-law, especially if the circumstances are tragic and the person is young. Poor Donal Kerrigan, our old postman, died of prostate cancer last week aged eighty-six, but he hardly got a mention in the weekly round-up. However, some poor woman I don't know, who has been diagnosed with motor neurone disease aged thirty-six, got huge airplay. Nora Munroe is the kind of person who sucks the joy from any situation. You know the type. You could be in perfectly good form, life trundling along nicely, and then you meet her and you come away depressed off your head. Nothing has changed in your life, but she just brings you down.

'Go off and get washed and dressed, pet,' I tell Kate.

'Will I wear my blue dress?' she asks, knowing it's not her favourite but Nora bought it for her.

'Wear whatever you like, love.' I wink. 'We won't please Nana Nora either way, so we might as well please ourselves.'

Kate runs to her room to get ready, and I follow her upstairs into my own bedroom to survey my wardrobe.

What will I wear? Kieran says I look lovely in anything, and to be honest, when I get dressed up with make-up and heels, he likes it less than me in jeans and a jumper. But that won't do for my monster-in-law. Orla, Kieran's sister, will no doubt be in a designer outfit, with matching Fergus… As soon as I've had that thought, I realise I'm being catty and regret it. Orla and Fergus are nice, and Kate is best friends with their daughter, Evie.

Catriona, another sister, is also always perfectly coiffed and dressed, but she'll be by herself because her husband, Seamus, is a top cardiologist and never comes to anything. They have an amazing house, but I feel sorry for Catriona really, as she never sees him. Everyone talks about him and how wonderful he is as a doctor. I don't doubt it, but he's an absentee husband and father, that's for sure. Kieran is so hands-on with our girls, always was, and they have a great relationship with him. I'm glad that he's a roofer and not saving lives. I mean, how do you give your fella an earful for not showing up to things if he's curing cancer? Or fixing hearts or whatever. See? You can't. You just have to be saintly and put up with it.

The third sister, Aoife, will be there with her lovely organic husband, Leonard, and they'll be perfect too, in a kind of wholesome way. They are both teachers – he's a principal – and they are so PC, it's a bit intimidating. Everything with them is responsibly sourced and ethically produced. Last Christmas they gave everyone a goat. Well, donated a goat on our behalf to Africa. I've no objection, it's a nice idea, but they looked so pious when they did it, glancing around at the new phones, toys, cosmetics and computer games we had given and received, nearly fainting with horror at their carbon footprint. No better than my own sister Dolores, although to be fair, without the weed.

At least Gearóid will be there; he's my favourite of Kieran's siblings. He has a fabulous job running the Irish language theatre in Galway and is always popping up in the newspaper, pictured with celebrities. I happen to know, because he whispered it to me, that he's in a new relationship with a Spanish flamenco dancer called Enrico, whom he met a few months ago on a skite to Seville, and they've just moved in together.

Nora adores Gearóid, but she doesn't know he is gay. In fact, none of the family do. I only found out by pure accident a couple of years ago, and Gearóid swore me to secrecy because he 'can't be bothered with all the family drama'. And knowing his mother, I can't say I blame him. But I really, really wish he'd tell Kieran. My husband wouldn't give two hoots, and I hate having this secret between us. Gearóid keeps on promising he will, but in his own time. And I suppose it's his right, but still, it's awkward for me when we all meet up.

Kieran and I are the only disappointments to Nora. The ordinary house and ordinary cars – very little to brag about with us. But nonetheless, we will turn up and Nora will give me that withering look up and down that she does.

I give up trying to think what to wear. Nothing will be right for my mother-in-law anyway, especially since as I spend my work life in uniform, wearing flat, kind of ugly Garda-issue shoes, my ability to wear a heel has gone out the window.

I swear Kieran wears his scruffiest jeans and a hoodie that is spattered with paint on purpose, just to wind his mother up. And while I admire that in him, that he doesn't bow down to her, the thing about it is she doesn't blame him for it, she blames me. In Nora Munroe's world, how well-turned-out a husband is, or is not, is due to the calibre of wife he has. Kieran's poor dad, Kevin, looks like a new pin all the time. He reminds me of a child who has been dressed before an event and told to sit on the couch and not move a muscle for fear of getting dirty.

I decide to strike a happy medium and pick out a pair of black jeans with a cream top that, according to my mam, skims the hips and hides a multitude of sins. Mam has a great eye for clothes and knows what women want to achieve.

As I jump in the shower, I hear Kieran come back. He walks into our bathroom, and I turn to face the wall, not because I'm shy in front of him but because I hate the look he gets on his face when he sees the scar from the bullet wound on my chest. It's like it all comes back to him, and I feel so guilty.

'Nice bum,' he says cheekily as he takes his hoodie and T-shirt off to have a shave. He's in great shape because his job is so physical, and I watch him out of the corner of my eye admiringly. At that exact moment, Ellie walks into our room and sees her father stripped to the waist and me naked in the shower, and she screams. Actually screams, like it's the most horrifying thing she's ever had to witness.

'Oh my God! What are you doing?' she demands.

Kieran answers her as he spreads shaving soap over his jaw. 'I'm shaving and your mother is having a shower in *our* bathroom, off *our* bedroom that *you* just marched into unannounced.'

'Urgh…' Ellie manages.

'Maybe learn to knock, Els.' Kieran smiles as he picks up his razor. 'Or you could stumble in on worse, you know.' He chuckles.

Ellie pales, looks horrified, mutters 'gross', shudders and retreats.

'Could you imagine?' I ask, rinsing my hair. 'She'd need therapy.'

'Well, since me holding your hand going down Pearse Street last Saturday was very high on the morto meter, anything more romantic would send her into a right spin altogether.' He laughs as he draws the razor down his face.

'Did you tell your mam we've to leave early?'

'I did.'

'And how did she take it?'

'Like a cut cat, as you predicted. She doesn't like us, but she doesn't want us to leave either. She's a piece of work, my mother, no doubt about it. I told her we had to collect Marie from a dance because she'll be legless on the sherry.'

'What? Please say you didn't!' But he's a messer, and I wouldn't put it past him. My poor mother has never been good enough for the mighty Nora Munroe with her detached house and double garage, so the idea of my abstemious mother falling around drunk at a dance would be something the old wagon would relish.

He finishes shaving and then turns and goes to our bedroom door, locking it from the inside. Then he strips off and gets into the shower with me.

'We'll be late,' I protest as he kisses my neck, but I don't stop him. Nora can wait.

CHAPTER 9

*A*s we turn in to Nora's driveway, I see to my astonishment the Stars and Stripes fluttering from a flagpole that is stuck into the front lawn. It would look nice, patriotic even, in Wisconsin or Maine, but it's just confusing in Ballycarrick. I know it's something people do, having flags in their gardens in America, but it's not done here. Probably something to do with nationalism and wars and death being so recent. And even over there I've only ever seen American flags, but perhaps they fly other ones too, who knows, but I can imagine the neighbours in some American town would be just as bewildered if someone filled their garden with Irish tricolours and harps and what have you. It's like she's trying to be something she's not.

Ellie groans almost as loudly as when she caught me and Kieran in the bathroom an hour ago, and Kate giggles.

Kieran sighs behind the wheel. 'Honest to God, Mags, I think she's losing it. I mean, I know she's a snob, and she's always crowing about the girls and Gearóid, but this takes the biscuit.'

'Can't you talk to her about it, Kieran? I mean, it's...' I struggle for the right word.

'Mortifying!' snaps Ellie, and for once I am inclined to agree.

'Orla and Catriona have tried talking to her about it already, Mags, and Fergus is bewildered. He only mentioned it in passing one day that some distant cousin of his father's was running. He'd no idea she'd get her knickers in a twist like this.'

'Surely Gearóid can talk sense to her?' Nora listens to her youngest son more than she does the others; he's her favourite.

'Maybe he can. He's not been home in a while, so I'll ask him and we'll see.' He parks next to the gently billowing Star-Spangled Banner. All his sisters' expensive cars are lined up in front of us, along with Gearóid's BMW. The front door to the house is wide open, and Nora is standing there waiting for us, wearing a scarf of red, white and blue.

Behind me, Kate dissolves into further giggles while Ellie moans into her hands.

'Girls, behave,' I say sternly. 'Get out, give Nanny Nora a kiss, then run off and find your cousins. And if you can't help laughing, tell her it's because Dad was telling you a funny story on the way here.'

They do as they're told, bless them, then get away as fast as possible, running off around the corner of the house to where they can hear their cousins' voices.

Kieran and I follow more sedately. As usual, Nora studies our clothes with a frown, but this time it's because, as she complains to Kieran, 'You're as bad as your sisters. Don't you children ever listen to anything I say? I wanted everyone to wear something red, white and blue, just for fun of course, but the only one who's done anything about it is Gearóid.'

'Sorry, Mam.' He kisses her briefly on the cheek. 'You look great in that scarf.'

'Anyway, you're late. I'm after figuring how to project the thing from Youtube to the telly, it took about four hours but I've mastered it. It's a town hall format, and Max is super at those. The pundits are predicting a shellacking for both the Democrat and the RINO...'

'There's a rhino?' I'm genuinely confused. I'm assuming Max is the lad we're all supposed to be shouting for. Himself and Nora are on first-name terms already.

She throws me a look of contempt. 'Republican in name only.' Am I imagining it, or is there a faint American accent?

In the drawing room, we find Orla and Aoife with husbands Fergus and Leonard, Catriona, predictably without her saviour husband, and Gearóid. Kieran's dad, Kevin, is looking very spruce in a red, white and blue tie. Gearóid is sparkling away in a crimson, silver and azure diamanté shirt, presumably stolen off his new live-in lover, the dancing Enrico. There is a big spread on the table, but instead of the usual bottle of Chardonnay and ham and cheese sandwiches, there are cans of American Budweiser, a bottle of Jim Beam, some Coke and a tray of hot dogs.

Conforming to the stereotype, Nora. She probably saw an American barbeque on the telly and decided this is what Americans eat. When Kieran and I visited the States a few years ago and met up with some of his old friends from his days there it was all craft beer from microbreweries, hors d'oeuvres and cocktails but she wouldn't want to hear that. I suppose American's have plenty of stereotypes about us too, it's harmless.

I start saying hello to everyone, but Nora shushes me fiercely as she turns up the television. Gearóid pats the sofa for me to join him, and Kieran plonks down beside Catriona. I'm not particularly up with American politics, but I listen and it's interesting. There's an audience asking questions, and the three candidates on the stage are answering them in turn. A lot of the questions are about taxation and legislation around job creation, and then it turns to gay marriage. Max McMahon is very non-committal on the subject. He's good, I have to give him that, keeping the middle ground, offending nobody, but I wonder what he stands for.

Nora nods. 'Max can't say it of course, but it's all gone too far in my opinion. I mean, let the gays do what they want, I suppose, but why do they need to be going on and on about it?'

I feel Gearóid tense beside me and glance at his face. Usually he ignores any homophobic nonsense from his mother, but right now he's frowning angrily. I wonder if he is serious about Enrico, and whether they've actually been thinking about marriage.

The next member of the audience asks about gay men adopting, and Max says there are a number of things to consider on that topic, that he's very glad the voter asked him that, but that the public should rest assured that it is something that deserves a full and frank discussion where all sides of the debate are heard and respected. Expert obfuscation from Max, but he's not unique in that, our own crowd above in Dublin do exactly the same.

'Poor children, having two mammies or two daddies. It's cruel,' says Nora, sipping her Jim Beam and Coke.

Which is when finally, after all these years avoiding drama and refusing even to tell Kieran, Gearóid snaps. 'Mam, look at me.'

Mildly surprised, she does.

'Mam, look at what I'm wearing.'

She smiles fondly. 'Red, white and blue, just as I asked...'

'Mam, I'm wearing a diamanté shirt.'

She's clearly puzzled, but his siblings are turning in their seats to study him closely. You can hear the pennies dropping everywhere, *ping, ping, ping.*

'Mam, I'm gay.'

She is still looking puzzled. Kieran stands up. Catriona grabs Aoife's hand. Both Leonard and Fergus take a big swallow of their Jim Beams and ginger ale. Orla laughs and says, 'Well, well, that explains it.'

Gearóid stands up, straightening his sparkling shirt and looking mainly at Kieran, who has remained silent. 'I'm sorry. I don't know what just came over me, to tell everyone like this. I wasn't even going to say it ever. I really don't want any big family hoo-ha about it, it just came out. And now I would like you all to forget about it and go back to thinking of me as your slightly flamboyant brother Gearóid, no drama...'

Which is when Nora comes over all dramatic. 'You're not a homosexual! You can't be!' She bursts into stormy tears, rocking backwards and forwards in her chair, clutching her heart. 'You can't be! You can't do this to me! I'm your mother. You're not like that...'

Everyone else is rigid with embarrassment, except Kieran, who snaps at her. 'Mam, stop carrying on like a lunatic. Dad, do something. Take Mam outside and calm her down.'

Kevin for once rises to the occasion. He ushers the weeping Nora from the room, and as he goes, he gives Gearóid a sly pat on the arm and a wink. 'Knew it all along, Son,' he hisses out of the corner of his mouth. 'You were always very neat.'

'Thanks, Dad,' says Gearóid uncertainly. Then, when they've gone, he walks over to embrace Kieran. 'Thanks, big brother.'

To my surprise, Kieran doesn't hug him back. Instead, he asks Gearóid coldly, 'Why didn't you tell me before?'

Gearóid looks guilty. 'It's just like I said, I didn't want any drama...'

'You thought if you told me, I'd make a big drama out of it?'

'No! Look, Kieran, it's not just you. I haven't told anyone in the family till now. You know yourself, a secret in Ballycarrick is something you tell one person at a time –'

'So you thought I couldn't keep a secret?'

'He was going to tell you,' I blurt out, because I can't stand this. 'He wanted to. He just hadn't got around to it yet.'

Kieran turns to me, stony-faced. 'You knew, Mags? And you didn't tell me?'

Gearóid jumps to my defence. 'Mags only found out by accident, and I asked her to keep it under her Garda hat.'

Kieran's mouth sets in a hard line. 'You trusted Mags to keep your secret, but you didn't trust me? Thanks, little brother. And thanks, my darling wife.'

I'd thought I'd been acting for the best, although I don't blame Kieran for being hurt. I found out about Gearóid when a lover of his got beaten up by homophobes two years ago. I happened to be in court at the time, and he was there as a witness. After that, I'd urged him to tell Kieran. I knew my husband would be fine. He'd support him and love him, and it wouldn't have turned a hair on him. Gearóid always said he would one day, so I'd thought it was the right thing to wait until that happened.

It's obvious my husband doesn't see it that way, though.

* * *

AFTER GEARÓID'S startling exit from the closet, the rest of the afternoon wraps up pretty quickly. Leonard turns off the TV, and we all raise a Budweiser or Jim Beam and toast Gearóid while he stands there rolling his eyes and eating a hot dog. He then collects his coat and leaves.

After he's gone, the general consensus among the sisters becomes that they've known all along, although I'm pretty sure that is twenty-twenty hindsight because they've spent their adult lives teasing him about one woman or another that he's been seen partying with in the celebrity pages.

Kieran and I drive home in silence, with the girls chatting happily behind us. In the house, I peel and boil potatoes and slap on steak and onions, because somehow we'd not got around to eating any of the hot dogs at Nora's.

The girls run off to amuse themselves upstairs, but Kieran remains in the kitchen, standing at the table. I know he wants to say something and is looking for the right words. I keep frying the steak.

'Why didn't you tell me, Mags?' he says at last. His voice is quiet and shaky.

I drop the spatula and turn to face him.

He looks pale and sad. 'I can't believe he told you and he didn't tell me. I thought he trusted me. He's my brother. Did he think I'd disapprove or something? Did *you*? I can't believe you would but...'

I hate to see such deep hurt in his eyes. 'Of course I didn't think that, love, neither did Gearóid. And he didn't *tell* me, I just found out by accident. A fella he was with before was assaulted a few years ago, and I happened to be in court the day it came up and so I saw them. He asked me not to say anything, and I told him then, and loads of times since, that he should tell you, but he didn't want his life being discussed back here.'

'And he thought I'd go spreading it around Ballycarrick.' Kieran's voice is suffused with flat disappointment.

'No, he didn't. I think he just got away from here, lived his life for years in Sydney and then came back to Galway. He found he loved the scene in the city, but the parish pump of Ballycarrick was too much for him. I don't think he wanted to cut you out or didn't trust you. It was just if he told you, he'd feel he'd have to tell your sisters, and then it was only a matter of time...'

'And you didn't think you should tell me either?'

I feel for him, I really do. He loves his brother and feels betrayed.

'Kieran, if I bumped into them in the street, or in a pub, I would probably have told you, but I didn't. It was in court, and so it was in the line of duty, which you know I can't talk about.'

'Ah, Mags, will you stop? You weren't even involved in the case. You just happened to be there.'

'All the same, I saw him in my capacity as a guard, and so I couldn't –'

'You could have and you didn't. And to hell with you being a guard. I don't like it, you being a guard – I don't want it.'

I'm seriously unsettled. I don't think I've ever heard him sound this angry. And why is all this about Gearóid spilling over into resentment about me being a guard? Unable to answer him, I get a bag of frozen peas out of the freezer and put water on to boil.

'Am I not who I thought I was, Mags?' he carries on furiously. 'I ring you and you tell me you're going to be at your desk all day, but you're lying to humour me, I can tell. I'm not stupid.'

'I'm sorry. I just don't want you to worry about me.'

'So you think I'll make a big thing out of it if you tell me the truth? And is that what Gearóid thinks too? I'm a pathetic brother, I'm a weak husband, I'm an emotional flake who can't be told hard truths in case I overact and make everyone's life difficult, is that it?'

I shake my head. 'Kieran, stop. You're an amazing man, everyone relies on you, me and the girls, all your family, the lads you work with. You take care of anyone...'

It's like he can't hear me. He slumps into a chair at the table, defeated. 'You're both right, you know. I thought I was strong, but I can't cope any more. I just can't cope.'

I look at him. Then I turn the dinner right down and step out into the hall to check the sounds from upstairs, making sure the girls are happily engaged and won't come bursting in on us. Then I close the kitchen door and go back to stand beside him.

'Of course you can cope,' I say. 'It's just a bit of a shock for you, Gearóid coming out.'

'That's not what I can't cope with, Mags, for God's sake,' he says in a muffled voice, burying his face in his hands. 'Why do you think I'd not be able to cope with that? No, it's...' He stops, breathing hard.

I pull up a chair and sit beside him, take his hands in mine and gently pull him around to face me. He looks up and I see it. His eyes are red-rimmed and irritated, as if he's been crying. I've seen him cry twice in all the years, and both times involved a football. I'm worried now. If it's not about Gearóid, what is this about? Is he sick? Has he done something illegal? Is he having an affair? I dismiss each idea out of hand. But something is definitely very wrong.

'What's the thing you can't cope with, love?' I ask, dreading his answer.

He shakes his head and gazes towards the kitchen window, where darkness is gathering.

'Kieran, what is it, love? Whatever it is, we'll face it together and it will be OK.'

He gives a deep, shuddering sigh. 'I...I know I said it was all right, I could cope, after the shooting. But, Mags, I can't. Every time you go out that door to work until you come home, I'm worried.'

'I know, and so is Mam, but –'

'No, you don't know. I'm a lot more than worried. If you don't answer my call, I just see you lying somewhere in a pool of blood, and I actually have a kind of a panic attack or something, I don't know. It sounds stupid, I know, but I find it hard to breathe. And I'm so furious, Mags, I feel almost out of control. I'm not just worried about you – it started out as that, but it turns into fury – I'm so angry at you for doing what you do. And I know it's not really dangerous, and why shouldn't you do it if it's what you want, but I...I just keep thinking what if that bullet had been an inch higher, to the left. You'd be dead

73

and me and the girls would be alone and...' His voice breaks into a sob then, and I don't know what to do.

I reach over and hold my lovely, hurting husband as he cries.

CHAPTER 10

On Monday morning I'm wading through the latest Department of Justice circular on the subject of the provision of interpreters for suspects' interviews in rural communities – riveting stuff, let me tell you – when the internal line buzzes. It's Delia on the public desk telling me there is a young man and his mother here to see me.

Delighted to have an excuse to get away from boring office stuff, I slam the file closed and head for the public desk.

'I've come to see the chickens,' bellows Phillip as soon as I appear behind the counter.

'If it's not too much trouble to the gentleman who owns them...' says Martha a bit stiffly. She's dressed in grass-stained jeans but a clean and ironed white blouse, and her fair grey-streaked hair is freshly washed.

Delia smiles at her. I've given her the heads up about Phillip, and she's already cleared it with Jerome. 'No trouble. The gentleman in question is expecting you. In fact, if you want me to take them up there, Mags?'

'No, I'll do it,' I say. 'I need a breath of fresh air, and I want to pop into Mam on the way back.' Both these things are true, but the real

reason I want to do this myself is that I haven't told Martha we are
going to a halting site and I don't want her saying anything in front of
Delia that might come over as offensive. 'Now, Phillip, would you like
a ride in the Garda car?'

'Yes, I would!' His grin practically splits his face in two.

I really shouldn't do this, but I let Phillip sit up front, and we take
the long way round on the back lanes behind St Colm's so he can have
a go at working the siren and flashing the lights. He would clearly love
to keep turning the siren on and off all day, yet he doesn't complain
when I say we have to stop. He really is a nice, well-behaved kid,
much better than a lot of the teenagers I come across in my line of
work.

Martha is sitting in the back, looking tense. I manage to catch her
eye in the rear-view mirror, and say, 'He's a credit to you.' I'm pleased
to see her relax and soften, just like Delia's mother softened when I
praised Delia.

She tenses up again when we stop outside the halting site. 'What
are we doing here?'

I take my seatbelt off and turn in my seat to look at her, holding
her gaze. 'You won't find a better small holding in Galway than
Jerome McGovern's,' I say firmly. 'Phillip will love it here.'

'But...aren't they...?'

'The McGoverns are a Travelling family, yes. But they've been
welcome in Ballycarrick for the past 100 years. That young guard you
were talking to in the station? That's Jerome's daughter, so you can
see there's nothing to be worried about.'

She relaxes a bit, and we all get out of the car. I do my usual thing
of removing my hat and pulling on a hoodie over my blue Garda shirt,
and we head into the site. Jerome waves to us from a distance, and
Phillip waves back and trots off towards the big man, trailed by a
crowd of interested kids.

'So, Phillip,' Jerome is saying as Martha and I catch up to them.
'What do you want to see first? The hens, the ponies or the ducks? We
have dogs as well, and one of them has puppies...'

Half an hour later, Phillip is in his element. He has fed the chickens and ducks, he's played with the puppies, and now he's riding one of the ponies, bareback like the Travellers do. One of the McGovern girls, fourteen-year-old Olivia, is leading the pony around by its halter, and several mothers have come to stand in the doors of the caravans, waving every time Phillip is led by. He waves back, slightly wobbly on the horse, but he's got a small boy holding him by the ankle on each side. It's lovely to see him accepted into the McGovern family without question or teasing.

It's not just Phillip either. It's not long before Jerome and Martha are deep in conversation about how to grow onions next to carrots because that gets rid of carrot fly, and setting beer traps for slugs, which apparently have a taste for alcohol. All her anxiety about Travellers seems to be dissolving in the face of the children's friendliness and Jerome's expert knowledge.

I'm not a gardener – in fact, that's an understatement; I'm actually one of those rare beings who can kill a Busy Lizzie – so I slip away to see Delia's mother for a cup of tea. Before I know it, it's nearly lunchtime, and I remember I've told Mam I'll pop into her with a couple of rolls from Teresa's. Apparently there's something she wants to tell me, and it can't wait till this evening.

'We're ready to go when you are, Mags,' says Martha as I join her and Jerome.

I smile apologetically. 'Sorry to rush. I promise we can do this again soon. Phillip, are you ready to go?'

'We don't want him to go!' There's a chorus of protest from the children, and Phillip looks both disappointed and hopeful.

'Ah, why don't you let him stay for a couple of hours?' suggests Jerome gently.

'He'll only be a bother to you…' says Martha.

'Ah, not at all. He can help me grub up some potatoes and carrots for the stew, and we'll feed him and keep an eye on him – we won't let him wander off by himself. One of the lads can drive him home later, or Olivia can walk him back. You're living up at Annette's place, aren't you?'

'Well, if you're sure…' Martha is pink with pleasure. Despite my doubts, I feel genuinely happy for her. She seems slightly lost to me, but she's come home to Ireland in search of a close community that will accept Phillip for who he is, and I hope she's pleased with what she's found so far.

* * *

IT'S ONLY two minutes from the halting site to Ballycarrick by the main road. I drop Martha to the station car park where she's left her battered old Opel Corsa, check in on Delia and let her know how well everything went with Phillip, then hurry on down the town to see Mam, picking up two chicken salad rolls from Teresa's Bakery on the way.

I realise I'm vaguely worried that Mam has something to tell me that 'can't wait', but to my relief, I find her beaming.

'Well, what's the story that can't wait? What has you so chirpy?' I ask as I unwrap the rolls and she makes a pot of coffee.

'Nothing.' She grins.

'Ah, don't go all coy on me now. Spit it out. You're going on *Dancing with the Stars?*'

She laughs. 'If I was doing that, you'd have found a note on the door, "Gone indefinitely".'

'OK, don't tell me. I'm a cop, I can work this out. Dolores has had to cancel her trip?'

'Mags Munroe! Don't you be so mean about your sister.'

I laugh. 'I know, I know, we love her and all of that, but you'd want to be in the whole of your health for her and her vegan tofu.'

'I don't know what you're complaining about.' Mam giggles. 'She's the perfect daughter. She's bringing me some devil's claw tea to help with my arthritis in my hands, and it will definitely work because she consulted an aura cleanser about it.'

'Ah, well, you wouldn't want to argue with an aura cleanser, Mam.' I wink and take a bite of my chicken salad roll. 'No good could come of that. Now come on, what is it you wanted to say to me?'

She adds milk to our coffees. Her cheekbones have a high spot of colour. 'I wanted to say, will you tell Ellie and Kate I won't be at home on Sunday for *Strictly*, but that I'll record it and we can watch it on Monday? And that they are not to watch it ahead of me because I'm hoping Emma stays in, but her foxtrot was a bit ropey last week so I don't know?'

I try to remember the detail of that message because the girls will want it word for word. Each week people are voted off the show to the howls of delight or dismay from my mother and daughters.

'I'll tell them. But you haven't dragged me down here just for that, have you? Come on, where are you going?'

'Ballinasloe.' For some reason, she looks embarrassed.

I'm puzzled. 'You don't usually go there, do you? Is Peggy going?'

The spot of colour on her cheeks spreads, and I wait, chewing my sandwich.

'I'm going with someone else.'

'Who?' But I think I know the answer, and a big grin spreads across my face. Hallelujah. Joe Dillon has finally made his move.

'It's a man I met at a dance in Killarney a few weeks ago,' says Mam. 'Remember I went down with the active retirement gang, though I'm not retired. But they're wild – you could only do a night a year with them. Nellie Keane got cautioned by a young guard for taking his hat off him and dancing on the table when the guards were called by the barman to get them out. But anyway...'

'What do you mean, "a man"?' I ask anxiously. This is all very disconcerting, not at all what I was expecting to hear. 'Who is this man? Why didn't you tell me about him before?'

She raises her eyebrows at my tone. 'There's nothing to say. I met him, we had a chat, he asked for my number, and he's been ringing. And one time he came up to Galway for work and we met for lunch.'

'Is he some sort of ancient twinkletoes? Should he be on his knees praying for a happy death?' Most of the men at her dancing evenings are much older than her, and the ones who aren't are often best avoided as gold-diggers.

'He's sixty-five.' She reddens even more.

'Seriously, a toy boy?' Mam is seventy although she looks way younger.

'Ah, Mags, will you stop,' she says in exasperation. 'I won't say another word if you don't cop on.'

'OK, OK!' I raise my hands in surrender. 'But I have to say, it's like some kind of weird mismatched love boat around here these days. Despite all Delia's protestations, I'm pretty sure I nearly walked in on her and Darren kissing the other day – they jumped apart very suspiciously. And Sharon's mad about that '80s mullet-man Trevor Lynch – Kieran and I have a double date with them next Sunday.'

'Do you want to hear about *my* date or not?'

'Sorry, yes. Of course I do, tell me.'

'Then stop changing the subject.'

'OK.' I sip my coffee and adopt my professional 'listening' expression. I do want to listen, and I've always wanted my mam to find happiness. It's just that it feels a bit odd to hear Mam talking about a man other than Joe, which is maybe why I want to change the conversation to something different.

'Don't laugh or react or say anything that will make me want to clout you.'

'Not a word.'

'Well, his name is Teo Valdez and he's from the Philippines. He's a consultant at the Bons in Limerick and sometimes in Galway. He's a great dancer. He came over here to work in 2001 with his wife, who was a nurse, and she passed away five years ago. He has one son back in Manila, and he decided to try dancing rather than just work and sleep. And so that's it.' It's clear she's had this little speech rehearsed in her mind. She adds, 'I haven't got a photo, but you can Google him if you like.'

I pull out my phone, and sure enough, there he is.

'Oh...' This is very disappointing – for Joe anyway. Teo has a full head of silvery-black hair, and a silver moustache and goatee. His eyes are warm and smiling, with crow's feet deeply etched. 'He's...umm...'

'He's very handsome, isn't he?'

'Yes.' Poor Joe.

'And he's very nice.'

'That's great.'

'And a famous oncologist.'

I sigh. Game over for Joe Dillon. 'When can we meet him?'

'How does 2026 sound?' She winks. 'I won't be bringing him to Ballycarrick, if that's what you're asking. That's the last thing I need at this stage, to have the whole town looking at him.'

Maybe she's not that serious about him?

'I really like him, Mags.'

OK. I take a deep breath. 'So have you told Joe?'

A shadow crosses my mother's face, and for a moment she looks annoyed. 'And why should I tell Joe Dillon?' she snaps.

I'm surprised. 'Because...well, he's your friend, Mam.'

'So? I haven't told Peggy yet, and she's my friend.'

'But Joe, he's...'

'What?' She's exasperated now.

'He's...'

'Mags. Joe is my once-a-week lunchtime friend who has no interest in me that way, and anyway, he wouldn't dance if there were wolves after him.'

I'm not sure about the no interest, though I can see why she's come to that conclusion. She's probably right about the dancing, though.

I kiss her and congratulate her, then leave her to go back to work. On the way up the town, I spot the poster by the Parish Council telling everyone about the special Mass and reception in the hall after to celebrate Bertie getting the pope's medal. No doubt Bertie himself is behind that.

* * *

KATE KNOCKS on the window of my office as she passes the station on her way home, waving in at me. I beckon her in.

'Hi, Kit Kat, how was school?' I ask as she arrives into my office via the back door.

'Grand.' She sighs, flopping down in the seat on the other side of my desk and dropping her bag unceremoniously on a box of court transcripts. 'But Mr Dorgan is so completely evil. Like honestly, Mam, I think he sleeps in a coffin or something, or drinks kids' blood. I can't wait for Mrs Donnelly to come back. She keeps having babies, and they land that vampire in on us whenever she goes on maternity leave.'

I laugh. Kate had Mrs Donnelly in second class, again in fourth class and now sixth, and each time she's gone on maternity leave. She's perfectly entitled, of course, more power to her. She has six kids already; this one will be her seventh. But Kate's issue is Johnny Dorgan, the local sub. He'll never get a permanent job because he's definitely a bit odd, but with all the teachers going to Dubai to earn thousands tax-free, beggars can't be choosers. He *is* like a vampire. He's sickly pale, with dead-black hair in a kind of widow's peak, combed back. And although he's only in his thirties, he's even more of a throwback than Trevor Lynch – he thinks he's teaching in 1956 and children should be seen and not heard.

Luckily for our kids, most teachers nowadays have a much more relaxed attitude to learning, and Mrs Donnelly, to be fair, when she's there is a great teacher. The children gently tease her about all the dings on her car – she must be a woeful driver – and she gives as good as she gets. It is lovely to see the smiling happy faces coming out each day.

Johnny Dorgan, though, puts the fear of God in them.

'He says that on Monday he's giving us a two-hour test on parsing sentences, and a huge sheet to learn off over the weekend. I don't have a clue what he's on about, subjects and adverbs and all of that. Like, we can speak English – we don't need to know what a conjunction is. And then straight after that, we've an Irish test where he's making us translate an entire chapter from some mad old book about an old woman on an island from the *aimsir chaite* to the *modh chionníollach*. That's from past tense to future conditional, if you don't speak Irish, which I know you don't so I don't see why I have to. He's a total tyrant, and Mrs Donnelly never makes us do awful stuff like that. I wish he'd fly back to his bat cave and leave us alone.'

I actually agree with her, but I can't say that. I'm the local guard and have to have a good relationship with all the schools.

'I am the count, aha ha ha!' I mimic the count from *Sesame Street*; she used to love that when she was small.

She would normally smile but isn't finished with her rant yet. 'It's grand for you. All you have to do is sit here filling in forms, but I'm stuck with him all day. It's torture, honestly. Can I be sick on Monday, and I'll help Granny Marie in the shop instead?'

'Definitely not,' I say. 'But I'll tell you what. Try to learn the things, and do your best with the test, and if you do well, Dad and I won't make you go to work in the Chinese coal mine for the summer.'

I laugh at my own joke, although it's really Kieran's; he's always 'threatening' the girls that if they don't pick their shoes off the living room floor or they leave the milk out on the counter instead of putting it back in the fridge that he knows a fella who owns a Chinese coal mine and he's looking for staff.

She shoots me a disgruntled look. 'Don't make jokes, Mam. You're not good at making them.'

'Hey! I made you, didn't I?'

And there it is, the lovely Kate giggle that she can't help when it happens.

I decide to call it a day and offer my youngest daughter a lift home. After the stress of the weekend, I think myself and Kieran need some family time. He or I would normally have to rush out again on a Monday night while the other one stays in with Kate, because Ellie goes to the Galway Youth Theatre. But their tutor texted earlier; he's been in contact with someone with coronavirus and is self-isolating. Or else he's decided to take a long weekend. No, that's not fair; Patrick is one of those keen bubbly theatre types, and he genuinely loves his job.

Either way, a night with us both at home suits me.

CHAPTER 11

'You're home early.' I can tell by the way his voice deepens slightly that he's pleased to see me. 'And what's that lovely smell?'

'Nothing special. Lamb chops from Bertie's.' Whatever you say about Bertie, his ghastly hypocrisy and weird romantic ways, you can't say he's a bad butcher, and Kieran loves his chops more than anything.

My husband drops his lunchbox on the table and immediately comes behind me, puts his arms around my waist and kisses my neck. 'Mm,' he whispers.

'I wonder would I get that reaction if I was serving you a kale salad?' I chuckle.

'You wouldn't.' He gives me a squeeze. 'But lamb chops make me want to eat and then drag you off into the cave.'

I crane around and kiss him. He smells of fresh air and slightly of tar; it's not unpleasant.

'I'm really sorry about Gearóid,' I whisper. 'I should have told you.' We've been stiff with each other ever since Nora's party, but he seems happier now.

He gives me another squeeze. 'It's me that should be sorry. I've been acting like a child, and I hate you seeing me like that...'

I hold him close. 'Don't let things build up in you again. Just talk to me in the future, OK? And, Kieran, good news – neither of us has to go to Galway tonight because Patrick's cancelled, so we can have an evening in together for once.'

'Thank God.' He smiles and kisses me, then pulls back hastily as the girls come pounding down the stairs. 'Right, I'll light the fire so we can relax after dinner, then I'll get cleaned up and that pair of lazy-bones can give you a hand. Kate! Ellie!' he calls. 'Come in and lay the table.'

We enjoy a lovely family dinner, and Kate has us in stiches with her impression of Mr Dorgan and his English grammar lessons. Ellie is a bit disappointed about theatre being cancelled because she loves it so much, but she cheers up when she hears there's caramel ice cream for dessert. She's planning to audition for Dorothy in the *Wizard of Oz* – it's going to be the youth theatre's big Christmas musical – so I hope she's as good as Patrick tells us she is and that she isn't too disappointed if she doesn't get the part.

After dinner, Kieran and I move to the sitting room with our glasses of Rioja, where the fire is crackling and the curtains are drawn, while the girls load the dishwasher.

I tell him about Martha and Phillip and Jerome, then apologise about Gearóid again, but he seems to have got over it, or my role in it anyway. 'It's fine, Mags. Gearóid texted that he was always promising you to tell me, so I realise it's his fault, not yours.'

I agree it's Gearóid's fault. I hated the position he put me in. But I like him, and I do understand his reluctance to mix his two lives, the Galway theatre circuit and little Ballycarrick. I realise Patrick from the youth theatre probably knows Gearóid is gay, but I don't say it out loud in case Kieran gets even more hurt about not being trusted.

'How is your brother, after Saturday?' I ask.

He shrugs. 'He texted he's going to stay away from Ballycarrick for a bit, until Mam calms down. Dad thinks she will. She's always worshipped Gearóid, and she'll work it out in her head somehow. She'll probably end up boasting he's the gayest man in all of Ireland.'

We both laugh. He stands up to put another log on the fire and then comes back to sit beside me on the couch.

'I never thought I'd hear myself say this,' he says, 'but at least she has that congressman in America to distract her.'

'Oh, did he win?'

'He did, it seems. He's now the representative of some state. I can't remember which one – California, maybe? And believe it or not, my mother got some sort of pro forma letter from him thanking her for her support. And though it's obviously the same one that gets sent to everyone, with a print of his signature' – Kieran gulps at his wine as if to fortify himself – 'she's showing it around the town like it's from him to her personally.'

I nearly splutter Rioja across the sofa. 'Oh, Kieran, no!'

'I'm afraid so, my dear.' He tops up our glasses. The fire crackles merrily in the grate as wind and rain whip up outside. It's great, being together like this. We're both so busy between work and driving the girls everywhere, it's rare to get time to ourselves. He leans back and I rest against him.

'Is the job on O'Grady's farm roofs almost done?' It has turned out to be a huge contract because the O'Gradys have an enormous dairy farm and their milking parlour and sheds were badly damaged in the last storm.

'Another month or three, I'd say, even if this latest weather blows over quickly. He wants everything replaced, not just the damaged sections. I might even take on some extra lads. They have some operation up there, in all fairness to them. Jack O'Grady was telling me how his grandfather was earmarked for the priesthood and his grandfather's older brother got the family farm below in Limerick. But Jack's granda had his eye on a girl, and even though he had nothing, no land or prospects, she wanted him too. They ran away knowing neither family would be happy with the match, and they built the farm up from nothing. Renting a bit of land, breeding a few cattle, then buying a bit, and a bit more. Then Jack's father took over, and now Jack.

They're milking 1,500 cows a day and plan on expanding further if they can buy more land. The whole place out there is a hive of activity.'

'And they are lovely people too, good to work for, I hear.'

'They are, and there's a great view of the town when I'm up on the roofs. Talking of which, I see there's polytunnels going up at Annette's.'

'Already? That must be down to Annette's new lodger, Phillip's mother. I told you about her, the Irishwoman back from Canada. She and Annette have great plans for expansion.'

'I know, I've met her. I called in on my way home to ask did they need a hand putting them up.'

'Well, you're the knight in shining white armour, aren't you, Mr Munroe?' I tease. 'I thought you hated gardening as much as I do.'

'Not me, you eejit.' He laughs. 'I've enough on. Wojtec's sons are just finished school, and they're looking to make a few quid over the summer. He asked me if I knew of anywhere that would hire them.'

'That's a great idea. I'm sure Annette will be delighted, and if they're anything like their father, they'll be great workers.' Kieran employs mostly Polish workers because they are reliable and efficient and, like him, will not take stupid chances. 'And it sounds like the two women are definitely going to need help.'

'That's what I thought,' says Kieran, 'but Martha wasn't keen. I explained the lads were only young, they would only have to pay minimum wage, and that they're like their father, mad for work, but Martha was adamant, said she could manage. Annette went along with her, so I just left it at that.'

'I suppose they're trying to keep every penny,' I say thoughtfully. 'Though how Martha can manage two polytunnels and the vegetable garden all by herself, I don't know. I suppose she has Phillip, if she can ever prise him away from Jerome McGovern...'

'And Annette.'

I shake my head. 'Annette's not able for it any more, sad to say. Her arthritis is very bad. That's why she advertised for a lodger in the first place, to help her because she couldn't do it herself.'

Kieran looks surprised. 'Annette, arthritis? Hardly. She was hopping around like a spring chicken when I saw her. She's in great form, very chatty. Whatever condition she had must have cleared up. I commented on it actually, and she said it was all thanks to Martha.'

I look at him, amazed. 'That's wonderful! I wonder what Martha did to cure it?'

'Maybe just gave her something else to think about, cheered her up a bit?'

'Maybe...'

But Annette is a trooper, and she wouldn't complain about her arthritis unless it was very bad. She's not the sort where it would be all in her head. I know she's happier now that Martha and Phillip have moved in, and happiness helps of course, it makes things more bearable, but I still can't imagine her going from the state she was in to hopping around like a spring chicken overnight. Now that I think about it, when I met the two women and Phillip in Teresa's Bakery, Annette had no problem holding her cup. I wonder briefly if Martha has given her some weird ancient herbal remedy. Maybe something native Canadians discovered centuries ago. I'm sure arthritis must be a problem in the Arctic, what with all that cold weather.

What was the cure Dolores had suggested for my mother's hands? Devil's claw tea?

Maybe they use it in Canada. I must ask.

* * *

SATURDAY COMES AROUND, and Kieran and I have our double date with Sharon and Trevor this evening.

But first there is the special midday Mass, where the town gets to celebrate their favourite butcher getting the pope's medal. I feel obliged to go. I'm sure Bertie would rather I didn't, but then what would that look like? The most holy man in Ballycarrick is being practically awarded a sainthood, and the local defender of the law declines to show up?

After the Mass is the reception in the church hall, which is decorated with yellow and white flowers and banners in the pope's colours. The ladies of the parish under Maura's directions are serving tea and coffee, and I bring a cup of tea and a plate of ham and cheese sandwiches to Father Doyle, who is sitting in the corner looking exhausted. He has just celebrated his eightieth birthday, and he really needs to retire, although there's no one to take over from him.

At least Father Doyle hasn't had to exert himself today. Bertie has his wife, Maura, and other ladies doing everything according to his directions: the flowers, the banners, the blown-up photos everywhere of the world's holiest butcher. The bishop is there talking to Bertie, who has the gold medal on its yellow and white ribbon pinned to the left side of his chest. Bertie is almost fainting with the pleasure; he even stays smiling when he notices me passing him with the plate of sandwiches. I smile brightly back, trying very hard to suppress the dreadful but hilarious memory of my torch shining through a car window onto Bertie's naked arse jigging up and down.

I eat far too many sandwiches while I'm talking to Father Doyle. He won't let me go because he needs me to protect him from Oscar O'Leary, who is hovering nearby ready to discuss what can be done to restore the Church to its former glory. So it's late afternoon before I get the chance to escape and head for home to get ready for our double date.

Mam is already here to babysit; she is watching television with the girls downstairs. I run up to our bedroom, jump in and out of the shower, then throw open my wardrobe and wonder what to wear.

Kieran arrives in while I'm standing there in my bra and the very unattractive but absolutely critical shapewear. I could never have imagined I'd let a man see my elasticated knickers, but Kieran doesn't take any notice of things like that. 'What will I wear?' I ask him.

'You look beautiful in anything,' he says unhelpfully as he heads into the bathroom for a shower and shave.

He's wrong. I'd met Sharon for lunch on Friday, and she'd had that loved-up look, skin glowing, beautiful. It made me conscious that Kieran and I are an old married couple with children, and we're not really glowing any more. Things are much better than they were before I started taking HRT, but our romance is not in its first flush. I'm worried I'll look old and tired beside her, and I wish I hadn't eaten so many sandwiches out of boredom at the reception.

'You'd swear 'tis you were going on the date, you're so skittery,' Kieran says as he dries his face on a towel after shaving and as I change into the fourth dress in twenty minutes.

'I'm going on a date with you, aren't I?' I say.

'You are, I suppose, but since I see you every day, this level of preparation must be for someone else, since I'm usually treated to the sight of my lovely wife in the very alluring uniform of An Garda Síochána or else a fetching combination of leggings and hoodies.'

'I dress up for you sometimes.' I'm indignant, but he's right. I don't really.

'Nope, only when we're going out with someone else. I don't care. I love you in leggings. You look very…flexible.' He laughs, and I throw a shoe at him as he pulls off his T-shirt.

'Do *not* wear that green shirt your mother bought you,' I warn as his hand reaches for it in the wardrobe.

'What's wrong with it?'

'It's got that stupid little symbol on the front that just screams, "Look at my very expensive shirt! It's much dearer than yours."'

'Does it?' He examines the shirt and the little embroidered symbol. 'I never saw that before in my life.'

'Well, that's because, my darling man, you are not a slave to branding, but your dear mother loves to show off, and those shirts are around three hundred euro each.'

'They are not!' He looks so horrified I have to laugh.

'They are, and she bought it as a dig at me, because she's always asking me why you look so scruffy all the time, asking have you no nice clothes, as if I'm at fault for not sending you up on roofs in a tuxedo like James bloody Bond or something.'

He guffaws. 'I'm scruffy 'cause my missus doesn't know how to work the washing machine. I told her that already…' The second shoe goes flying then, but he ducks. Kieran lives in those kind of work pants with all the pockets, and T-shirts in summer and hoodies in winter. At the weekends he wears jeans and this grey Aran jumper that the girls and I have tried to kidnap around eight times, but he always finds it and restores it. It is soft and cosy, fair enough, but it's full of holes and drives his mother insane.

'That's really helpful, Kieran, thanks so much. Give your mother more ammunition, why don't you.' My husband loves saying things like that to Nora to wind her up, but as a result she scowls at me even more.

I pull on the green dress I bought in the sales after Christmas at Sharon's urging, that I worried at the time made my boobs look huge. It is one of those crossover things, and when I check the mirror, my boobs don't just look huge, they look enormous. As I go to pull it off in exasperation, I see Kieran watching me in the mirror, still shirtless.

'Wear that one,' he says, all messing gone.

'I think it makes me look very...' I gesture to my 'ample', as they say in all the old books, bust.

'It does. It makes you look gorgeous, which is what you are, so please, wear that one.'

Normally I'd say something self-deprecating, but something about him just then, in our bedroom, the bed piled high with discarded clothes, stops me.

'All right, I will.' I smile and go to his wardrobe and pull out a lovely blue linen shirt he's had for years. He takes it and pulls it on, but before he can start closing the buttons, I put my arms around his waist and kiss him.

'Do we have to go?' he murmurs into my neck.

'No, of course we don't. We can stand my best friend up,' I joke, and he groans.

'All right, but can we come home early so? Because I'd really like to take that dress off you.'

He kisses me then, passionately, and I love the feel of his strong arms around me. I wish too that we didn't have to go. God bless HRT for waking that bit of me up again; I thought it was dead. We pull apart hastily as my mother calls up the stairs for us to hurry up and leave or we're going to be late.

* * *

THE RESTAURANT where we're meeting Sharon and Trevor is a lovely old pub near Mountbellew, and it has a great reputation.

On the way, we pass through a commercial forest, and before I know it, Kieran has pulled off the main road and down a broad track, driving into the heart of the fir trees.

'What are you doing?' I complain in alarm. 'It's not this way. This isn't even a proper road.'

He says gruffly, 'It's no good. I won't be able to concentrate on the conversation if I don't get to take that dress off you first.'

My first thought is that we'll be late; the second is that the shapewear is not a glide-off, sexy kind of undergarment. But then I decide he's right. We're only middle-aged once.

We arrive to the pub fifteen minutes late, mumbling something about Kieran having to take a work call, but really fifteen minutes in Ireland doesn't count as late at all. Sharon comments enthusiastically on my 'lovely glow' while Trevor and Kieran shake hands, and then we get down to ordering drinks and food.

Over fish and chips, I realise what Sharon sees in Trevor. He's funny and has some great anecdotes about his days touring with Tequila Mockingbird before coming home to care for his late mother.

Also, he's very attractive in a quirky way. I can see Sharon's influence, because the mullet is gone, which must have been quite a concession on his part. It's been replaced by Lydia's signature cut – short sides, longer on top – and it suits him because his hair is thick and glossy. He has a stubbly beard and piercing blue eyes, and while he isn't a big man, he is fit and athletic looking.

He's also got rid of the spurs on his boots, although he's still wearing snow-washed denim jeans and hoop earrings. I suppose he can't leave the '80s behind altogether; it's part of Tequila Mockingbird's brand. And sure enough, when I ask him how the music's going these days, he tells us his re-formed band is headlining an '80s festival in Leitrim in a couple of months.

'I'm going as Cyndi Lauper,' says Sharon excitedly. 'I'm going to get

Gerry the hairdresser to give me really, really big hair.' So Trevor isn't the only one making concessions in this relationship, and I really hope that means these two have a future.

While Sharon shows me pictures of Cyndi Lauper and we discuss which of Cyndi's outfits she would look best in, Trevor engages with Kieran about English soccer and then in reminiscing about New York, where Kieran lived for a few years before coming home and marrying me, and where it seems they used to go to some of the same places.

I'm delighted the two men are getting on so well together. In the past when we went out with Sharon and Danny, it was always me dragging Kieran by the hair of his head because he couldn't abide Danny Boylan. And my friend seems so relaxed in Trevor's company, something she never was with her ex-husband. Back then, she would have one ear and eye on the conversation and the other ear and eye listening and watching for Danny flirting with passing women.

'I suppose you'll be practising in the run-up to the festival,' I comment to Trevor as we study the dessert menus. Sharon shoots me a look. She knows Trevor's drums are a sore point with me, not because of Trevor himself but because of his next-door neighbour Nell McNamara. After Trevor's mother died and he stayed living beside Nell, she tried to get a judge to make him stop playing the drums. The judge ruled he could practise, but only between certain times. Trevor has always stuck to the rules, but still Nell has me and every guard in the station, and my poor mother for that matter, driven up the walls with her constant complaining.

Trevor looks embarrassed, and I feel bad for him – I didn't mean to put him on the spot.

'Sorry, forget I said that,' I say. 'It just slipped out...'

'I'm the one who should be saying sorry,' he says apologetically. 'Sharon tells me Nell McNamara has a path beaten to your door.'

I make a joke about it to set him at ease. 'Off the record, are you deliberately trying to drive her daft? Like you've been drumming for years, so surely you don't need to practice every single day?'

He smiles, then looks around the table at the three of us. 'Nell McNamara has been our neighbour all of my life,' he says quietly. 'And when I left, back in 1989, she had a parrot, remember him? Ernie, she called him, and Ernie never stopped, like all day, screeching and wailing, and my poor mother was too nice to say anything. Anyway, one day I went in and politely asked Nell if she'd cover the cage at night so that the bloody thing didn't start up with the racket when the sun came up, but she refused and was very rude about it. Then when I came back, Mam was very ill, Ernie was dead, and what did Nell do the minute I arrived? Get another, even louder parrot. Mam had terrible trouble sleeping, and Nell used to keep the bird in the conservatory at the back so we could hear it perfectly. It drove me mad that the stupid bird would wake Mam every morning, so again I asked, fairly politely, that she cover the cage, but no way.'

He takes a sip of his wine. 'Then when Mam's Alzheimer's got worse, she started to think the parrot was a woman being murdered, or sometimes it was the man who was murdering the woman, and it would really upset her. And I swear if I'd had a pistol, I'd have shot the damn thing and to hell with the consequences. So, Sergeant, you're right, I don't need to practise every day.'

If I'd had any lingering doubts about Trevor Lynch being a suitable man for my best friend, they would have vanished immediately.

There's such a thing as natural justice, you know, and law enforcers, lawyers, even judges, love it when it happens. Because to be honest with you, justice and the law often haven't much in common. I've seen situations in court where people who are guilty as sin get off scot-free on a technicality, and other situations where someone is convicted of a crime they committed but the extenuating circumstances made it impossible for them to do otherwise. The law is not bad, or corrupt; it's just a bit of a blunt instrument, subject to manipulation, and it can't really deal with nuance.

I remember a case a few years ago where a man who had a business importing furniture from Europe was approached by the leader of a very violent gang. He was told he was to use his trucks and his furniture to hide and import drugs. Naturally he refused, but then he got an envelope in the post with pictures of his car, his wife's car, his kids' school, his children, his elderly mother's house, and he felt he had no choice. At the time, this gang were ruling the roost, so he knew the threats were real. We were doing our best to stop them, but again, the law was being manipulated by clever barristers, even if we could get them into court. So the furniture importer said he would do it once, and they agreed to leave him alone after that. They wouldn't have, of course, but he did it and was caught. The volume of drugs was huge, Class A, and so the law said he had to go to prison. He's serving a long sentence now, and those who intimidated him are sunning themselves in Spain. Nobody in court that day felt good about the result, but the judge said if he didn't hand out a custodial sentence, it would be a free-for-all and lead to increased intimidation. He was right. But that didn't make watching that poor man's wife sobbing in court any easier to witness.

So when even a little thing happens, where natural justice wins out, we love it. And Nell paying for her cruelty to poor old Mrs Lynch makes me smile.

CHAPTER 12

'*And* he's very well connected, you know. His wife actually knows Oprah. And I really think RTÉ...'

Kieran has his mother on speaker as we clean up the kitchen. He rolls his eyes at me. 'Listen, Mam, I've to bring Kate to the dancing and Mags is cutting the grass, so I'll let you go.'

I point out the window at the rain.

'Mags is cutting grass in the rain?' Nora sounds dubious.

'No, not cutting it. She's in the garage checking the lawnmower. She's going to cut it tomorrow, I think, if it's dry.' Kieran shrugs at me. He can't even be bothered to make up believable lies to get her off the phone.

'Well, it's badly in need of it. I'm surprised the neighbours don't complain, that and all the weeds and the flowers dying in their pots...' Nora, when she visits, looks at our garden with a mixture of horror and sympathy.

'Bye, Mam.' He presses 'end'.

'You'll pay for that,' I warn as he boils the kettle for tea while I get the dishwasher going.

'Probably.' He couldn't care less. He opens the treat box, beams when he finds some of my mother's chocolate cake and cuts big slices for both of us to go with our tea.

I join him at the table. My mother is a wonderful baker, and her chocolate cake is so good, I reconcile to the diet beginning again tomorrow.

'I met that boy Phillip coming against me up the hill today when I was leaving O'Grady's place,' Kieran tells me as he scoffs his whole slice and then takes a big bite out of one of buns the girls made this afternoon. Unlike me, he never gains weight. 'He had Olivia McGovern with him, and they were carrying a bucket of eggs between them. I offered to turn around and give them a lift up to Annette's, but they said they were happy to walk. We had a great chat, though. Phillip's very knowledgeable about hens these days, silkies and bantams and Rhode Island Reds. Jerome McGovern is breeding them, and he lets him bring some of the eggs home. Olivia is a nice kid. She's only fourteen, but she seems to have appointed herself as his minder. They go everywhere together.'

I'm happy that Kieran likes Phillip, and I'm even happier that it's helping him see the good side of the McGoverns, how kind and gentle they are to the disadvantaged. Delia is the same. She's so warmhearted and helpful with children and old people, and they all love her, although it's taking her a bit longer to show her good side to the likes of Olive Moran, who is still raising complaints about the McGoverns at the neighbourhood watch meetings. After the horror of the chickens running across the sports fields, it's now a problem that the Travellers leave their bins for collection once a fortnight by the side of the road. Though where else the McGoverns would leave them is hard to say. Apparently the wind blew one of the bins over last week, and there was some disaster involving a tin can.

'I know,' I say to Kieran. 'Phillip's so excited by Jerome letting him help out. Imagine there was a time when people like him were just left in institutions? So cruel. And look at all the joy he brings, not just to Martha and now Annette but to the whole town. Everyone is starting to know him and look out for him. Ellie said he started a chant at the Ballycarrick minor camogie final, the women's version of hurling, and by the end of the match, he had everyone chanting and singing, and the girls won 2 goals and 13 points to 6 points. They carried him on their shoulders around the pitch afterwards, and he was in great form.'

'He must be a worry for Martha, though, isn't he?' muses Kieran. 'Like, our two will grow up and hopefully go on to have happy lives, study, work, maybe get married and have kids, and we just need to look after them till they're old enough to do it themselves. But imagine if you had a kid with special needs that would always need caring for. The worry of who would do it when you're gone must be huge.'

'I know. But look, maybe Annette and Martha will be able to make a real business out of the potatoes and other vegetables for them both, and at least that way, Phillip might have some financial security.'

He nods. 'I know they can't afford to pay for help, but tell them if they need a hand with any heavy lifting, just to give me a shout.'

I smile. He's a nice man, my husband.

He goes off to bring Kate to the dancing, where Deirdre Hickey, who taught me herself and must be 100 years old by now, bellows instructions from her armchair to small girls hopping around like frogs. Neither Kieran nor I can endure the Irish dancing – it's absolute torture – but Kate loves it. It should be my turn tonight, and it's very kind of my husband to do it for me, because although I took his turn last week, it was only on condition he went to the garden centre (he'd rather have bowel surgery) to buy some bedding plants and put them in outside the front door. I love the look of flowers, but I can't grow anything to save my life, as my mother-in-law has correctly noticed.

Ten minutes later Ellie appears from camogie training, having been dropped back by one of the parents we carpool with. 'Rachel Mahony's father got a ginormous gold medal from the pope for being the best Catholic in Galway or Ireland or the world or something,' she says, dumping her gym bag in the middle of the floor. 'He had a big celebration at the weekend.'

'I know, I was there,' I say. 'Put your bag by the washing machine.'

'How do you know everything? I can never tell you any news about this place that you don't know already. Why didn't you tell me you were going?'

'I thought I did. It was only a Mass and tea and sandwiches afterwards, nothing that exciting.'

'Rachel said the pope was at it and everything.'

'I suppose she meant the bishop.'

'Well, she said the pope. She was going on and on about it at training, like, it's actually a bit mortifying, but she doesn't seem to care about that. And Jenny Walsh was making faces behind her back when she was talking, and everyone was trying not to laugh because Rachel is a bit of a weapon and nobody wants to be on the wrong side of her.'

I know all about Rachel.

'I'm starving.' After moving her bag next to the washing machine, she roots in the fridge, despite her only having just finished dinner before she went out the door to camogie. She tears at a packet of ham and begins eating the slices.

'There's a portion of chicken curry in a bowl if you want it,' I say.

'Did you make it?' she asks, abandoning the ham and taking the tin foil off a bowl.

'No, Dad did.'

'Oh yum,' she says. 'No veg in it then.'

I sigh. Kieran makes dinner by frying meat, adding sauce and serving it with chips, rice or pasta that can be microwaved in the little pouches. I try to make things using nutritional ingredients and without packets and jars, but I'm under no illusion – they prefer his efforts.

She microwaves the curry and plonks down with it at the table. Ellie is whippet thin, but even if she wasn't, I'd let her eat all the healthy stuff she wants. She's in a growth spurt, so she's always hungry.

'So what do you have to do to get the gold medal then?' she asks through a mouthful of curry.

'It's for services to the Church over a lifetime.'

'Is Bertie very holy?'

'That's what you get the medal for.' I keep my voice non-commit-tal. Ellie is sharp-eyed and can sense it if I have an opinion on some-thing. I can't afford to have her quoting me having a bad opinion about anyone in Ballycarrick. A guard has to be seen to be impartial.

'Is it actual gold? The medal?'

'I think so.'

'Rachel said it's worth loads, like enough to buy a plane or something.'

I can't help smiling. Ellie stops and looks questioningly.

I say, 'I think the idea is that you keep it, not flog it on Done-Deal.com as fast as you can.'

She chuckles.

'And I doubt very much it would raise enough to buy a plane, though what a butcher might want with a plane, I don't know.'

'I thought he'll probably sell it and use the money to buy a new bacon slicer because Granny Marie said the slicer in Bertie's was cutting the rashers too thick last week.'

She says this as if that's a normal thing for someone her age to say. I love my daughters, and Ellie is so creative and artistic, but some-times I wonder how she fares in the world at all. Kate is younger but much more practical and sensible, and sometimes Ellie comes out with things that would have you scratching your head.

She moves on from the medal to other things. 'You know that lady Annette, you know, the one that wears the mad clothes and red shoes? Well, she fell outside SuperValu.'

'When did that happen?' I ask, alarmed. I'd only seen Annette yesterday; she'd been on her way into the bank. And like Kieran had told me, she'd been skipping around like a spring lamb.

'This evening. We went in before training to get sweets, and she was coming out. We were going to help her up, but the manager came out and two of the fellas that work there, and they helped her instead. She wasn't that bad, though – she was laughing about it.'

Poor Annette. Clearly she was putting a brave face on her pain, but it sounds like her arthritis is still serious, despite whatever Martha has given her. Probably the remedy didn't work any better than a placebo.

And yes, I know placebos help with pain – it's why mothers kiss their children better after they skin their elbow or knee coming off their bikes – but if the pain is long-term, eventually the brain works out it's being tricked.

At eight, Kieran returns with Kate, who runs upstairs to play on her Nintendo for the allocated hour a day she's allowed, and he goes into the sitting room to watch soccer. Ellie is doing her homework. I decide to drive up and see if Annette Deasy is all right.

'Just popping over to Annette. She fell outside SuperValu earlier. I won't be long.' I kiss Kieran on the top of his head.

'OK, love,' he replies absentmindedly, glued to the soccer match.

The lights are on in Annette's little cottage as I pull up outside.

Martha Turner opens the door. She's in gardening clothes, a pair of jeans that have seen many better days and a jumper with holes. As soon as she sees me, she gets that slightly hunted look about her. 'Sergeant Munroe?'

Although to be fair, maybe it's not a guilty reaction on her part; maybe it's just fear. That's one of the hard things about being a guard – people think the worst when you arrive on their doorstep unannounced. I realise I should have texted ahead. In fact, I wonder why I didn't? It strikes me that maybe I wanted an excuse to drop in on these women unannounced. Maybe I still think there's something else to find out about Martha, although what it is, I can't imagine.

'Not Sergeant Munroe tonight, just Mags.' I smile. 'It's not an official visit, but my daughter said Annette took a tumble earlier this evening, and I thought I'd check up on her.'

'Oh…right.' She moves back to allow me to enter.

Annette is in an easy chair by the fire, eyes closed, clearly tired. There are a few crumbs of biscuit on a plate on her lap. The room smells sweetly of turf smoke from the fire. I stand looking at her for a moment. The only sounds are the clock ticking and some distant snoring, which I assume is Phillip in his room, early to bed. Annette doesn't have a television, and only turns the radio on once every few days. She lives simply, but there is something lovely about it. The aroma from the fire is combined with something else. I can't place it.

A Yankee Candle maybe, or Indian incense. I look around but can't see any candles.

'Annette?' says Martha from behind me. 'Mags is here!'

Annette opens her eyes with a start. She looks anxious, and says slowly, like someone waking from sleep, 'Is everything all right?'

'Everything's fine, Annette. Just Ellie told me you had a fall, and I thought I'd look in and see how you were.'

'Oh goodness.' She sits up straight and laughs a little giddily. 'I'm fine. I was just hurrying too fast and tripped over my own feet. Bouncer Brennan's young lad that works in SuperValu wanted to call an ambulance, but I'd no need of that. I'm like a young one these days, thanks to Martha.' She smiles warmly at her lodger, who colours.

'I'm glad to hear that,' I say, looking at her closely. She seems in the pink of health and not in any pain, although her speech is a bit slower than usual.

'Will you have a cup of tea, or a coffee, Mags?' Martha offers. She says coffee like a Canadian, 'caw-fee'.

'I'd love a tea if it's not too much trouble.'

Martha goes into the small back kitchen off the living room, and Annette gestures for me to sit opposite her. ''Tis a lucky day the day she arrived, Mags, honest to God,' she says with a huge smile. 'She's a Trojan worker. You should see the manners she's put on the place already, and she's only here a few weeks.'

'How are you getting on with Phillip?' I ask.

'Oh, he's wonderful. I love him to bits already. Do you know, I was talking about needing some hooks the other day, and the next thing, he comes back from the Traveller site with some metal hooks for me, which old Johnny B. showed him how to make.'

'That's so kind of Johnny B.' Jerome's great-uncle must be well over eighty now. He has always been a bit simple, but he's skilled in the old Travelling crafts and still does a bit of tinkering, fixing pots and pans and making small items out of iron. When he was younger, you'd see him at the Ballycarrick craft fair, demonstrating his skills.

'He's made such good friends among the Travellers. There's Jerome, of course, and one of the cousins, Olivia – she's fourteen and adores him. She often walks home with him, and they both love Harry Potter, would you believe, so the two of them spend all their time discussing Hogwarts and Azkaban and spells and horcruxes. Don't ask me, but they love it. They even bought a Harry Potter Trivial Pursuit game in the charity shop last Tuesday from the money Jerome gave them for cleaning out the chicken coop, and they're going to play it up here in the cottage this weekend.'

'That's lovely to hear. It sounds like he's really fallen on his feet. I'm glad Martha's come to the right place for community.'

Annette nods enthusiastically. 'To be honest, Mags – she was telling me a bit about her life – she has no real family to speak of, she's never married, and she met lots of people in Canada but it never felt like home. I think she's looking to put down roots someplace, and I'm just glad she picked here.'

Martha arrives with tea and cake, and we chat easily by the fire.

'So, Martha, how's life back in Ireland treating you?'

'Great, I'm loving it. And so's Phillip. Canada feels like a lifetime ago.'

'I've never been there myself. I hear Toronto is a nice city.'

She nods. 'It is, but I'm not a city person. I like the quiet, nature.'

'It must be a complete culture shock to be back in Ireland after so many years all the same.'

Martha shrugs. 'In a good way.'

'I suppose there's no place like home, no matter how long it's been.'

'That's exactly right.' She softens and smiles tenderly at Annette.

When Irish people talk about coming home, they usually mean home to Ireland as a whole, but when I see the way Martha looks at Annette, I see such warmth there, I realise she's referring to this actual place, this lovely cosy little cottage, as her home. Despite the fact she's still evading my questions about Canada, I find myself warming towards her and wishing her well.

We chat about this and that for a while, the issue of the McGoverns possibly being moved, which has both of them outraged and anxious for Phillip as well, and the potential for building up a cut-flower business if all goes well with the vegetables.

'Well' – I stand up – 'I'd best get home. Kate has to dress in yellow tomorrow for a school cake sale. It's for the Cancer Society, and we'll make the donation with a heart and a half, but now I've to go rooting for yellow clothes. If I wear anything yellow, I look like a fried egg, so I tend not to buy that colour for the girls either. I'd swear her teacher dreams this stuff up on purpose to wreck my head.'

'I've a yellow dress she can borrow if you like?' Annette offers. 'It might be too big and too long, but if you put a belt on it?'

Kate would probably rather die than go to school in one of Annette's mad-looking hippy dresses, but I haven't the heart to refuse.

'Thanks so much, Annette. I will, if you don't mind.'

Martha offers to get it, but to my amazement, Annette springs to her feet and trots off to her bedroom to search for the dress. She's slightly wobbly on her feet, but again I see no evidence of pain.

I catch Martha's eye, my eyebrows raised. 'Annette keeps saying it's all thanks to you, but how on earth have you made her so much better? And can I have some of whatever it is for my mother? She's a small touch of arthritis in her hands.'

She hesitates. 'Well, it's an herb, I don't know what you'd call it in Ireland. But I'm so sorry – I haven't that much left until I grow some more...'

'My sister is bringing over some devil's claw tea from the States for Mam. Is it anything like that?'

Her face lights up. 'That's exactly it. What a coincidence!'

'I'll send Dolores up to see you when she's here, and I'll tell her to bring extra for Annette as you're running out.'

She smiles enthusiastically. 'Great!'

Annette reappears with a yellow long silk dress, and I take it. 'Thanks, Annette.'

'No problem, thanks for calling.'

She walks me slowly to the front door. Wobbly, but no pain.

I step out into the star-filled night.

CHAPTER 13

The internal line buzzes. It's Delia, who is on the public desk with Nicola. Apparently Nell McNamara is here to see me. My heart sinks.

'Ah, well,' Nell starts as soon as I appear. No hello, no preamble, just straight in. 'You did nothing up to now, and after this I suppose I can throw my hat at it entirely.'

I compose myself because I know what she's insinuating, and I try to never react emotionally at work. I don't always succeed, but I try. It's a constant struggle, like yesterday when Dave Coo-Coo (no idea his real name), the local pigeon fancier and owner of Jules Verne, a racing pigeon of some fame, turned up to the station asking if we'd drive around looking for a pigeon that had flown off course. Honestly, he thought we've nothing better to do with our time and resources. The first three seconds of the conversation, I thought it was a child who had gone missing, he was so distraught, and so I was trying to calm him down to get the details. But when it became clear it was a bird, well, it would test you. He's a right bore. Apparently one of his birds won a medal for itself over in England, as if getting an engraved metal disc from humans means anything to a flipping bird. Some people are bonkers.

I take a breath.

'Mrs McNamara, as I've explained, *many times*, the judge has ruled that Trevor Lynch is allowed to play his drums for a designated period of time during the day. There is nothing more I can do.' I used to feel sorry for her, but now that I know the true story, all sympathy has evaporated.

She's not going away, though. She stands fuming in front of me, psyching herself up for the latest onslaught.

'There is nothing more you *want* to do, more like, especially now that he's sniffing around your friend, the one that's married to Danny Boylan.' Her face is pinched with undisguised satisfaction that she's caught me out.

Right, Nell, if that's how you want to play it, game on. I change my tone slightly but enough to make her realise this isn't a friendly chat now. 'Are you making an official complaint that I or the officers in this station are not doing our jobs?'

She's taken aback, I can see, but not enough to shut her up, unfortunately...for her.

'All I'm saying is that my human rights are being violated, and that I'm entitled to peace and quiet in my own home. And if I have no recourse to the law because the local guard is socialising with the enemy...' Her voice fades a little. She's seen the expression on my face.

I can be stern when I need to be, and Nell McNamara is going to get it both barrels now. The idea of her deliberately tormenting poor old Mrs Lynch, who wouldn't say boo to a goose, has enraged me.

'An accusation such as the one you made here, in front of witnesses, that my personal friendships dictate how I apply the law, is an extremely grave one and one that I take very seriously indeed. I would like to point out, *Mrs McNamara*,' – I emphasise her surname; we are normally on first name terms – 'that I *have* applied the law, to the *letter*, in your case, as I do in every case. Every "i" was dotted, every "t" crossed. So if you would like to make a complaint, I will ensure it gets to the correct authorities, but I will warn you that spreading malicious, unfounded rumours of collusion or favouritism on the part of a member of An Garda Síochána is not something I or my colleagues will take lightly. And while we're on the subject, anything you have to say to me in my capacity as the most senior officer in this station, about this or any other case, please do so through the correct channels. Bringing your grievances up with other people, such as my mother or my daughter, is something I will not tolerate either.'

Nell had stopped Ellie the other day on her way home from school to listen to Trevor playing the drums, with instructions to tell me how loud it was, and she is always bothering Marie in her shop, as if my poor mother could change the law of the land.

Her narrow face looks even more sour now, and a high colour has formed on her powdery cheeks.

'So?' I press. 'Would you like to make a formal complaint?'

'Of course not, Mags, you're being ridiculous. I just meant that...' She falters.

'You meant what exactly, Mrs McNamara?' I ask, and I can see Nicola and Delia watching, their faces deadpan as they've been trained.

'Well, it's not fair is all, it just isn't. And all I want –'

'I think you've made it patently clear what you want. However, the district court in Galway has ruled in this matter. You are within your rights to seek legal advice regarding an appeal, but you would have to prove that some aspect of the case was not dealt with in the appropriate manner. Simply not liking the verdict is not grounds for appeal.'

'Well...' She tries to find something to say that would allow her to depart with dignity. ''Tis a sorry state of a country we have if this is the way law-abiding people are treated, while the likes of musicians and Travellers and criminals in general have all the law on their side.' And she sweeps out of the station, her nose in the air.

There isn't a horse high enough for her, as my mother says.

I turn to find Nicola and Delia staring at me.

'What?' I ask.

'Well, she's been tormenting us for over a year, and I don't think we'll be hearing from her after that, so well done, Sarge.' Nicola smiles.

'Era, we've enough to do. I won't tolerate any accusations of corruption, even if it's snide or under the breath. We need to operate at all times to the letter of the law, but once we do that, then we don't have to put up with people trying to cast aspersions on our integrity.'

'Lesson number one received loud and clear, Sergeant.' Delia grins.

'Good.'

I go into my office and shut the door. I should have put the run on Nell ages ago, but I suppose I felt sorry for her. Just goes to show, doesn't it, there are two sides to every story.

Five minutes later, as I'm writing up a report, the outside line rings. It's Mam, and I get a fright. She knows my shifts better than I do and, unlike Kieran, never calls me at work, so I'm afraid something serious has happened.

'Sorry to ring you now, love. Nothing is wrong, but I'm all a fluster and don't know what to do. Teo's wife's anniversary is on Sunday, and he said to me yesterday that it's always a hard day for him to be alone, so far from home and family, and their son especially. And I can't decide if that means I should invite him for Sunday lunch or not, whether it would be a nice thing to do for him or just tactless.'

While I'm relieved no one has died, I can see she is in an awkward spot.

Teo, who we've yet to meet, seems to really like Mam's company. They've had plenty of lunches out together, and he's already invited her to his own house for a meal – she said it was lovely, very posh of course – a big detached place in Ardpatrick. Not surprising, what with him being a high-ranking consultant oncologist. So Sunday wouldn't be the first lunch date they've had, and it does seem to me from what Mam's saying that Teo is angling to be asked, but she's clearly finding him hard to read. Which is peculiar for her, because she can usually tell exactly what people are thinking.

I remember I was in her shop once and Joe Dillon came in looking discombobulated, stared at a small pink dress on the toddler's rack and left again without saying a word. 'Oh, how lovely, his daughter must be pregnant,' says Mam, completely unfazed. 'His first grandchild and he's hoping it's a girl.' Spot on, as it turned out. So I'm surprised she's having such difficulty reading Teo.

'Well, I think you should invite him, and if he doesn't want to, then he can make some excuse about having something to do, and at least you'll have offered.'

'Yes... No... I don't know... Mags, supposing he does come? Your dad lived there, you were reared there. It feels...not wrong exactly, but... And my place is so different from Ardpatrick...and everyone...'

This problem is knottier than I thought.

Mam feels she's betraying Dad in some way, and maybe me and my sisters as well, and on top of that, she's probably a bit nervous about inviting Teo to her small terraced house in Ballycarrick after having been to his mansion. Not to mention that the whole place will be only dying to get a look at him.

The word is out that Marie is courting. Peggy, her dancing partner, is, I suspect, the source, and Mam is a bit put out by the whole thing. I've heard through the grapevine a variety of rumours: that he is French, Black, a dentist, has a prosthetic leg and is still a champion dancer. And bizarrely, someone asked Kate if her granny was going with a bird expert. I was puzzling that one for a while until Kieran made the connection between an oncologist and an ornithologist.

As I say, you can do nothing in Ballycarrick without a full-scale tribunal of the natives.

'Right. I'm coming over. It's almost tea break time anyway. This needs one of Teresa's cream slices.'

'Ah, there's no need, love. I shouldn't be bothering you, you've enough –'

'I'm on my way,' I say, and hang up.

Nicola is still managing the public desk, Michael and Delia have gone out to do a road safety demo in the primary school, and Darren is in court. They can manage without me for half an hour.

As I pass Joe Dillon's menswear shop, Joe himself suddenly pops out at me, as if he's been lying in wait. 'Ah, Mags, I was wondering, how's your mother these days?'

'She's in great form, Joe. I'm on my way to see her now, and I'll tell her you were asking after her. But why don't you go and ask her yourself?'

He twitches and looks awkward. 'Ah, 'tis hard to leave the shop right now. I've a young fella from Transition Year doing work experience, so if I leave him on his own, the place will be full of young ones from the convent flirting and spilling Coke all over the clothes.'

'Well, ask her when you see her for your lunch in the Samovar.'

He twitches again; he's like a hen with an egg. 'Yes, yes, of course. That is, if she still, you know... Well...the thing is...'

I wait for a minute to see if he's going to say what's on his mind but then give up. 'Sorry, Joe, I've only half an hour to spare. Can we talk some other time?'

'Yes, yes, of course.' He hurries back inside the shop.

Something odd is going on with Joe. I'm very fond of him, but I haven't got time to work it out right now. Maybe I'll drop in on him later.

I arrive at Mam's shop and turn the sign in the glass door to CLOSED.

'Come on,' I command.

Mam is shocked. 'I can't close the shop in the middle of the morning!'

'You can and you will. If Biddy Maguire has to wait twenty minutes for her tights, she won't die for the want of them. We are going for a coffee and a cake, and we'll make a plan.'

'Ah, Mags...'

'No arguing. If the head of law enforcement in Ballycarrick, County Galway, can take twenty minutes off to talk to her mother, then that mother can take those twenty minutes too.'

Mam smiles and gets her coat.

At Teresa's Bakery, we sit in one of the booths to get a bit of privacy and she spills all her worries. Normally it's the other way around – me moaning to her, and she has all the answers – so this is a new development. She doesn't want people talking, the house is too small, what if he thinks she's after his money, what if it's insensitive to invite him to lunch on his wife's anniversary, what if she doesn't and he's all alone thinking she doesn't care, and – the absolute crux of the whole thing, and she's squirming telling me this, by the way – what if he wants to move the relationship out of platonic and into something else.

I stifle a laugh. This so reminds me of Sharon when she was inviting Trevor over for the big night. Even though there's thirty years between Sharon and my mother, the conversations are interchangeable: How to get up the guts to have sex with someone after a long period of celibacy.

OK. I address each thing, one by one, the easy stuff first.

'People talking. Well, I hate to tell you, Mam, they're already talking. That's what they do. Mostly they're nosy or jealous, or else they're cheering you from the sidelines, wishing you well. And anyway, what other people think of you is none of your business, Mam, you taught me that.'

She smiles.

'Next, the house is fine. It's small, but presumably he's not the Hulk. He doesn't think you're a gold-digger because he's an intelligent man and has eyes and ears. You are one of the most independent women I've ever met and you don't need anything from anyone, and Teo can see that too. It gleams out of you like a beacon.'

'Well, that's good, I suppose,' she concedes.

'Now as to whether it's insensitive to ask, probably not. Say you completely understand if he'd rather not on the day that's in it, but if he'd like to come for lunch instead of being alone, then he'd be welcome.'

I see her weigh this up. 'Well, he can just say no, I suppose, and at least I'd have asked.'

'Exactly. Now as to the other thing...' I lower my voice. My mother and I are typical Irishwomen, so very little time in our lives is spent discussing private matters such as bedroom activities, but I can tell she is tying herself in knots over it. 'I doubt you'll need to worry about it on Sunday anyway. He's hardly going to jump your bones on his wife's anniversary now, is he?'

'Mags!' Mam is genuinely shocked, and I try not to laugh. She's puce, and her eyes are darting nervously left and right for fear I've been overheard.

'Ah, Mam, you know what I mean.' I lay my hand on hers. 'Do you think he wants to get more physical than a dance?'

'Well, yes…I think so…' She blushes again. 'Ah, this is ridiculous, a woman of my age acting like a silly little bobby-soxer over a boy. I should cop on. Maybe I'll say I can't see him any more. Sure this is stupid, only making a show of myself…'

'Ah, don't.' I immediately regret my gentle teasing. 'He likes you, you like him, and you are doing no harm whatsoever. He wants to have a relationship with you, so why not stop overthinking it and just see how it goes?'

'I just don't know. What if he… I… Mags, it's been so long. Your dad, God rest him, wasn't well for years before he died, and there's been nobody since. I don't think I even…'

'Mam, it's like falling off a bike. It will come naturally if it's right, and I'm sure he's not the type of man to push you into anything you're not comfortable with, so stop worrying.'

'Oh, he's not, Mags, he's lovely. Such a gentleman and so considerate. He's very old-fashioned, opening doors and that kind of thing.'

'See? So you're not going to be compromised. Take it at your own pace. Ring him and ask him if he'll come. We can pop in for a few minutes if you like, just to meet him, or we'll leave you at it if you prefer. Whichever you'd rather.'

She thinks about it, then shakes her head. 'No, don't pop in this time. It might seem a bit much, introducing him to my family at this stage.'

'Like "meeting the parents"?'

'Mm.'

'We'll stay away so.'

She laughs. 'Look, I probably took him up all wrong in the first place and he doesn't want to come at all. I will ask him, but I'll text him. It's less awkward if he doesn't want to, and he'll have time to think up an excuse.'

I laugh as well. 'Look at you, the professional dater, Mam.'

'Ah, you pick up all sorts at the dancing.' She winks.

'Men included. Talking of which, Joe stopped me outside his shop to inquire after your health. He seemed a bit agitated, to be honest. Says he can't come down to see you because he has some Transition Year kid in the shop who he's scared will make a mess of things. Aren't you still going to the Samovar with him?'

She says something inaudible and stabs her cake with her fork, looking annoyed.

'Mam? Is something wrong between you and Joe?'

She snorts. 'To be honest, I've no idea. People keep telling me that he is asking after me, but the last two times I was expecting him to call down about lunch, he never even showed up, so is he still my friend or not? I went in to see him myself the other day, and he was all cool and stand-offish. I don't know what to make of it.'

'Is he jealous, do you think?'

She looks at me, startled. 'Jealous? I think his shop is doing just as well as mine?'

I can't tell if she's being disingenuous or has genuinely misunderstood me. 'No, I mean of Teo.'

'Teo? What? Joe, jealous? God no.' She stabs her cake again. 'If Joe felt that way about me, he would have said it a long time ago. I used to think he might... But it seems I'm not as good at understanding him as I thought I was.'

'Would you have been interested if he had asked you out?' I ask, purely out of nosiness.

She shoots me a rather sour look. 'Does it matter, Mags? That ship has sailed. Now, back to the matter in hand. What will I cook for Teo?'

I think about it. Luckily, unlike Sharon, my mother is a wonderful cook, so I don't have to persuade her out of the kitchen. With Marie, the problem is which of her many fabulous dishes would be best. 'Your free-range chicken, with herb butter under the skin and lemon stuffing? And those fabulous roast potatoes?' I suggest.

She nods, pleased. 'And I'll do my port gravy, and we'll have my chocolate cake and ice cream for dessert…'

'After a feed of all that, he definitely won't be trying anything on,' I say, and she cringes and rolls her eyes. These days my mother seems to find me as 'mortifying' as Ellie does.

CHAPTER 14

*M*am is as happy as a pig in muck when I see her again the following Monday. The Sunday lunch with Teo was a great success apparently, especially the chocolate cake.

'Except when he arrived, Anne McGreavy had to deadhead a single petunia in her window box, and Mary had to call the cat in, and Barry Molloy suddenly felt the urge to give his filthy old car a wipe down with a hanky. And it was the same when he was leaving, everyone doing the exact same thing, it was...'

'Mortifying?'

'Exactly. Anyway, Teo wants to take you and Kieran out to dinner in Galway.'

'Ah, the big "meet my parents" moment has arrived!'

'Oh, stop it.' She's blushing like a schoolgirl.

'When's the big day, so I can put it in my calendar?'

'Not until after Dolores has been and gone. He was happy to bring her too, by the way, but I told him she's shy.'

'Shy? *Dolores?*'

'No, of course I don't think she's shy, don't be silly. That was just my excuse to Teo. The real reason is she would definitely lecture him about how chemotherapy and radiotherapy are worse than cancer, and if we only all lived on whole grains and never drank milk, then no one would ever get cancer at all, only the doctors don't want to tell us that because they're in league with big pharma.'

'Mam, you're right as ever.'

* * *

THE FIFTEENTH of the month rolls around, and I and Mam go to fetch my sister Dolores from Shannon. As soon as she's in the car, and has reorganised her beads and dreadlocks, she explains she's only going to be here for a few days because she's heading for a commune in Germany where they're going to do Ancient Egyptian moon dancing or some such thing, although she might favour us with her company again on the way home if we're good.

'That's lovely, Lori,' says Mam cheerfully, and Dolores throws her a suspicious glance, clearly unsure whether Mam is pleased she might be coming back again or pleased because she'll be leaving in a few days.

'I see Ballycarrick hasn't changed a bit,' she says sniffily as we drive into the town.

'I know. Isn't it lovely and old-fashioned?' I say, deliberately misunderstanding her.

'Even if it's not as ancient as Ancient Egyptian moon dancing,' says Mam brightly.

'Oh, stop it,' says Dolores, but she laughs and relaxes a bit.

One of the first things she does when we arrive at Mam's is complain about all the poison in the fridge (for poison, read milk, butter and cheese and, horror of horrors, ham), and then she prepares a pot of devil's claw tea, which smells absolutely horrible and, judging by Mam's expression, tastes worse. But Lori assures her it's wonderful for arthritis.

'I've brought over two extra packs of seeds for that woman you were telling me about,' says Dolores. 'I know you said she's going to plant some, but it needs dry conditions, like, originally it's from the

Kalahari Desert, so I'll be surprised if she can grow it in the west of Ireland.'

I'm delighted she's remembered. I'd only told her about Annette in passing when she rang last week. 'That's so kind of you, Dolor...Lori. I don't know about growing it, but they have polytunnels, so maybe that's dry enough conditions? There's two of them – Annette who has the arthritis and her lodger, Martha. She's an Irishwoman who's just moved back from Canada, and she was the one who gave Annette the devil's claw tea. It's worked miracles for her, I have to say.'

'That's great to hear. Where do they live? I'll take a stroll up there if you point me in the right direction.' Dolores totally brightens up at the thought of finding not one but two kindred spirits in Ballycarrick. The sort of people who understand ancient herbs have far more to offer than big pharma, which just wants to keep people sick.

'Kieran works up beside them at the moment – he's reroofing O'Grady's farm. He can bring you up tomorrow morning if you like.'

She grins at me, noticing that I've decided to forgive her for what happened the last time she was alone with Kieran and I came home to find them stoned and giggling like idiots. Ah, well, hopefully she's learned her lesson and won't bring any more weed to Ballycarrick.

* * *

THE AMAZING THING IS, after Kieran introduces them, Dolores and the two women become firm friends. She genuinely adores Phillip, and she thinks Annette and Martha are the best thing since sliced bread (although of course in her book, sliced bread isn't a good thing at all, just more poison). In fact, Mam and I barely see her again for the rest of the visit. Apparently, my little sister isn't just all talk when it comes to organic vegetables and healing herbs, because she gets completely stuck into the polytunnels and starts calling herself a WWOOFer, which means something like 'worldwide opportunities on organic farms'.

'Are they an item?' she asks me one day, on a rare visit to my house.

'An item? What?'

'An *item*, Mags. I know this is Ballycarrick, but surely even you –'

'Oh, you mean…Annette and Martha? Oh… Do you think they are? I thought they were just friends. Like Mam and Joe are friends.'

'None so blind as those that will not see,' Dolores says, and I feel like an old-fashioned fool.

I feel even more of a fool after Joe arrives into the station a few days later and says he needs to speak to me in private about something. I bring him into the room where we hold the neighbourhood watch meetings and make him a cup of coffee, then sit down opposite him. 'What is it, Joe?'

Just like outside his shop, he spends a ridiculous amount of time saying nothing, until I very pointedly glance at my watch and pretend I'm running out of time. 'Is there something wrong, Joe?'

'It's about your mother,' he blurts out.

I suddenly wonder if he knows something I don't, and my stomach turns over. 'Joe, is there something wrong with Mam? Something she hasn't told me about? Is that why you keep asking me about her health?'

'No, God no, your mother is perfect. Wonderful. Beautiful. Never better.'

'Oh, thank God…' I breathe again. 'Then what is it?'

'It's just…' And to my astonishment, his brown eyes fill with tears. 'Oh, Mags, I thought she and I had a… I thought we had an…well, an understanding, if you know what I mean. And now she… It's all so… I mean, I'm not surprised, she's the perfect woman, so obviously there are going to be loads of men falling at her feet. I just thought we had…'

Oh God. Poor Joe. And also, as much as I like him, I'm frustrated at him being so backwards in coming forward, as they say.

'And now this man –'

I interrupt him firmly. 'Joe. Listen to me. For a start, you shouldn't be having this conversation with me, you should be having it with Marie. I mean, what do you expect me to do? Tell her to break it off with him and go back to her once-a-week lunch at the Samovar with you?'

He mops his eyes. 'I don't know. I'm a foolish old man. I suppose I thought you might tell her how I feel.'

I sigh. What a mess. 'You're the one who needs to do that, Joe.'

'But I don't know how...'

'And isn't this whole problem caused by you not knowing how to tell Marie how you feel?'

'I thought we had an understanding...'

'No, Joe. You had a *mis*understanding,' I say, strongly emphasising the 'mis'. 'I actually had a conversation with her about you the other day, and I can tell you she has no idea you look on her as anything other than a friend, if even that these days, because apparently you're being cold to her and she doesn't know why or what's going on with you.'

He looks amazed. 'But isn't it obvious what's going on with me?'

'No, Joe, it's absolutely not obvious. For three or four years now, the two of you have been having lunch once a week, and in all that time, you have never once suggested you have any interest in her beyond the occasional friendly chat. You've never taken her dancing –'

'I've two left feet!'

'Or asked her to the cinema, or on a day trip to Galway, or anything at all. So why would she imagine you were interested in her that way? Why would it be obvious you're jealous of Teo?'

'Oh, *Teo*...' His face darkens and he nearly grinds his teeth. 'Teo, Teo. I've been hearing all about him around the town. He's handsome, he's young, he's rich because he drives a Bentley, he's an ornithologist –'

'Oncologist actually.'

Joe's face darkens even further. 'Right. Wonderful. A cancer specialist. So he's also got the most important job on the planet. Hooray. If I wasn't ready to give up before, that puts the tin hat on it. I won't take up any more of your time so.'

He heaves himself out of his chair and heads for the door. I stand up as well. I can't let him go looking so dejected.

'Joe, wait. Is that it? Are you really going to give up without a fight?'

He pauses at the door and nods miserably. 'I'm afraid I am, Mags. I should have said something long ago, but I was scared she'd turn me down. And now...'

'I don't think she would have turned you down, Joe,' I say gently.

The tears fill his eyes again. 'I wish you hadn't told me that, Mags, not now it's too late.'

'Maybe it's not too late?' This is mad. I shouldn't be saying things like this – I can't interfere in Mam's life – but I'm so fond of Joe.

He looks despairing. 'It *is* too late, Mags. Even if that...that...*man* didn't have all those other advantages, he's a fabulous dancer. A veritable Rudolf Valentino, according to Peggy. How could I ever match up that?'

He's right. I shake my head sadly. 'Oh, Joe. Why didn't you ever learn to dance, just to please her? That would have shown her how serious you were about her, even if you couldn't tell her in words. Nothing says "I love you" like learning to do something your partner loves to do.' Even as I say this, I feel a stab of guilt about never showing an interest in English football, but then I remember that I used to go hiking with Kieran before the girls were born, even though it's my idea of a bad time, and he used to come sea swimming with me, even though he detests cold water.

Joe is staring at me. He opens his mouth, and then, just as I think he's going to say something else negative and defeatist, he abruptly leaves the room. I follow, but by the time I reach the public desk, he's left the station and is pulling away in his car.

'What on earth's the matter with Joe Dillon?' asks Darren, who has just arrived back into the station from court. 'Did you say something to him?'

'Not really.' I'm genuinely puzzled by his speedy exit. 'Only something about learning to dance?'

He laughs. 'He must be rushing off to see Deirdre Hickey so.'

I roll my eyes. What a thought. Deirdre sitting in her armchair with her crutches at her feet, shouting instructions at the poor man and occasionally tossing him a fizzy sweet like she does with the young girls at the Fèis.

I have work to do, and I turn to go into my office, but Darren follows me. 'Sergeant, do you mind if I have a word?'

'Of course.' I hold the door open for him, then close it behind us. 'What is it?'

'I wanted you to see this, Sergeant.' He takes out his phone and holds it out for me to see what's on the screen.

I peer at it. It's a picture taken in a pub, one of those lovely old ones with nooks and crannies, low ceilings and open fires. At first I don't know what he's asking me to look at, but then he turns the phone sideways and enlarges the picture.

There are five men in one of the snugs between the bar and the toilets, sitting around a table. One of them has just popped a bottle of champagne, and three of the others are waving their glasses at him. The fifth man is holding open the door of the snug, as if he's just walked in. His hair is so blond, it's almost white, and he's looking sideways so I can see he has freckled skin and stubby eyelashes.

I look at Darren, my eyebrows raised. 'When was this taken?'

'This lunchtime. I popped into Langan's for a mineral and a toastie, and I saw this lot celebrating something.'

I frown at the photo again. 'So you took this?'

'I was on my way back from the gents, and the man you see there at the door was in front of me coming out of the toilets. He walked into the snug, and that's when I saw them all. I had my phone in my hand because I was texting...' He stops and clearly decides not to tell me who he was texting, though by his shy smile, I'm guessing it was Delia. 'And I took this picture.'

I'm impressed by the speed with which he acted to take the photo, but also troubled by what I'm looking at.

The man popping the cork is Duckie Cassidy. With him is Richard Moran, the chairman of the board of St Colm's, who wants to expand into Drumlish and have the McGoverns evicted. The man on the other side of him is Andy Maguire, county councillor and estate agent, who will make a nice profit from the sale.

'Did they see you, Darren?'

'I don't think so. Too busy guffawing at each other's jokes like braying donkeys. Do you know the man sitting opposite Duckie? I recognise Moran and Maguire, but not him or the man by the door.'

'I don't know the one standing up, but the man opposite Duckie is James Delahunt, the new inspector who goes around the halting sites. I don't think he's directly employed by the council, by the way, just contracted in.'

'So if there's a negative report on the Drumlish halting site, he'll be the one making it? I wonder if his boys go to St Colm's. I know the others all send their sons there.'

I frown. I don't like the idea of one guard accusing another of being involved in corruption, even if it is the awful Duckie Cassidy, but I strongly suspect that's what Darren is after here.

And then he comes right out with it. 'If they're all together celebrating, surely that proves corruption? Shouldn't I show this to the McGoverns?'

I indicate for him to put away his phone. 'Darren,' I say firmly, 'for all we know, these five men know each other *because* their sons go to the same school, and they're celebrating, I don't know, a win for Raymond Moran's team or something. James Delahunt is a second cousin of Andy Maguire's, which is a perfectly innocent reason for him to be out drinking with Andy and his friends. There's no indication this is anything to do with the McGovern halting site, and if you go around accusing these men of corruption, you will not only be undermining a fellow guard, you'll open yourself up to a charge of defamation and probably lose your job.'

'But –'

I raise my voice, just slightly. 'Darren, I'm your superior officer, and I'm instructing you to not, under any circumstances, make this picture public knowledge. In fact, I'm ordering you to delete it, right now. And if I find you have disobeyed my instruction, you will be immediately suspended pending an enquiry.'

He goes white. I've never spoken to him so harshly before, but it's necessary. He's close to endangering his career. I'd watched in horror as a brave officer called out wrongdoing within the force a few years ago. He was victorious in the end, and exonerated of all wrongdoing, but not before the forces from within almost destroyed him. Not alone him, his wife and family too. It's a sobering thought.

Also, there's my own reputation to consider. Do I want to be the sergeant who allowed a subordinate to break ranks and blow the whistle on a colleague? Even if Duckie is in the wrong, should I let Darren side with the Travellers against one of my colleagues? Many of my friends on the force would say no, I shouldn't. After all, as those same friends would say, it's not like the Travellers respect the guards – they hate us.

'Have I made myself understood, Darren?'

'Yes, Sergeant,' he mumbles, fiddling around with his phone, then showing me the picture has been deleted.

I soften my voice. 'Darren, I know how hard it is when being a guard means you can't follow your heart, and I know how fond you are of Delia, but you mustn't let your feelings cloud your judgement. Delia manages to separate her loyalty to her family from her duty as a guard. If she can do it, so can you.'

He sighs. 'No wonder they hate us, though,' he says.

'Who hates us?' I ask, as if I don't know.

'Travellers. It's terrible the way we treat them, and the way they're treated by everyone. Delia told me she and her cousins were booked into the Carrick Arms Hotel for a hen do. They booked it under the name of one of the girls that wasn't a Traveller name, but when they turned up, they were refused entry to the hotel. The manager had some story about them needing a credit card rather than a debit card, but it was just an excuse. He saw they were Traveller girls and didn't want them. They had a whole day booked in the spa, treatments and dinner, and there was a band playing that night. They'd all saved up for ages and they were so excited, but they found themselves out in the car park.'

I'm not surprised Delia never mentioned it to me. She doesn't expect or want sympathy, so it was a real sign of how much she trusts Darren that she told him.

'I'm sorry to hear that,' I say. 'That must have been very upsetting for them.'

At the same time, it's not unusual. Most places don't want groups of Travellers; it's not their image of themselves. And I'm going to be totally honest here – if myself and Kieran went away for a weekend to a hotel and then realised a Traveller hen party was on there, we wouldn't be best pleased.

Why, you might ask. Well…and I have to think about this, to be fair. Because they party in a way we don't. They dress in a way we find unsuitable. They love to dance and drink, they wear a lot of make-up – and I mean *a lot* – they have elaborate hairdos that look like they have so much hairspray in them you'd be fearful of a naked flame, and they'll be fake tanned and show lots of bare flesh, regardless of age or size. There. That's the truth.

Would they harm us or say anything we'd find upsetting? Very unlikely. It's just not our idea of a nice night away in a hotel. I know I might sound prejudiced, and the truth is I am. Most settled Irish people are when it comes to how they dress and behave.

I got a call from one of our local pubs last year. One or two Traveller girls had gone in and got a drink, and then others came to join them, and before the elderly publican knew it, he had ten Traveller women in his pub. He rang me, terrified it was going to turn into something. Was he being racist? Yes. Is it illegal? Yes. But last year a family of Travellers had a funeral after-party in his pub, and another rival family came in and a fight broke out, and 10,000 euro worth of damage was done.

You see the problem. Not every Traveller is like that, but some are, and they give every one of them a bad name. You can't blame people. But at the same time, I know Delia's cousins would have just wanted a nice night out. So you see, it's complicated.

CHAPTER 15

J bump into Martha and Phillip in the town and stop to talk to them, partly to make sure my sister hasn't got the two women driven demented.

'How are you, Martha? I hope you don't mind Lori spending so much time with you.'

For once, she doesn't flinch at the sight of me. 'Not at all. She's been a fabulous help and won't take a penny for it. She's an absolute pet.'

I suppress a grin. I can't wait to tell Mam that Martha Turner thinks Dolores is 'an absolute pet'. Maybe that's why her opinion of me seems to have gone up as well. 'That's great to hear. Phillip, are you well?'

'I'm perfect and Mam is too. Everything is super!' Phillip sports his usual broad beam. 'Isn't it a beautiful day?'

It strikes me that we could all learn a lot from the likes of Phillip. He's mindful without even trying. He lives in the now, the thing that has the rest of us nearly bankrupting ourselves to be able to do. If I showed you all the books, CDs, guided meditations, affirmation cards and vision boards I've invested in over the years, you'd be laughing, I'm not dismissing that stuff. I'm a bit of an old hippie under it all, you know, and it works, kind of, sometimes. But it's Phillip we should all be emulating. I've never seen him down in the dumps or worried. He's always cheerful, and he'd put you in good form. No wonder everyone loves him. I sometimes think it's more to do with who he is than the Down's syndrome. If he didn't have it, he'd probably be naturally happy too, although maybe then he would end up weighed down by a mortgage and kids and all the other things that the rest of us worry about.

'Phillip and Olivia have entered Jerome's hens for an award,' says Martha, smiling fondly at her son.

'Yes, and we're going to win!' He digs in his pocket and produces a newspaper page, well worn on the creases because it has been read so often, and hands it to me. It's an advert placed by the Galway City Council, announcing a competition for the marketplace on sustainability and environmental awareness.

'Well, what a good idea, Phillip,' I say. 'What did you and Olivia put on the entry form?'

'Olivia wrote that the feed for our hens is made by Jerome, so that's local, and our coops are made with recycled timber from old caravans and have wire and hooks made by Johnny B. McGovern, and the hens are outside all the time except when we shut them up at night to keep them safe from the foxes.' He's clearly learned Olivia's words off by heart and is so proud it would melt a snowman.

I make sure to look impressed. 'The hens are really outside all day? Well, do you know Kieran was watching something on telly, and he told me that some of the free-range eggs you buy in the shop are from hens that aren't really free to roam at all. The farmers only leave them out for a very short time so they can say they are free-range.'

Phillip looks at me, his trusting brown eyes sad. 'The poor hens. Ours love being outside. They love the sun and seeing their friends and pecking away at the ground.'

'Well, I bet you that the McGovern hens are the happiest in Ireland.'

He turns to his mother, his beam restored. 'Are they, Mam? The happiest hens in all of Ireland?'

Martha chuckles. 'We have to be careful with definitive state-ments, Sergeant, because a certain pedantic young man I know will want to visit every hen in the country to check, if we say things like that.'

'Well, I'd say they are very, very happy. Sure don't you and Olivia take such good care of them, Phillip?'

'They love Olivia. One of them got into a fight with another one and got pecked, but Olivia made her better.'

'Do hens fight?' I ask, genuinely interested. I know nothing about things like that.

Phillip nods enthusiastically. 'They do, and they get jealous. So you have to be very clever.' He taps his temple.

I chuckle. 'Well, if anyone is smart enough for them, it's you, Phillip.'

'I really am,' he says, and giggles, his hand to his mouth. 'Who tells the best chicken jokes, Sergeant Munroe?'

I've heard from Dolores that Phillip is great for jokes.

'I don't know, Phillip, is it you?' I smile.

'No, not me. It's comedi-hens!' He laughs uncontrollably, and Martha and I can't help but join in.

Across the street, Jerome McGovern is coming out of the hard-ware shop. He waves to Phillip, who calls back, 'Hi, Jerome! Mam, I must ask him something.' And the next thing, he is gone across the road and is deep in chat with the Traveller man.

Martha smiles. 'Jerome's so good to Phillip. Phillip spends hours following the poor man around. I've told Jerome to tell him he has to go, but he never does.'

'I suppose Jerome knows what it's like to have people make assumptions about you without even knowing you. They have that in common.'

'True. It must be so hard for them, facing so much prejudice. And they're lovely when you get to know them properly. Paddy and Niall McGovern have a van, and they do a bit of driving for us, dropping off vegetables to the supermarket. We pay them a bit, but they charge next to nothing, a fiver at the most. I think it's because they love

Phillip. They're always giving him rides here and there, when he's not with Olivia.'

I'm really pleased to hear about Paddy and Niall. I always thought those two were cheeky scamps, but they're obviously turning out well. Now the thing to do is make sure they're kept away from the Carmodys.

'They're so worried about the council moving them on,' Martha continues, echoing my thoughts. 'I heard from Annette how Olive Moran and the rest of them are hell-bent, and it's very unfair. That family have been here for years, and why should they have to leave all they know because some posh school wants even more land? And then Paddy says this latest inspector, Delahunt, he turns up at all times of the day doing what he calls "routine inspections". The place is always immaculate, as you know, but he swears your man is just looking for reasons to recommend they be moved.'

'It's very upsetting for the McGoverns,' I say, as non-committally as I can. I wish I could tell her how Duckie, Andy Maguire the county councillor, and Olive's husband, Richard Moran, who's the chairman of the school board, had been seen meeting with James Delahunt and a mystery man.

'And Paddy says they see him dropping his boys off at the school every morning, so they obviously go there too. I mean, that's not fair, is it?'

Ah, so Darren's hunch was right. I try to again look non-committal. 'Well, just because his children attend a school doesn't mean he's behaving inappropriately, I suppose.'

Martha eyes me knowingly. 'I know you can't say so, Mags, in your position, but you know as well as I do that if it looks like a duck and walks like a duck, the chances are it's a duck.'

'You're right. I can't say so.'

Even with someone I trust, and I still don't trust Martha, I can't go making unsubstantiated accusations the way other people can. But it's very dodgy indeed. The county councillor who stands to make a packet on the deal, the chairman of the board and the inspector whose recommendations will sway the council are all united by the fact that their children attend the school that wants to buy the land. And Duckie Cassidy sends his son to school there too, so it doesn't surprise me one bit that he's clearly somewhere in that particular food chain as well. It stinks to high heaven, but without proof...

And on the other side are the poor McGoverns, who have no pull with anyone whatsoever.

At the end of the day, it's up to the council to make the decision. And the reality is, nobody will really object if the McGoverns are moved. Well, maybe a few will, but people are selfish and think about the price of their property and not the human lives that will be impacted.

I've already heard people in the shops suggesting that it would be best if they all lived together, the Travellers, I mean. But that's like saying, 'You're a family, so why don't you go and live with this other family because you all have dark hair?' It's mad. They're different people, and they are united by being Travellers, but that's all.

'I hope it plays out fairly for them, I really do,' I tell Martha. 'Especially for the older members. They've always lived there, it's their home, and they can walk into town, get their messages, go to Mass. If they put them out where the Carmodys are, on the Tuam road, it will mean they'll have to be driven in. The younger Traveller women drive, but many of the older ones don't.'

Martha nods. 'You know, Mags, when I was young, I never took too much notice of older people. They were there, but it never occurred to me that they might have plans or dreams or things they wanted other than what they already had. But as I get older and I see the potential for life, I'm so glad to be able to embrace it all and have new things happen.'

'I know what you mean, not that you're anywhere near old. Sure you're not even fifty.'

'Fifty-six.' Martha grins, and I don't have to pretend to be surprised.

While we're waiting for Phillip to finish talking to Jerome, she starts telling me about the business. She and Annette have got contracts for four new places for the microgreens and sprouting seeds, and they are putting up a third tunnel for the fast-growing, high-volume plants. 'We have raised beds the whole length of them, and we're flying. Annette has such green fingers.'

'And can she get up the hill to the tunnels?' I ask. The lane behind Annette's is really just an old sheep track and very steep.

'Oh, she's flying around.'

'That's wonderful. It was awful to see her in such pain. The devil's claw is working wonders for Mam as well, or so she tells Dolores...Lori.'

Phillip appears at our side once more. 'We have to go to get extra-long cable ties, Mam,' he announces. 'Jerome says they're the right job for securing the trellises for the runner beans. He thinks they have them in the hardware shop, but if we can't get the right ones, we're to ring him 'cause he can get them. His number is 085 33033021.'

'You can't remember my number, but you can remember Jerome's,' teases his mother.

'Priorities, Mam.' He grins.

'Well, I have my orders.' She laughs as Phillip links her arm. 'Extra-long cable ties, here we come. Bye, Sergeant Munroe.'

'Nice to see you, Martha.'

'Bye, Mags.' Phillip waves.

'Good luck with the competition, Phillip. I really hope the happiest hens in Ireland win!'

CHAPTER 16

*D*olores asks me to bring her to Shannon airport at an unearthly hour of the morning because *of course* her flight is at 6 a.m. and she needs to be there two hours ahead of time. I grumble about it to Kieran, but I find myself enjoying my sister's company on the drive, especially as for the first time since she was a little girl, she is saying nice things about Ballycarrick.

'I must say, the town's really coming on,' she announces as I drive carefully down the N18, through the dark and pouring rain. 'It's wonderful how everyone in Ballycarrick is getting into organic foods and herbal stuff. Martha and Annette are especially fabulous, and Phillip too. It's great how accepting everyone is of him. Best visit ever.'

'I'm so glad you enjoyed yourself. Will you be staying with Mam again on your way back from Germany?'

'Defo. Can't wait. I met a couple of nice people in the town as well, just even when I was sitting in the park.'

I'm delighted by her enthusiasm although still surprised by her complete change in attitude to Ballycarrick and its residents. 'Who were they?'

'Mm...I think they were called Denny or Lenny, and John or Joe or something. Only kids but cool. Yeah, the whole town has really light-ened up, starting with Annette and Martha, of course – they're totally the best.'

'What is it you love about those two women especially?'

She says nothing. I glance at her, and she's smiling to herself.

'Dolores…I mean, Lori?'

She starts. 'Oh, sorry, my mind wandered. OK…what do I love about them? I suppose it's because they're just, well, clued in, y'know? I mean, Annette's a wonderful old hippy, and Martha, she's really been around.'

My Garda antennae spring to attention. 'Been around where?'

'Oh…here and there.'

I shoot her another glance, but she's clearly not going to reveal any more. All very puzzling, but we're having a nice time together, so I let it go.

* * *

I CAN'T SLEEP after getting home, so at six o'clock, I'm already showered and in my uniform. I leave Kieran to get the girls off to school and go into work earlier than normal, hoping to get through the usual pile of reports before the rest of the world descends on me.

Before turning into the station car park, I take a short drive around the town to check all is well. Nobody is on the move yet, only a couple of builders' vans passing through. The only thing unusual is that Deirdre Hickey's front door is open. Not the door to her house, but to her dance school, which is the former railway station.

I slow to a crawl as I pass by, worried she's been broken into or just forgotten to lock up.

She must be in, though, because her car is in the dance school car park. I know it by the blue disability sticker on the windscreen, which shows a person in a wheelchair. Deirdre isn't a wheelchair user and the sticker is not the best look for a dance teacher's car, I sometimes think, but nobody seems to notice; they all send their children to her anyway, including me.

There's a black car parked next to hers, and I slow down even more. Surely that belongs to… No. It can't be. I mentally slap myself. Anyway, if Joe had listened to me about taking dance lessons, he'd have gone to a proper salsa teacher, not to Deirdre Hickey, who just barks out instructions from her chair because she's too lazy to get up.

If he's here, it must be to discuss costumes. Mam does all the girls' Irish dancing costumes, but there's boys who dance too, well into their teens and even beyond, so Joe's menswear shop handles that side of the business.

Even so, I stop the car completely and wind the window down and listen carefully, while feeling a bit guilty for snooping. It's tough sometimes, trying to walk the fine line between making sure everyone is safe and well and butting unnecessarily into someone's private business. All is quiet apart from little birds singing…and the *clump, clump, clump* of heavy feet hopping around on Deirdre's sprung floor. And the familiar roar of Deirdre's voice. '*One*, two, three, *one*, two, three…'

I drive on, my head spinning.

* * *

I HEAR Delia arrive into the station at eight o'clock and go out to chat to her. She looks visibly upset.

'Is everything all right?' It's unusual to see Delia McGovern this shaken; she's normally so stoic.

'It's fine, Sergeant.'

It's clearly not fine. 'Well, you don't have to tell me, of course, but if someone has said or done something to upset you in the course of your work –'

'Nobody's said anything to me, Sergeant.' She walks in behind the public desk and starts leafing through the diary without really looking at it.

Nicola arrives at that moment, so I leave her in charge and call Delia into my office and sit her down on the chair in front of my desk.

'Now, tell me, what is it?' I take my own chair. 'And please don't tell me everything is fine.'

'It's nothing to do with work, Sergeant.'

'Delia, if you're this upset, this has everything to do with work. If any one of us here in the station is in trouble, it affects everyone, so I want to get to the bottom of it and help you if I can.'

She looks directly at me then, with tears of frustration in her eyes. 'We always keep our place nice, you know? Nana always made sure the place was clean and there were flowers and all of that.'

I nod. She's right. Dacie McGovern kept that site neat as a new pin, and woe betide anyone who dropped a paper or didn't have their flowers watered and up to standard.

'And Dad has kept it the same way, in honour of her.'

'I know he has.'

'Well, this fella from the council has been coming around, checking, and every time he comes, he can't find anything to complain about, even though he tries. There isn't a blade of grass astray 'cause Daddy says maybe if we give them nothing to complain about, they can't sell the land on us. And since…well, since Daddy took over the family, everyone is still behaving right. My cousins are all working and staying out of trouble. We had a meeting, y'see, Sergeant, and we said we'd make sure we gave them no cause to evict us.'

My heart breaks for her family. Why should they have to be on their best behaviour like schoolchildren? It is so demeaning and unfair.

'Well, last night, a lot of us were away. An aunt of ours died, God rest her, and she was being buried in Athlone. She'd be a bit like Nana, one of the older generation, and everyone liked her, so most of the family went and they stayed up there.' She stops, a catch in her voice. Even telling me this is upsetting her.

'Go on,' I say gently.

She clears her throat. 'Well, there's only a few of us didn't go to the funeral, and when my cousins Paddy and Niall got up this morning, the place was destroyed. Dirty rubbish everywhere, and the sinks blocked in the washing unit and water everywhere. There was horse dung and everything, and empty cans and bottles of drink. And the chickens were let out of the coop and running across the sports fields again. And your man from the council arrived while Paddy was still staring in shock at it all and took a load of pictures.'

I'm horrified. 'You're telling me someone came in and did this deliberately?' I'm kicking myself that my early morning patrol of the town didn't take in the Drumlish halting site.

Her face tightens and she juts out her chin, like the old defiant Delia. 'I thought you of all people wouldn't blame it on us, Sergeant...'

I sigh. It's annoying when she gets snippy around me without justification. 'I don't, Delia. Of course I believe you. So don't get all defensive when I ask you this next question. Why didn't you hear anything in the night?'

She shrugs, avoiding my gaze. 'I suppose it was done very quietly, not to disturb anyone. I only found out when Paddy rang me after your man was gone with his photographs.'

'Paddy didn't wake you when the man from the council came?'

'No.'

'No?'

I'm not sure why I keep pushing her like this, but as I've said before, when you're trained as a guard, you learn how to tell when someone is...well, not lying exactly, but not quite telling you everything you need to know.

She blushes furiously. 'No. The thing is...I...I wasn't there.'

'Oh, I see.' I wonder if her absence has anything to do with Darren.

'It's all my fault, Sergeant,' she says forlornly. 'Daddy left me behind to keep an eye on the place. He asked me to make sure that there was nobody sniffing around. But I...I... Well, I didn't think anything would happen after it got dark, so I went...somewhere else. And that left only my Auntie Nonie, who's in her own van and deaf as a post, and my cousins Paddy and Niall, who'd promised to do some deliveries for Mrs Deasy this morning, but they were playing the Xbox with headphones on and heard nothing. And anyway, they thought I was there keeping watch, and I should have been. I'm supposed to be a guard...'

'You *are* a guard,' I remind her.

'Well, I'm not much of one if I can't even protect my own family, our home. And now Daddy's going to want to know why I didn't do what he asked me to, and...' – her voice chokes on the emotion of it all – 'and they'll be able to throw us out now, saying we're drawing rats or something.'

My heart goes out to her. Obviously the inspector's photographs were staged somehow, but if they get made public, they will play into every stereotype some people have about Travellers. And she's right – they will probably be enough to get the town to rally behind the eviction. It's a horrible trick to play.

'Delia, don't despair. We'll figure this out. Is there any CCTV on the site?'

She shakes her head. 'And nobody will have seen anything, Sergeant, you know they won't. Sure it's only fields and woods and the school football pitch beside us. And Daddy will be so upset with me. I'll have to tell him the truth, that I wasn't there.'

Poor young woman. On top of the stress of feeling responsible for getting her family evicted, she'll also have to answer questions about where she was, which is something I'm sure she's dreading. I know Jerome McGovern would never hurt her, but still, a girl's virtue is highly regarded in that culture, and I don't like to think of the consequences for Delia if her father discovers she was out all night.

'I was with Darren, Sergeant. I might as well tell you the truth.' She is scarlet with misery and shame. 'I was at his place watching a film, and we fell asleep, on the couch like, not in his bed or anything, I swear to you. But I know my family won't allow us to be together, and whatever hope there might have been, a very slim one that they might understand, there's none now because they'll blame him for what happened last night, even though it's not his fault. And they'll think that we... But we didn't. I just... I... We love each other. And I don't blame you if you want to suspend me.'

'Delia, stop.'

She goes quiet but still won't meet my eyes.

'First thing is, what you do in your free time and who you spend it with is entirely your own business. You're a grown woman, and you can decide who you want to be with, and who you want to sleep with too, for that matter, so that's nothing to do with me or anyone else. There's no rule to say people don't meet on the job – of course they do. It happens all the time. I know lots of couples where they are both guards, so you've done nothing wrong. I've never seen evidence that either of you allowed this to spill into your professional lives, so there my input ends.'

She's listening to every word, I'm glad to see.

'The second thing is this. I can see that this is a difficult situation given the way your family would feel about you and Darren, so if you want to tell them that you were working last night, I won't contradict you. I won't make a habit of covering for you – this is a one-off, you understand – but if it would help, you can say I sent you to do something. I don't know what – you can figure that part out yourself.'

The relief is so obvious on her face, I have to smile.

'It's not a crime to have a boyfriend, Delia, and Darren is a nice lad. I know it's complicated, I do. And your family have a lot to contend with just now, so introducing the idea of him and you as a couple under these circumstances wouldn't be ideal, I get that.'

'Thanks, Sergeant. I...I'm really grateful. I just couldn't bear them to think that I...'

It's pointless me going into how that kind of outdated thinking is precisely why women have been oppressed for so long. Honour and virtue and being the property of just one's husband is such a patriarchal notion. But now is neither the time nor the place. Delia has been brought up to believe it, and while I won't bring my girls up with the same ideas, I have to respect her culture.

'Right, we'll say no more. But I will finish with this, Delia. Your mother and father have their lives. They've had choices and options, and they've made whatever decisions they did. But this is your life, and you'd be foolish to allow anyone to live it for you. I know family and tradition are important to you, to all of us, but you're the master of your own ship too, you know?'

She nods and gives me a weak smile. 'There was this poem the master, Mr Hartnett, taught us,' she says. 'I forget who wrote it, but I remember thinking a lot about the last four lines. I wrote them on a bit of paper and stuck them over my bed. "It matters not how strait the gate, how charged with punishments the scroll. I am the master of my fate, I am the captain of my soul."'

'"Invictus", by William Ernest Henley,' I say.

'That's it. I forgot his name there for a minute. Anyway, my nana saw it one day and asked me what it was about, and I explained about it and how Nelson Mandela had it in his cell on Robben Island and it gave him courage and hope. She had great time for him, all he put up with for what he believed in.

'She told me that I should always try to be respectful to my parents and be a good girl, but that God put each of us here for a reason and it's up to each person to find out what that is. She backed me to join the Reserves, and she convinced Daddy that the lad they had picked out for me to marry wasn't going to do at all. I was so sad when Nana died, and I miss her every day. But she kind of sent me you, Sergeant, and I'm really grateful.'

I'm so touched, I don't really know what to say. Delia is deep, often unfathomable. She's a very unusual young woman. 'Thank you, that's lovely to hear. Now go and dream up some reason I had you working all night.'

'But what can we do about the inspector's photographs?' she asks, looking worried again.

'I'd say your father needs to make a formal complaint so we can officially investigate, although if there are no witnesses and no CCTV, and if nobody saw or heard anything, I'm not sure what we can do.' I wish I had something more cheerful to tell her, but I don't.

Before Delia leaves, Nicola puts her head around my office door. 'Annette Deasy is here, Sergeant. She says they can't find Phillip. Martha's gone up to your place, Delia, to see if he's around nearby, and Annette's come in to talk to you, Sergeant.'

Delia looks worried. 'They still haven't found him? Sergeant, I should have said. It was Martha who woke Paddy this morning, looking for Phillip. That's when he realised about the damage, because he went to check the chicken coop to see if Phillip was there. He didn't hear anything else about it, so we thought they'd found him.'

'Don't worry, I'm sure he hasn't gone far.' Phillip doesn't strike me as the sort to stray. He probably went out for an early walk and got picking mushrooms or something.

Annette is at the public desk, her usually well-brushed silvery hair in a mess. 'Mags, I'm so sorry to bother you, but we can't find Phillip. I got Mary Coughlan to drop me in here. He went to bed last night, but when Martha got up for a drink of water, he wasn't there, and he hasn't come back home, and he's not picking up his phone.'

She is trying not to panic, I can see, but failing. I know how she feels. It's terrifying when a child goes missing, even for a short while. It happened to me with Ellie once when she wandered off a little way into the woods while we were having a picnic and got so interested in watching a spider spinning its web, she forgot to come back again. I also know that despite everyone's immediate jumping to the worst possible outcome when a child goes missing, there's almost always a reasonable conclusion.

'Maybe he's somewhere in the fields, picking mushrooms? I know Jerome has been teaching him which mushrooms are safe to pick, and dawn is a great time to look for them?'

'No, I'm not explaining this properly. It was still dark when Martha got up, maybe not even five o'clock. She looked for him all over the cottage, even in the attic, and then we went out with torches and searched all the fields and the polytunnels. And the O'Gradys were up at five thirty with the cows, and we called to them, and they searched their own place, the barns and everything. And as soon as it came light, we rang Jerome to ask if Phillip was at the halting site, but Jerome was on his way back from a funeral. So we called one of the lads who does the deliveries for us, Paddy, and he went to check the chickens and found the place had got destroyed overnight, and Phillip wasn't anywhere to be seen.'

I don't like the sound of this, although at the same time, I don't want to alarm her. I take out my notebook and rest it on the counter. 'OK, I'm sure there's a good explanation and he's not gone very far, and it's nothing to do with what happened at the McGovern place, but I'm going to open an investigation. Have you any idea what he might be wearing?'

Annette looks ill, and I know being asked about his clothes makes her feel like Phillip is going to turn up in a shallow grave or something. 'Well, we think he was wearing his Ballycarrick GAA top, and tracksuit pants, and his red and green ski jacket. That's what he was wearing yesterday, and they weren't in his room, and he left his pyjamas on the bed.'

'Nicola, call Darren and Michael to come in. I want them to take the car out looking for Phillip. Delia, make a note of what Annette just told me. Phillip is likely wearing a Ballycarrick GAA top, tracksuit pants and a red and green ski jacket. Then both of you go down the town to every establishment with CCTV outside and ask them to look if there's anything on it that would let us know if he passed by.'

Relieved that I'm doing something and not just soothing her with platitudes, Annette grabs and squeezes my hand. 'Thank you, Mags. I know it's probably nothing, but he normally would never do this. He always texts us at least every half hour to let us know what he's doing and where he's going, and he always answers his phone.'

'He definitely took his phone with him?'

'Yes, it's not in the house. We keep calling it, but he doesn't answer.'

'Is there a chance he's put it on silent, even by accident? That's happened to me in the past.'

'I suppose he might have.' Annette's brow furrows. 'But he would know we'd called him even so, because he's always checking his phone in case he's missed anything.'

She's right; I've seen him do it. 'Do you have Olivia McGovern's number?'

'Yes, they're together so much, Martha asked her for it, just in case his phone ever went out of charge. But Olivia wasn't there. She went to the funeral as well.'

'Even so, why don't you go and sit in my office, plug your phone in if you need to, and call Olivia to see if she has any ideas about where he might have gone. Maybe Phillip said something to her, and to be honest, she's more likely to tell you what he said than to tell me, because I'm a guard. Write down what she says – there's pen and paper on my desk. While you're doing that, I'll bring you a cup of tea.'

After I've settled Annette, who is clearly relieved to have something useful to do, I go into the room where we hold the neighbourhood watch meetings and put the kettle on. Then I scroll down to Detective Inspector Ronan Brady's number on my mobile. Maybe this is using a hammer to break a nut, but Ronan owes me one since the time he refused to go with my hunch that Natasha McGovern was in danger, and that ended up with me being shot and a dangerous human trafficker almost getting away. Plus poor Annette is out of her mind, and to be honest, and I wouldn't say this to her, I now think she's right to be afraid.

I ring Ronan's number.

'Mags! Great to hear from you. How are things? We have to meet up...'

I'm glad Sharon isn't around to hear the enthusiasm in his voice. Sharon always calls Ronan Brady 'your gorgeous boss' and 'the George Clooney of the west of Ireland', and she claims he had a notion of me before. Kieran's as bad; he can't stand him, mainly because he blames him for me getting shot but also because he agrees with Sharon about Ronan having an eye for me. Utter codswallop. Unlike Duckie, the man does indeed look like George Clooney, and I look like some exhausted mother out of a washing powder ad, and he no more fancies me than the man on the moon; he just thinks of me as a work colleague. But try telling that to my pig-headed husband and my best friend.

'Fine altogether, Ronan, but I'm wondering if you could do me a small favour? I know I should have probably rang traffic, but I figured it would be quicker to go straight to you.'

'If I can help, I will. What's up?'

'There's a local lad, Phillip Turner. He's seventeen but has Down's syndrome, and he's been missing from at least five this morning. He's not answering his phone, and his mother and the other woman he lives with are very worried. They and the farming family next door to them have already done an extensive search. So I was wondering, could you find out if any Garda cars from the towns around here are or were out on the road this morning, and have they seen anything, and can they look out for him? We think he's probably wearing a Ballycarrick GAA top and tracksuit pants under a red and green ski jacket. Look, I know it's probably just that he's gone off for a long walk or something, but I don't know, call it gut instinct, I am a bit unsettled about it.'

He doesn't push back at all. 'If this job has taught me anything, it's to trust your instincts. Leave it with me. I'll log into the Garda system and put out a notification to all Gardaí to be on the lookout for this lad, and I'll be back to you shortly.'

'Thanks, Ronan.'

I make the tea and bring it into my office to find Annette saying goodbye to Olivia and ending the call. 'We've got lots of guards out looking for him now, Annette. I know it's easy for me to say, but try not to worry – we'll find him. Did Olivia have anything useful to say?'

'Only that he was anxious about the hens because she and Jerome were both going to the funeral and Paddy and Niall have no interest in them. He was worried they'd be hungry or a fox might get them if nobody shut the door of their coop after dark. But we knew that already. He was on about it last night, and we let him ring Paddy, who promised the hens were fed and locked in. Then when I rang Paddy this morning, he and Niall went straight to the hen coop to check, and that's when they found the whole site had been trashed and the chickens escaped across the sports fields. I was worried they would think Phillip had done it, but they didn't of course. They know him too well for that.' She shivers. 'I mean, it couldn't be anything to do with Phillip disappearing, could it? I mean, he'd never do anything like that.'

'Of course he wouldn't. Annette, I wonder if I should get Michael and Darren to run you home in the car as soon as they get here. There's no point in you going to the McGovern place as well – Niall and Paddy will have that end covered with Martha, and Jerome will be back soon.'

'But I want to help…'

'Of course, but the best way to do that is to go home. You don't want the house to be empty if he turns up, and there's no point to you both haring off all over the place. I've a very senior guard on the case, and I'll keep in touch with you by phone. Use your landline if you need to make a call, to keep your mobile free.'

Michael arrives in the next moment with Darren, who looks almost as upset as Delia did earlier. He must have heard from her about the site.

'Lads, will you run Annette home and then go driving around searching for Phillip? Annette will tell you what he was wearing, and where she's searched already.'

I walk Annette out to the car with them, and she turns to me before climbing in, distraught. 'He'd never go with someone he didn't know, Mags. Poor Martha is so worried. I wish I could go back with better news. And he wouldn't have anything to do with damaging the coop or letting the hens escape.'

'I know, and honestly there's almost always a simple explanation. But we'll have some information for you very soon, and if he turns up at your house, let us know right away, OK?'

'I will. Thanks, Mags.'

The lads and Annette drive away, and I stand on the steps of the station, collecting my thoughts. If Phillip couldn't sleep and went out walking at night, any local person coming home late could have stopped to see if he was OK, and since everyone knows him, that could be anyone. Maybe they took him home with them because it was raining and he needed dry clothes, and he and whoever it is are still asleep. But I know in my heart of hearts that I'm grasping at straws, that that's not what has happened. There's something worse behind this, and it's very hard to think it's not to do with the halting site being vandalised.

I ring Kieran. 'Hi, love. Can you get home earlyish today? Something's come up and I've to work late. I don't know how long I'll be.'

'What's happening?' I hear the panic in his voice.

'Please don't worry about me, I'm fine. It's just that Phillip Turner has gone missing, and as well as that, the McGovern place got trashed overnight, and I need to find out who it was and what's going on.'

He makes an effort to stay calm. 'Oh, the poor lad. Martha must be sick with worry. Can I help at all?'

'No, not really. Just take Ellie to the youth theatre later and make sure Kate has her Irish homework finished – she got a note from *Bean Uí Mhurchú* yesterday to say it wasn't done properly, so just check it, will you?'

The mention of the fearsome deputy principal that was in the school since God was a child was enough to strike fear into every Ballycarrick heart, young or old.

'How is that auld bat still alive? I might as well be looking at hieroglyphics, Mags, but I'll try.'

'Send a picture of her homework to Gearóid if you don't know,' I say, anxious to get off the phone. Gearóid is a fluent Irish speaker, but Kieran hated it at school and spent a lot of years abroad once he left school, so he forgot all his Irish.

'I'll figure it out,' he replies coolly. I'd forgotten things were still frosty between those two, and I feel like knocking their heads together. Gearóid no doubt imagines his brother's cold shoulder is because he's gay, when Kieran couldn't care less about that; he's just still hurt because Gearóid didn't confide in him. Anyway, I've promised Kieran I'll stay out of it, so I will.

'OK, love, see you later.'

I go to end the call, and he says, 'Mags, I love you. Be careful, all right?'

I fight down a surge of frustration. When will he get over the shooting? Since he broke down after his mother's party and his fight with Gearóid, he's gone back to not talking about the way he feels, just ringing me at work and being worried about me. When will I get my strong, calm husband back again? Will I ever get him back?

'I will be careful,' I say irritably. 'And please don't ring me again at work today unless you really, really have to. I have enough to worry about without worrying about you worrying.' Then I realise I'm a horrible wife and relent. 'Forget I said that. I'm just under a lot of stress. I love you too.'

* * *

THE REST of the day is a nightmare.

We speak to anyone and everyone we can think of and draw complete blanks. Phillip seems to have vanished into thin air. The CCTV from the one or two shops and pubs that have it is so patchy and of such poor quality, it's no use at all. Ronan has alerted all the Garda cars in the area, but none of them have seen anything. Ronan keeps phoning me up to talk, but he has nothing useful to say so just annoys me by tying up the line. Also, I can't seem to convince him that the damage to the halting site was done by outsiders, and so it's hard to get him to take on board that Phillip might have run into a bunch of criminals.

I call in to Annette's to see if they've heard anything but no news. People keep bringing casseroles, although Annette, her hair limp and greasy, her face grey from stress, wants nothing but the news that Phillip is alive and well. Martha spends the day searching the fields and woods.

Everyone in Ballycarrick is on high alert, checking their own sheds and gardens, while Jerome McGovern and his sons and nephews are driving slowly up and down every back road and byway. Frustratingly, people keep phoning the Garda station complaining about 'a white van full of Travellers obviously looking for things to steal', and the St Colm's caretaker, Charlie Walsh, keeps getting on to me about the chickens, which must be the size of dinosaurs they're allegedly doing so much damage to the sports pitch. Still, at least he says he's done a thorough search of the school and grounds for Phillip, so that's something.

My heart sinks lower and lower as the day creeps towards evening.

Phillip is so vulnerable and young. Wherever he is, he must be very scared. I can't bear it, thinking what might be happening to him. My worst fear, which I don't voice to Martha or Annette, is that he went to check on the chickens and came across the vandals wrecking the place, and got hurt by them.

Or worse.

CHAPTER 17

*I*t's one in the morning when I finally get home. I would have stayed longer, but having had only two hours sleep the night before, thanks to having to drive Dolores to the airport, I can't go on without another couple of hours at least.

Kieran looks up from the TV as I come in.

'Sorry I'm so late. I hope everything went all right?'

'Everything was fine, Mags. Don't you worry. Do you want me to make you a sandwich?'

'No thanks. I'm going to have a shower.' I'm too tired to even eat.

I drag myself upstairs, go into the bathroom and strip off my uniform, turn the shower on and step in. The hot water cascading over me, the drumming of the jets on my head, is oddly soothing. I try to stop my mind racing. Annette, Phillip, Martha, Darren, Delia, Jerome… They scrabble for space in my exhausted brain.

Where is Phillip now? What is the link between Phillip and what happened at the McGovern site, if any? The last time we called his phone, it was dead.

I stand there for another few minutes. Bone-weary. I know people think that police don't get involved personally in the things that happen, but I can't do that; I just can't walk away. The crowd up in

Dublin are blue in the face sending us on courses on coping in a stressful job, but it doesn't help. Some people are better at it than others, the disconnecting. I'm terrible at it. And this case particularly, you'd want to be made of marble not to worry about poor Phillip.

I rack my brain for the millionth time. We've spoken to everyone, trying to find anyone who might have any inkling that he was maybe friends with people nobody knew about...and nothing.

I finally turn the shower off, wrap myself in a towel and sit at the dressing table to dry my hair. I look ancient. Tired, stressed, puffy eyes, and surely that chin wasn't always there? I lift my head, jutting my chin out, but no, decidedly double-chinned these days. Brilliant. All I need. I'm fifty and I look it.

I put on my pyjamas, a lovely, comfy brushed-jersey pair that do nothing for me but I don't care. They're cosy. I'm half lying in bed looking through my phone for a message from Ronan or anybody to see if there has been any update when Kate and Ellie appear at the bedroom door.

'What are you two doing awake?' I ask, secretly delighted to see them. 'It's the middle of the night!'

'I know, but Ellie woke up for the loo, and she saw you were home and woke me to come and see you,' Kate says as I draw her in for a hug. Ellie just stands beside the bed, as tall as me now.

'I'm sorry I wasn't here at all today. Did Dad cope all right with everything?'

They exchange a glance, an unspoken conversation.

'What's up?' I ask.

'Did you talk to Dad yet?'

'Yeah, well, not really. He was watching television and said everything was fine, not to worry. Did something happen?'

Another look.

'Girls, you're scaring me now. What is it? He didn't...get upset, did he?' I have a vision of my once-strong husband breaking down in front of his daughters, scaring the life out of them.

'Well...' says Kate.

'Not upset, but...forceful,' says Ellie. The word 'forceful' sounds old-fashioned coming out of her mouth, and I worry that she really means 'angry'.

'With you two?'

She looks startled. 'What? No!'

'So tell me what happened.'

Ellie glances again at Kate. 'Matthew Corcoran was making fun of Nana Nora's garden with all the American flags...'

'Oh dear.'

'And he and all his bully friends were ganging up on Kate and jeering her, and then they took her school bag and flushed it down the toilet...'

'Oh, darling...'

'All my books and my pencil case and calculator and everything, and all my beanie babies...and it was in the boys' toilets too,' says Kate furiously.

'And when she shouted at them and tried to get it back, one of them grabbed her and ripped her school shirt, and the boys saw her chest.'

I'm wide awake. 'Why did nobody ring me?'

'The school couldn't get you, so they rang Dad instead.'

'I'm so sorry...'

'No, it worked out great!' Ellie beams. 'Dad just sort of transmogrified into absolute Dad Hero! He roared up in his van, and instead of being all even-handed like you have to be in public because you're a guard, he flat out ordered our head teacher to suspend all the boys for a week or he'd sue the school for enabling the assault, and to charge the parents for all of Kate's damaged things or the school could pay for them, he didn't care which. Then he rang Matthew Corcoran's father – Dad knows him from school or something – and told him to tell his son to stay away from Kate or he'd have bigger problems than replacing a school bag. And after that he drove both of us over to Nana Nora and told her that she was not American and that she didn't know that politician fella from Adam and to take down all the flags and to stop making a complete show of us around the town. And that while she was at it, she had to talk to Gearóid and apologise for being so horrible about him being gay or she was going to lose him.'

Kate takes up the story, not to be outdone. 'And then in the middle of that, Wojtec rang. He'd cut his hand nearly off on a saw and had to go to the hospital to have it stitched back on, and so Dad had to bring him to Galway but he brought us along as well, so Ellie got to her audition after all and she got the Dorothy part. And then when we got home, he helped me with my Irish homework by sending a photo of it to Gearóid, and then he cooked the best chicken curry ever, a proper packet one with just chicken and no vegetables. If you're lucky, there'll be some left.'

I'm stunned. Why did I think my strong, calm husband had vanished on me forever?

'Kate, it doesn't sound like those boys will ever bother you again – their parents will be furious at them. And, Ellie, so many congratulations on being Dorothy! That's wonderful news! Right, I'd better go down and talk to your dad – he's had quite a day – so how about you two go to bed and I'll tuck you in, OK?'

Kate nods and gets off my lap.

'You can sleep with me in my bed if you want, Katie,' Ellie says, putting her arm around her little sister, and my heart fills. They might fight and steal each other's stuff, but for the rest of their lives, when the chips are down, they'll be there for each other and that's wonderful.

I go downstairs. Kieran is putting the milk back in the fridge. The TV is off. He looks shattered but happier than he's been for a while. I stand looking at him, marvelling that I thought he'd become unable to cope with life.

'So,' I say, 'I hear you've had quite a day.'

He winks at me. 'I thought I heard you talking to the girls.'

'They say you turned into "Dad Hero".'

He laughs. 'I wouldn't quite say that.'

'Well, I would. It's wonderful you got those boys suspended, and as for Nora, I can't wait to hear about that. But listen, first, Wojtec – how is he, and did he really cut his hand nearly off, like Kate says? I'll ring Mariola in the morning, see if she needs anything.'

He grins. 'No, they're being a bit overdramatic there, I'd say, but he did cut through a tendon. They'll be able to reattach it, so no long-term damage, and my insurance will cover his wages and all his hospital bills. And don't worry about Mariola. I organised one of the young lads to do a week's shopping for her and her boys, and her mother lives with them, so they won't have to think about anything but visiting him in hospital.'

'Oh, well done. But poor Mariola. It's so unlike Wojtec to have an accident.' I know the older Polish man well, and he's as much a stickler for health and safety as my husband.

'He picked up the saw without the safety guard. He's furious with himself. Says he was distracted by his brother phoning him and telling him all about his impending divorce. That's how accidents happen, Mags. With other people distracting you about their own worries. Like I've been doing to you, and making your life harder.'

I run across the kitchen and throw my arms around him. 'I'm sorry. I was horrible on the phone to you earlier. I didn't mean it. I know your worrying is all out of love for me.'

He hugs me back, then strokes my hair. 'No, you were right to have a go at me, Mags. I had a good think after that phone call and realised what if you kept calling me while I was on a roof in a strong wind, and telling me how worried you were about me falling off? How does that help me? It just makes my life more dangerous, having to deal with you worrying.'

'But your panic attacks –'

'Are my problem to fix. If it happens again, I'm going to go to the doctor and see what he says. I'm going to treat it like I have high blood pressure or something, a physical problem to be cured, not something we have to run our lives around.'

'I'll do anything I can to help. I love you so much. How are you feeling now?'

'Better than I have for a long time, to be honest. Just getting it sorted in my head today, realising it's not about you, it's about me, that's ninety percent of the battle, I think.' He holds me close and starts to kiss me as I lean against him.

My mobile rings upstairs.

'Leave it,' murmurs Kieran in my ear.

But I can't leave it. It has to be about Phillip. He's been found. I pull away and race up the stairs. I grab the phone before it can go to voice-mail. It's Delia.

'Delia?'

'Oh, Mags…'

'Is he alive?'

'Yes, he is. He's shaken up, but he's alive, Mags, he's alive!'

'Oh, thank God.' I fight back unprofessional tears. 'Has Martha been told?'

'My dad just phoned her, and she and Annette are on their way with a change of clothes.'

'Where was he?'

She makes an angry noise. 'In St Colm's. Dad would have found him a whole lot earlier if the school caretaker had let him come into the sports field instead of claiming he'd searched it himself and just going on about the chickens ruining the grass and how he was going to get the council on us. Dad had to wait until after dark to search the grounds, and even then it took hours because of the dark, but he found him in the end. The poor boy was hiding in a ditch full of brambles, and he was scared and wet and cold.'

I'm dizzy with relief while being furious with Charlie Walsh. 'So did Phillip tell you what happened?'

'He said he couldn't sleep because he was so worried about the hens not being shut in properly, even though Paddy told him they were. So he walked all the way to check, and then he was so tired, he crawled into their coop and lay down on the hay. Then he says a "bad man" woke him by bashing the coop with a hammer. Phillip tried to stop him, but the man pushed him and chased him, and he says he ran and ran until he found a ditch to hide in. And he was too scared to come out again in case the man was out there waiting for him, and he'd dropped his phone in the middle of the sports field so he couldn't call his mam or us.'

Instantly I go into investigation mode. We can't help it; it's bred into us in Garda College. 'Did he see this man? Can he give a description?'

'I asked him, but he's too scared and sad right now. I don't want to push him.'

'No, you're right. Can you put him on to me?'

'He's here in our caravan, wrapped up in a blanket. Phillip, I've someone here who wants to speak to you. It's Sergeant Munroe.'

A shuffle and then I hear his voice. 'Can you get my mam?'

The tears flow now, and I realise I've been holding my breath almost since he was taken. 'I will of course, pet. Your mam's on her way, Phillip, she'll be there any minute. Are you all right?'

'I'm starving, and I want my mam,' Phillip says matter-of-factly.

'But you're not hurt?' I ask.

'I have a sore foot because I had to run away from the bad man, and I cut myself, and I'm scratched all over with the brambles, and a nettle stung me. But I kept quiet as a mouse so the bad man wouldn't find me.'

'You're a brave, clever boy, Phillip.'

'Yes, I am. Does Mam know I'm here? I'm with Jerome and Delia and Olivia. Will you come too?'

'Of course I'll come. You stay there, all right?'

'OK. Can you find my phone? I dropped it in the field.'

'Of course we can, don't worry. Can you put Jerome on for me?'

Another pause and then, 'Hello, Mags?'

'Oh, Jerome, I can't tell you the relief. Thank God you found him.'

"Tis no bother. The school caretaker, that Charlie Walsh, wouldn't let me in to search. I'd have had him a lot sooner if I hadn't had to wait for it to get dark. The poor lad was scared to death.'

'I know. I'll be speaking to him in due course. Anyway, he's safe, that's the main thing. I'm coming over now, Jerome. Sit tight.' As I dress again, I glance at the clock. Two o'clock. Twenty-four hours since I've had any sleep at all, and it was only a couple of hours then. Still, I feel like I'm firing on all cylinders, and I couldn't sleep if I tried.

I see Kieran standing at the bedroom door. 'I'm sorry, I just need to go over there, figure out what on earth happened. Whoever scared Phillip was trying to cause trouble for the McGoverns, but I suspect I'll have my work cut out to make anything stick.'

'Go. Get Phillip home. We'll be fine. But, Mags?'

I turn from the door.

'You'll do great, whatever happens.'

I laugh with pleasure. 'Why, thank you for your confidence in me, Mr Munroe.'

* * *

THE ROADS ARE quiet as I drive through the town. It's a cloudy night without a chink of moonlight. As I reach the site on the far side of the playing pitches, Annette and Martha pull up in Martha's little old banger.

'I thought I'd lost him, Mags,' sobs Martha.

The three of us run together to Jerome's caravan, where the big man is waiting for us on the doorstep, holding Phillip's hand.

'Oh, my darling, are you all right, pet? I was so worried...' Martha hugs her son tightly, while Annette beams and hugs Jerome.

'Jerome, we can't thank you enough.'

'I'm hungry, Mam,' says Phillip in a squashed voice. He has a blanket draped around his shoulders, and he's wearing a ridiculously big tracksuit of Jerome's, the legs and sleeves rolled up as far as they will go but still too long. Someone has cleaned most of the mud off his face, and he has a plaster on a cut. But on the whole, he seems none the worse for wear. 'And Jerome's clothes are too big.'

'It's OK, darling. We brought your Man United tracksuit pants and your new black hoodie, so you can change, and I've two big chocolate cakes in the press at home waiting for you.'

'And he's already had two ham sandwiches and a pot of tea.' Jerome grins.

'I'm really, really, really, really hungry...'

'Don't worry, Phillip, we have any amount of casseroles and cakes and bread that people brought up to us today, and we'll have you as full as a bus and tucked up in your own bed at home in no time. Now, Jerome, if there's somewhere to change, we'll get his own clothes on him and then get out of your way.'

'Dora! Delia! Olivia!' calls Jerome into the caravan. 'Can you show these ladies where they can get Phillip changed into his own clothes?'

Dora emerges shyly and beckons them in, and Delia and Olivia are there in the background, smiling and eager to help.

I'm smiling as well, with relief. If all Phillip's worried about is his belly, he can't be too badly hurt.

While Phillip is being looked after, I step away to make a call. 'Ronan?'

'Oh, Mags, it's you...' he answers sleepily. 'It's good to hear from you.'

I doubt it is good to hear from me at half past two in the morning, but I applaud his politeness. 'It's just to let you know Phillip Turner has been found alive and well, by Jerome McGovern, so you can have everyone stand down.'

'That's great...' I can hear him yawning, and then he comes a bit more awake. 'Jerome McGovern, the Traveller?'

'That's right. He found him barely twenty minutes ago, hiding in a ditch in the grounds of St Colm's, and he'd have found him a whole lot sooner if that caretaker had let him in to look instead of claiming he'd searched the place himself.'

'And he was there in the ditch from early morning till now?'

'Apparently so. He was worried about Jerome's chickens and went to make sure they were locked in, and he fell asleep in the coop. And then the vandal or vandals I was telling you about started wrecking the site, so he tried to stop them. They pushed him and chased him, and he got away into the school grounds and dived into the ditch for cover and lay as still as he could. He was scared to get out again.'

'And does he know who attacked him?'

'He's not said anything about that yet. All he wants is food. I'll interview him in more detail tomorrow.'

There's a long pause, and just as I think I've lost the connection, Ronan says slowly but alertly, 'Listen, Mags, and you know I trust your instincts, but the story about the site being vandalised… I mean, I met that new inspector, and he says it's not new, how messy it was. They were on their third warning.'

'What? Ronan, that's just not true!'

'They were, Mags. There were ponies out one day, and rubbish on the road another day, and then they let their chickens run free all over the sports fields of that school next door. So those were three warnings. So to be honest, even if McGovern's story is true, I'm not surprised the caretaker didn't want a bunch of them stomping all over the place.'

I can't believe what I'm hearing. 'What do you mean, *even if* Jerome's story is true?'

He sighs, like I'm being naïve. 'Mags, I'm just saying, it's a strange coincidence, isn't it? Phillip going missing on the same night the site got trashed?'

'But it wasn't a coincidence. The reason he went missing is because he got chased by whoever did it.'

'But his being there in the first place? That's what I mean, Mags. Maybe the young McGoverns who got left behind when everyone else went to the funeral, maybe they even encouraged Phillip to join in whatever was happening, and something went a bit wrong? I do trust your instincts, Mags, but maybe they're blurred by having young Delia on the team. Seriously, I wouldn't just believe all that I'm being told here. You know as well as I do what they're like.'

I bite my tongue, literally, so hard it hurts. Chief Inspector Ronan Brady is my superior officer. I can't afford to have a go at him. Instead I say stiffly, 'OK, Ronan. You're right. I'll keep an open mind.'

'Good for you. And interview the lad as soon as possible, and get him seen by a doctor tonight.'

'We'll get our local GP to have a look at him in the morning. To be honest, he needs to be at home with his mother now, and I can speak to him tomorrow.'

'Well, Mags, if there's DNA, we need to take it,' he says, and I know what he means. If there was physical or sexual contact, that evidence is vital to secure a conviction, but I go with my gut on this.

'I'll make sure the clothes he was wearing are kept bagged and unwashed in the station with a list of the people known to have handled them, and I'll tell his mother it's very important to listen to everything Phillip says, even if it seems irrelevant, in case we can pick up any clues to this man's identity. And in the morning, I'll see how he is and hear the whole story. I'll be in touch then, all right?'

'OK, Mags, do it your own way.' He yawns again. 'And don't get me wrong, I'm delighted he's been found. It's really, really great.'

* * *

AN HOUR LATER, and I'm finally in bed, my husband's arms around me, and I turn to him, my eyes half open. 'I'm never going to be able to sleep, Kieran, my mind is going nineteen to the...'

The next thing I know, it's mid-morning.

CHAPTER 18

I've barely made it to the station when a call comes in that there's some kind of a disturbance up at the graveyard. Myself and Delia go to check it out and find a group of young Carmodys gathered around Blades Carmody's elaborate marble grave, drinking and smoking and playing loud music.

Blades was shot dead two years ago, trying to protect Natasha McGovern from human traffickers, and it is the anniversary of his death. Poor Blades is after gaining some kind of cult hero status among the young lads, a symbol of bravado or something. He was always in trouble with us, in and out of court, and to be honest, it was his fault the traffickers were drawn to Natasha in the first place. But he died trying to save her, and that's what's remembered.

The graveyard has a corner of magnificently ornate Traveller graves, and the party has spilled over from Blades Carmody's grave to others, leaving the place littered with cans and cigarette butts and flowers crushed. One of the graves they've managed to desecrate is Dacie's. The McGoverns won't take kindly to that.

Delia is furious and so am I, but that isn't what's needed here. We need calm. There must be ten or fifteen young men, all aged late teens to mid-twenties, and they are clearly under the influence of something. Weed, by the smell of it – and strong weed at that. Where on earth did that stuff come from? I'd thought Ballycarrick was fairly clean of drugs. I radio to Michael and Darren to come as backup, in case things turn nasty. Often the presence of even one guard is enough to disperse a crowd, but this feels different because these young men are all either drunk or high or both.

'You have to leave,' I say firmly, approaching them. 'Come on, everyone out.'

'Or what, shady lady,' says one of them, staggering to his feet. 'We don't have to do nothin' you say. This is our grave, he was our kid, now feck off and leave us at it, grieving our dead in peace.'

This young man is a cousin of Blades, though which one I can't say. His head is shaved, and he's got a livid scar on his neck. He's wearing a very expensive-looking tracksuit and runners that I know cost hundreds. His blue eyes are glassy, and he has a bottle in one hand and what is clearly a joint in the other.

'Lenny, you shouldn't be smoking weed in a graveyard...' Delia begins.

He slurs something at her in Gammon, and whatever it is, it stings her. They see her as a turncoat, I know that. To her credit she doesn't react angrily, just answers him in the same language, after which he simmers down a bit. I'm not exactly sure what she says, but I've picked up a bit of Gammon over the years and I think it's about how I'm the sergeant who saved Natasha after Blades was shot, and Blades would want them to show me some respect.

Despite Lenny backing off, I decide we're out of our depth. Most of these are kids I've dealt with for years, many of whom have been in tears in the station, but in a pack like this, teenage boys can turn dangerous. And they're all very high indeed and will need to be escorted out of the graveyard so they don't do any more damage.

I give Delia a look, and we turn, saying nothing further, and walk back towards my car, the whoops and yells of laughter and victory ringing in our ears.

As we reach the cemetery gates, Darren and Michael pull up in the Garda car. I quickly brief them, and they put the siren on. Police in

Ireland are usually unarmed, but we carry extendable batons, pepper spray and handcuffs as standard. I hope none of that will be needed here. We re-enter the graveyard to find the siren has sent most of them scrambling over the cemetery wall, which is usually the way it goes; teenage thugs stop being brave very quickly once they hear sirens.

We run and catch Lenny; he's slow because of whatever he's taken. And Delia and Michael easily catch and cuff two more cousins and march them out of the graveyard.

We will take them in and charge them for public order offences, destruction of property, possession of a controlled substance, threatening a police officer. The two boys Delia nabbed are underage and will get a warning, but Lenny Carmody is nineteen with form; he will have a preliminary hearing at the district court and will probably get bail pending the hearing. I wouldn't like to be any of these three once their family get hold of them. Death and gravestones are intrinsic to Traveller culture, and defiling them will not be taken lightly. For once Lenny might be crying to be kept in jail rather than let out.

I see Delia texting and call her aside. 'This is a Garda matter, not a Traveller one. You understand that, don't you?'

She nods. 'But, Sergeant, everyone has to know they've made a mess of Nana's grave and it needs cleaning up.'

By the time we've got the lads in the car with Darren and Michael, and have waited around while Darren reads them their rights, several of the McGovern women have arrived and are cleaning the graves, replacing the broken flowers and picking up all the beer bottles, cans, takeaway wrappers and joint butts. Within an hour or two, the place will be restored.

* * *

I DRIVE BACK to the station in my own car, dropping Delia off at the halting site as it's the end of her shift.

'How did it go talking to your dad about the night before last?' I ask before she gets out of the car.

She colours. 'I told him I was working, that we got a call about a drunk and disorderly and so I was doing that.'

'And he believed you?' I raise an eyebrow. Delia is not a good liar.

She nods. 'He did. I think he would never consider the alternative, and anyway, he was so vexed about the mess and the photographs and so worried about Phillip and all the rest of it. He nearly ate the head off of Niall and Paddy for not hearing anything because they were using gaming headsets with the Xbox. I feel terrible because it's way more my fault than theirs, and I was lying about where I was.'

I look at her. 'Do you think you'll ever tell your father about Darren, Delia?'

'You're not going to tell him, are you, Sergeant?' She looks like a rabbit caught in the headlights.

'Of course not,' I say. 'But I think maybe you should.'

'I can't, Sergeant. Please don't make us…please. He'll kill us both.'

I smile at her. 'Do you honestly think your father would harm a hair on your head? Or Darren's for that matter?'

'Not like that, but he'd be so… Well, he wouldn't allow it.'

'So what?' I gaze at her. 'You'll marry a Traveller man that he picks for you just to be the obedient dutiful daughter?'

'No, I'd never do that.' Her eyes flash with determination. 'If I can't have Darren, I won't have anyone.'

'So a lifetime of sadness for the two of you?' I rest my head back against the seat, suddenly shattered tired again. 'Listen, Delia, your nana saw something in you, and so did I. That's why we helped you break the mould and become a guard, and when your father saw how happy you were, he accepted it. I saw the photo up on the sideboard in his caravan, a big one of you on the day you passed out of Garda College. If he was shocked or against it, he wouldn't have that in pride of place now, would he?'

'This is different.' She is adamant.

'Maybe it is. But maybe it isn't.'

'What do you mean?'

'I think sometimes people, and men in particular, object to the concept of something when it's in the abstract. Just like Kieran didn't want to go to an Airbnb on our holidays – he said he'd rather go to a hotel where you knew what you were getting. Reviews and all of that. And so I left it, but then I booked a place in Spain. It was an Airbnb, but I never told him that, and now he'll tell anyone who'll listen that you're much better off with a privately owned Airbnb than a hotel. See? The one we went to was lovely, and so I didn't tell him how I booked it till I got there. It's the same with your father and the Garda. Once he got used to the reality, it was so much better than he'd imagined.'

'So my dad might hate the idea of me having a settled boyfriend, but if he gets used to Darren…'

'Exactly. And Darren got into Jerome's good books before, after he was so helpful minding the site when Natasha was in danger. So maybe we should give him the same job, to protect the site from being vandalised again.'

She looks uncomfortable. 'I don't know. I'd feel like I was tricking Daddy somehow, pushing Darren in front of him.' She's so honest; she hates lying even for the best reasons.

'It would be me doing the pushing. So you don't have to feel guilty. And, Delia, we all just get one life to live, just the one. And you have to please yourself. Make yourself happy. To be honest, when you arrived into the station two years ago, Darren was like a sick calf gazing at you, and I warned him off, told him he was wasting his time. I would have said more or less the same to you at the time. But you want to be together, any fool can see that, so I'm going to go back to the station now and tell Darren he's on patrol duty.'

She shivers and looks scared and pleased in equal measure. Then she gets out of the car and makes a run for the safety of her father's caravan.

CHAPTER 19

*N*ow that Dolores is gone to Germany, Teo decides to make good on his promise to bring myself and Kieran out to dinner in Galway. We treat ourselves to a taxi, and I can't resist wearing my green dress again, the one that got Kieran dragging me into the forest the last time. At least he can't do that when we're in a taxi, so we won't be late this time.

'So your mam and the doc are officially an item?' he asks, holding my hand as we drive into the city.

'She really likes him, but she's in the horrors about things getting more...' – I glance towards the taxi driver, but the glass screen is closed – 'intimate, God love her. It's been years and years, and she's got herself in a right twist about it. I told her it's like falling off a bike. There hasn't been any sleepover yet, so I don't know if she'll ever make the leap.'

'If she does, there's hope for us all then, I suppose.' He winks at me. 'I hope we're still at it when we're their age.'

I smooth my green dress, watching him watching me. 'There's hope for you now anyway – I can't promise anything else. I might take to the knitting, or the bingo, and lose interest in you completely. It happens, you know. The men of Ireland losing their marital rights because their women have more interest in some fella calling "legs eleven" and "two fat ladies" in a draughty hall.'

'Ah, now…with a sexy man like me by your side? You'd never swap me for bingo.'

'No, I wouldn't.' But he's got me thinking. 'It's not that complicated, is it, knowing if you fancy someone or not?'

'Not for me, anyway,' he says, squeezing my thigh.

I absent-mindedly put my hand on his. 'I mean, I know everything went haywire around the menopause for me, but that didn't actually stop me fancying you underneath it all. And Mam's well past her menopause. Do you think all this reluctance on her part is because she doesn't like Teo that way but doesn't realise it's about chemistry and thinks it's just because of her age?'

He is taken aback. 'If not Teo, then who does she want? I mean, he's an oncologist, he dances, he's handsome, he's rich…'

'Yeah, all that.'

'He's even years younger than Marie, so she's not going to end up pushing him around in a wheelchair. What more can she want?'

'I don't know, Kieran. What more does any of us want? Yet if someone like that had come along while you and I were courting, I wouldn't have looked twice at them.'

He smiles. 'I don't know, Mags. I mean, we were mad in love. She's seventy and this guy is perfect for her. Who else has she met over the years who's ticked all the boxes like this?'

'But the heart doesn't add up lists of good and bad points like taking a test. It just knows what it needs to be happy.'

'And who has made her happier than this guy?'

'I don't know…' I hesitate to say it. 'Joe Dillon?'

He roars with surprised laughter. 'Joe "lunch once a week" Dillon? He was never going to get off the starting blocks. After all these years?'

He's still laughing as we draw up outside the restaurant, but as I gather my bag and coat, I can't seem to get that sound out of my head…a man's heavy feet, clump, clump, clumping around on Deirdre's sprung floor.

Mam looks lovely in a pair of black trousers and a scarlet-red blouse. Her hair is silky and cut beautifully, and she's even wearing light make-up.

'Marie, you are looking gorgeous.' Kieran hugs her. He loves my mother and she loves him.

'Teo, this is my daughter Mags and her husband, Kieran.'

Teo looks even better in real life than in his pictures, his hair a lot more black than silver and his skin golden. His eyes are dark brown and twinkly, and his crow's feet are laughter lines.

'It's lovely to finally meet you both,' he says. 'Marie talks about you all the time. Can I get you both a drink?'

'I'll give you a hand, Teo,' Kieran offers, and both men go to the bar.

'Mam, he's gorgeous!' I say.

'He is, isn't he?' Mam grins proudly.

'So is tonight the night?' I tease.

She gives a sharp shake of her head. 'No, it is not. And please don't joke about it in front of him. He's already wondering about when he's going to pass the test.'

'The test?'

'My list of pros and cons. But, Mags, he'd pass anyone's list, wouldn't he?'

'He would, Mam. So what are you waiting for?' I'm genuinely curious, especially after my conversation with Kieran in the car. I get a sudden urge to tell her about Deirdre Hickey's door being ajar the other morning, and again this morning, but then the men return with two pints of Guinness and two gin and tonics, and the moment has passed.

We have a lovely night, and Teo is great fun. He's got a mischievous sense of humour, gently teasing Mam about not allowing anyone to meet him up until now, and she seems really relaxed around him. He shows us pictures of his son, Fabio, with his little daughter who looks about Kate's age. We talk about anything and everything, and I can't believe how quickly the night passes.

Teo insists on treating us all, and I offer Mam a spin home in the taxi with us so Teo doesn't have to bring her to Ballycarrick and then drive back to Galway by himself, where he has a clinic in the morning.

'So I've still not passed the test?' he teases my mother. 'You're abandoning me?'

Kieran pats Teo's shoulder sympathetically. 'I have to warn you, Teo, they're hard-won, these women of ours. Worth it once you manage it, every day of the week, but very hard to get.'

I look at him in surprise. I don't seem to remember playing hard to get. But maybe men see things differently from their side of the fence.

CHAPTER 20

$\mathcal{I}$'d rather have a root canal than have the neighbourhood watch meeting this Tuesday. After my phone call with Ronan Brady when Phillip was found last week, I've got a fair idea the sort of nonsense I'll be hearing about the McGoverns.

And it isn't just Ronan. I'm picking the rumours up from all around the town.

First rumour, overheard in Teresa's Bakery: The McGoverns were smoking weed in the graveyard. (It was the Carmodys, but who can be expected to tell one Travelling family apart from the other?)

Second rumour, overheard in Gerry's while getting my hair done: The older McGoverns went to a funeral, and the young ones, Niall and Paddy, had a massive party and smoked weed and God knows what else besides and trashed the place. (Worryingly, I catch a whisper about photographic evidence, so it sounds like the inspector's pictures have indeed been leaked.)

Third rumour, overheard in the Samovar while lunching with Sharon: The Travellers had to have had something to do with Phillip going missing. They probably had him locked up in a caravan. (This despite the fact that Phillip's own mother says Jerome is a hero for saving her son.)

Fourth rumour, and this one originates with Duckie, because Kieran heard him testing it out in Lydia's Turkish Barber's: Drumlish used to be a fine site when Dacie McGovern was alive, but since Jerome took over, he's too weak, and everything has gone downhill and they're no better than the Carmodys now. (Complete lies, the McGoverns have not been in trouble since Dacie's death.)

Can I stand to listen to it all being parroted by Olive? I toy with the idea of cancelling the meeting entirely, but I suppose I'd better not. It's better to let people say what they have to say, get it off their chest, and maybe I can put the other side of the story.

At twelve o'clock, the members of the committee start to arrive. The first in are Derry, Olive, Oscar and Joanna. Annette isn't coming because she and Martha are still not letting Phillip out of their sight. And there are a couple of new faces – two young blond women I think I've seen waiting for their sons outside St Colm's but whose names I don't know yet.

'Celine and Mairéad, I'm not sure if you've met Sergeant Munroe?' Olive twitters. God but she's one irritating woman. All tinkly and tight smiles and as fake as they come. She'd stab you in the back as quick as look at you.

I smile at the newcomers. 'Would you like coffee?'

'Yes, we'll all have coffee, thank you, Sergeant,' says Olive, as if I am set on earth to be her personal servant. 'Now, as I was saying, this is Celine Davitt and Mairéad Cullen. We were chatting at the school gates last week, and they were saying how they were new to the area. Their boys have just started in St Colm's, and I suggested they join us as a way to become involved in the community.' She gives a tinkly laugh.

'Welcome to you both,' I say politely. 'Anyone is allowed to join this committee, and I hope you'll be regular attendees. Oh, thank you, Derry. I was hoping someone would offer.'

The former headmaster winks at me, and I smile as he boils the kettle and unscrews the lid of the coffee jar.

'And this is Joanna Burke,' continues Olive, for all the world as if she's in charge of this meeting rather than me, 'and Oscar O'Leary.

And the man making the coffee – how very progressive of you, Derry – is Derry Hartnett. We're usually one more, but Annette isn't here, is she, Sergeant?'

'No indeed.' I nod. 'Now, I wonder if we might keep today's meeting quite short as I'm a bit under pressure at the moment.'

'Oh, I'm sure you're very busy, Sergeant, so we'll do our best to keep it brief,' says Olive, still acting as if she's running the show. 'It's just we have an important matter to discuss, so if you can bear with us…'

At that point the door opens, and I think, *Perfect. Just when I thought things couldn't get worse.* Nora Munroe has arrived. I have never seen her in my station before, and I wonder for a moment if I'm under too much strain and I'm seeing things. But no, it really is her.

I stand up quickly. 'I'm sorry, this is the neighbourhood watch meeting, Nora. If you want to see me, can you take a seat outside by the public desk?'

'I will not wait outside. I am here for the neighbourhood watch.' My mother-in-law smiles, a smile that strikes nothing but alarm in me. 'And I'm sure I have as much right to be here as anyone else.'

'You have of course, Nora. Mags was just saying that herself.' Olive beams. 'Are you here to discuss moving the halting site?' She thinks she's spotted an anti-Traveller ally, and she's not wrong.

Nora plonks herself down next to Olive, her handbag in her lap. 'I am always willing and open to discuss anything that improves the town,' she says to the room at large, 'and that's why I am here today, with a wonderful announcement which I am sure you will all want to be the first to hear.'

'Coffee?' asks Derry, who is circulating with a tray.

'Thank you, Derry.' Nora takes a cup.

Olive does as well. 'Thanks, Derry. And what would that announcement be, Nora?' It's quite clear Olive is prepared to humour my mother-in-law in anything if she can get Nora's support to move the McGoverns.

Everyone takes a seat, and Nora scans the gathering. She pauses theatrically, and then she speaks again. 'Well…' She fishes in her bag and produces an envelope with an American stamp, brandishing it around. 'As you may have heard, my family is directly related to a very important congressman in the United States who may well run for President one day. As he has relatives in Ballycarrick, I thought it would be only polite to invite him over for a town celebration, just as Mr Obama was invited by his cousins to Moneygall. And the Blewitts invited Mr Biden to Ballina, Mr Reagan went to Ballyporeen, and Mr Bush's seven-times great-grandfather came from Cork. We here in Ballycarrick are following a long and proud tradition of filling the halls of American power with Irish blood.'

I cannot react. I must keep a straight face, and I silently chew the inside of my cheek. She's nothing if not dramatic, my monster-in-law, I'll give her that.

'So I wrote, and this is the congressman's reply...'

I brace myself. Kieran has told me about this pro forma letter she got thanking donors for their support, referring to Nora as an exemplary American citizen, and not even physically signed by Congressman Whatever His Name Is, who incidentally she's never clapped eyes on and he wouldn't know her in a blue fit. Ellie's word pops into my head again. *Mortifying.*

Nora begins reading. '"Dear Nora, how wonderful to hear I have Irish cousins with my own name of McMahon. My great-great-grandfather, Frank McMahon, sailed to America from Galway in 1849. My Irish constituency is very important to me, and I will be delighted to attend a street party in your great little country, and to reconnect with my ancestors. My press secretary will be reaching out to you to arrange a date in June of next year. Yours sincerely, Max McMahon."'

Nora lowers the letter and beams triumphantly around the room. 'Now that's going to put Ballycarrick on the map, isn't it? So I've already emailed all the local papers, and I've told Tessa Merrion too, and she's agreed it's an excellent story and will be here personally to cover the event.'

I am unable to believe what I'm hearing. Maybe my first hunch was right and I am having delusions. Tessa Merrion is the Western correspondent for RTÉ, the national broadcaster.

Joanna Burke sits forward in her chair. 'So if we hold a street party for Congressman McMahon, RTÉ will be here to cover it? Can I see the letter, Nora?'

'That's right,' says Nora proudly, passing the letter over. 'And I have plenty of American flags in storage for the event.' She shoots me a narrow-eyed look. She clearly blames me for Kieran's outburst. 'I suppose *some people* will be glad I bought them now.'

'Well done, Nora.' Joanna passes the letter on to Derry, who studies it with interest. Oscar is crossing himself, and the two young blond women are clearly impressed.

'Thank you, Joanna,' says Nora, with another pointed glance at me. 'It's so nice to have one's community efforts recognised. And of course, this committee is going to be very important. We will need to paint the houses, and make sure everything is clean and tidy, with lots of flowers, and put up proper working CCTV for the congressman's security...'

Olive notices Joanna looking at her and jumps in. 'Yes, and of course the Travellers will have to go as soon as possible so we can get the site cleaned up. We can't have ponies and rubbish and drug raves bringing the town down, not when the congressman is coming to visit.'

'Of course not,' says Nora, and everyone except Derry nods, like it's a simple non-negotiable matter.

'So what we need to do,' says Olive, striking while the iron is hot, 'is draft a letter from this committee to the council saying that the local neighbourhood watch committee supports the removal of the halting site from the edge of the town.'

I finally find my voice. 'But I've told you before, Olive, this is not neighbourhood watch business. It's council business.'

She smiles sweetly at me. 'Then there's no need for you to sign the letter, Sergeant. It will be going from us, not from the Guards.'

I can feel the blood travelling up my neck. Any minute now I will look like a beetroot. I can't afford as a guard to get angry, but I'm afraid I might. I look around the room, and Derry meets and holds my eye. He hasn't said much at meetings before, except occasionally murmuring 'hear, hear' after Annette has said something sensible. I pray he'll jump in and say something now.

I like Derry enormously. He is a good man, and he commands respect in Ballycarrick for all his years as principal of the primary school. He can be gruff and impatient, and he gives the impression that he'd rather you got on with whatever you're telling him, but there's hardly a household here that hasn't been touched by his humanity and common sense. He knows every seed, breed and generation of families for miles, and his handling of awkward situations is exemplary.

He's also the reason the Travellers around this part of the world fare better in school. Delia and her siblings, for example, all finished primary, and most went to halfway through secondary at least. They can read and write. The trouble is it's hard to motivate them to work hard at school and achieve qualifications when nobody would employ them anyway. But Derry never lets that influence him. He doesn't segregate them, or make them feel anything but members of the school community.

Now I look at him, begging him with my eyes to help me.

He clears his throat. 'Well,' he says, looking around the room, 'I think the McGoverns are a very interesting family. They have all come through my school, right back to Jerome, and they're intelligent and capable, and very interested in their own history. As the principal of a school for decades, I like to view everything as a teaching moment. If the McGoverns were part of the town celebrations for Congressman McMahon, they could show off their way of life, blacksmithing, singing their songs, maybe have a sulky race down the high street.' Sulkies are small, light, horse-drawn carriages, and the Travellers race them with great skill.

'That sounds interesting?' ventures Celine, one of the newcomers.

'But they're drug addicts!' gasps Olive.

Derry looks at her with his eyebrows gently raised. 'No, you're mistaken, Olive. I know there was a spot of bother with the Carmodys recently, but that's a completely different family from some way off, so not to be confused, and Mags ran them straight out of town and they haven't come back.'

'What about the ponies and chickens?' she asks desperately. Joanna is sending her covert signals, cocking her head and tightening her lips, urging Olive on to say the nasty things that Joanna won't say herself in public.

'The animal welfare officer has consistently given the McGoverns a clean bill of health on their care of animals,' I say firmly. 'The ponies are always tethered, and the chickens are in at night.'

'They have ponies and chickens? Oh, how sweet!' chorus Celine and Mairéad. They are clearly city girls, and of course ponies and chickens would be just what they moved to the countryside for. 'Would they let our younger kids see them?'

'Of course. They're absolutely charming to children. They've been taking wonderful care of a young man with Down's syndrome who recently moved to the town,' I say, and when Olive opens her mouth to accuse the McGoverns of kidnapping Phillip, I shoot her such a look that she doesn't dare go there.

'Oh, how lovely...' coo the young women.

'They take drugs!' Olive almost shouts at her new friends, realising she is losing them.

They crease their foreheads and look at Derry in puzzlement. 'But didn't you say that was a different set of Travellers altogether, who don't live here?'

'That's right,' he says, and I could kiss him, because the gruff old fellow has the new women eating out of the palm of his hand.

'But it's quite clear who's supplying the drugs,' says Joanna suddenly. Normally she leaves the dirty business to Olive, but Olive is clearly forgetting her lines and so reluctantly Joanna has been forced to step in.

Olive takes her cue and nods furiously. 'Yes, I forgot to say, everyone knows it's the McGoverns who are the suppliers. They visit other Travellers all over the country and bring back the drugs in their big cars, which have secret compartments.'

'Oh goodness!' Celine is open-mouthed.

'Why haven't you done anything about this?' Mairéad asks me directly, clearly astonished at how badly I'm falling down on the job. 'We were assured by the estate agent that Ballycarrick was a nice place to live, and now we're discovering it's a crime-ridden village?'

I take a moment before I answer her, waiting for my boiling blood to settle. 'Because, Mairéad, this accusation has never been made before in my hearing. Olive, if you have indeed witnessed or have evidence of a criminal act, and for some reason have not reported it to me before, then you need to stay behind after the meeting and I will take a witness statement, which will form part of an investigation that will then, if necessary, be sent to the DPP for assessment.'

She looks alarmed. She's a bully and a snob, but even she doesn't want to take on the Director of Public Prosecutions, and wasting Garda time is an offence. 'Well, I haven't witnessed anything myself, of course...'

'Then you know someone who has?'

She flounders, speechless.

'I have a proposal,' says my mother-in-law loudly, and I turn to her in relief. I'm actually hoping she's going to start talking about her precious US congressman again, which shows how desperate I am. Instead, she says, 'What we need is a town hall.'

'A town hall?' Celine is confused. 'Ballycarrick is a bit small to have a proper town hall?'

'No, a town hall meeting. Just like they do in America,' explains Nora. 'When people have ideas or run for election, then they have a town hall meeting where everyone can ask questions of the people on the platform, and the community make up their minds one way or the other about what's being suggested. It's very informative and inter-esting and democratic, which is the way all politics should be.'

I stare at her, stunned. I'm not completely sure, and it's going to take a while for me to process this, but I think my mother-in-law might have just made a brilliant suggestion. I've often thought that if the townspeople of Ballycarrick actually knew all the ins and outs of

Traveller life, and listened to a few of them talk about it, then maybe, just maybe, we could begin to break down barriers.

Olive and Joanna share an unspoken conversation in a glance. They're rattled by the idea of not operating behind closed doors, but they want Nora on their side so have to be nice to her.

'That's a great idea, Nora.' Joanna's brittle smile betrays her discomfort. I know she was hoping to get this done under the radar, but a change of tack is now clearly needed. 'So will there be speakers, or what's the plan?'

'There will be speakers,' says Derry, suddenly jumping in on Nora's side. 'We can ask someone from the council, and someone from St Colm's, and of course someone from the Travelling community, and allow the people of Ballycarrick to make up their own minds.'

Joanna chokes slightly on her coffee.

'I know the new principal of the primary school well,' he carries on, 'so I'm sure I can arrange to have the hall for the first Tuesday of next month at 7 p.m., and I'll make sure there are posters printed to say all are welcome, and I'll chair it myself. I'll get Annette to help as well. Now let's wrap up the meeting, because I'm sure we all know that Mags has more important things to deal with at the moment.'

Well, I wasn't expecting that. Instead of all this behind-the-doors poison and innuendo, there's going to be an open public meeting where the Travelling community finally gets to speak. Though it might have been inadvertent, and God knows that woman has never done anything to help me in all the years, I find myself congratulating her. *Well done, Nora.* I love it.

CHAPTER 21

*A*fter a mercifully quiet week, Delia and I have to give evidence at the district court trial of Lenny Carmody. The case gets adjourned until later that morning as the first hearing has gone on longer than expected, so we decide to go for a coffee while we wait.

There's a place around the corner from the courthouse where more deals are struck than inside, and we find a table at the back. I realise as I sit down that behind me is Chief Inspector Ronan Brady.

'Ah, Mags, how are you? I've been meaning to text you to see how you're getting on.' He stands up, his coffee finished, and comes over.

'Grand, Ronan, thanks.' I smile, but I've not forgotten what he said the night Phillip was found.

'Well, you're looking well…and in fine spirits.'

I give him a look. That's a peculiar thing to say and he knows it. Delia casts a side-eye at him.

He flounders. 'I just mean, it's good to see you looking so…'

I let him off the hook. 'Busy?'

I know what it's like; I have a bit of verbal diarrhoea too sometimes in awkward situations. Never at work, weirdly – I love nothing more than a long awkward silence when I'm questioning someone –

but socially I'm bad at it, and I come home and I berate myself for the babbling out of me to fill the gaps.

One time at one of Kieran's mother's awkward lunches, I told the parish priest, who had a rash on his hand, that I often get rashes. Just trying to make conversation. And then went on to explain that sometimes the rash turns out to be thrush. I actually told the parish priest that, that I had thrush. I thought the poor man was going to choke. Can you believe it? I blush every time I think about it. So I feel for people who are like rabbits in the headlights.

'Yeah, I'm sure Ballycarrick is keeping you all flat out.' He's relieved to be rescued.

I hope he doesn't ask me and Delia why we're here. He's not completely against Travellers, but I spend a lot of my time trying to rid the guards around me of an ingrained prejudice, so telling him I'm giving evidence in a case against a member of the Travelling community isn't something I'd enjoy. It could be worse, I could have run into Duckie, but still.

Instead, he asks, 'And what's happening about the council and the sale of the Drumlish site and all of that now?'

I realise he hasn't recognised Delia, who is in her new uniform. He first met her when she was a Reserve, and he owes her because it was Delia who saved my life when Ronan inadvertently sent me into harm's way.

'You remember Garda Delia McGovern, don't you, Ronan? She came to my rescue in Spiddal.'

He colours. 'Ah, Delia. Wonderful you're with us. I'm…ah… I hope your family is well.'

She fixes him with a steely look. There are certain things for which she's never forgiven him, including assuming her cousin Natasha would willingly run off with a strange man. 'My parents are sick with worry, Detective Inspector. The council are meeting next month, but it looks like we're to be moved. The photos the new inspector took that morning straight after the mystery vandals wrecked our home look very bad, and somehow they've got out on social media. They make us look like we're filthy, and nobody will believe we didn't do it to ourselves.'

He flushes deeper. 'That…that's terrible, Delia. I wish there was something I could do. Hopefully it will all work out for the best.'

'Thank you, Inspector,' she says, her innocent words somehow conveying deep contempt.

He turns to me for respite. 'How's Kieran and the girls?'

I feel for him. Delia's gimlet gaze is not a pleasant thing. 'Great, thanks. Kieran is fierce busy, and the girls are growing up. They've a better social life than myself.'

'Well, make sure you look after yourself too, Mags. You've a lot of people who rely on you.' His blue eyes meet mine for a moment, then he nods nervously at Delia and is gone.

When the Lenny Carmody case finally gets going, it is short but sweet. Delia stays cool and factual during her cross-examination, explaining about the amount of weed we found, Lenny's threatening behaviour and the damage done to the graves. The prosecution drags up her Traveller background and suggests she is vilifying the Carmodys because she is a McGovern. Her eyes flash, but she answers calmly that her personal circumstances have no bearing on her work, and the judge rules the lawyer out of order. His rudeness doesn't help his client anyway. Lenny Carmody gets a four-month sentence, half of it suspended. As he leaves the courtroom, he shoots Delia a furious look.

She is still stiff with annoyance as we exit into the sunshine, and when I praise her for being cool under fire, she glares at me like I'm Ronan Brady. 'Just doing my job, Sergeant,' she says sharply. 'Like you tell me all the time, I can't let who I am influence what I do, and I won't be told I do anything otherwise.'

We walk for a minute in silence, back towards our car, and then she says in a much more cheerful voice, 'Well, look who's outside Supermac's.'

It's the two younger Carmody lads she handcuffed in the grave-yard, Patrick and Kenneth. They seem to have been in a bit of bother, because Patrick is on crutches and his face is bruised. Kenneth has a black eye that is going purply-yellow.

'Had an accident, you two?' she asks conversationally as we pass.

They stare at their feet.

'Well, looks like you two came out the wrong end of whatever scrap it was.'

Kenneth gives a non-committal mutter.

'Right, well, try to stay out of trouble, won't you?'

'We will,' Patrick replies sullenly. Both of them remain with their eyes downcast, a long way from the cocky lads squaring up to me in the graveyard.

I wait until we're well out of earshot before commenting. 'Well, if I'm not very much mistaken, did someone put manners on that pair of young pups?'

Delia smiles. 'Apparently them damaging Nana's grave was a bridge too far. Graves are sacred to us, and Nana was related to many different families. Her mother was a Carmody. The older Carmodys have been getting sick of the young ones carrying on all these years, drawing the guards on them and giving them a bad name, so they decided a good hiding was all they understood. And so those two are quiet boys these days. Lenny actually refused bail to avoid the same fate.'

I say nothing, because I can't be seen or heard to approve of violence, but like Trevor's drumming, I can't help thinking it's natural justice and no bad thing. One beating from those lads' uncles will hopefully put them on the straight and narrow, saving them a lifetime of misery in and out of jail. It's a pity that it's probably too late for Lenny.

Delia continues. 'A lot of the older ones in that family are decent people actually. Martin Carmody is helping old Kitty O'Brien to look after her two donkeys. She can't manage them since Neilus died but she can't bear to part with them, so Martin and his daughter call and feed them and look after them for her. Nobody ever hears those things about the Travellers, unfortunately.'

We have arrived at the car, and I still haven't spoken. She looks at

179

me before we get in. 'One more thing, Sergeant. I hope you'll under-stand I'm speaking to you in confidence, that this is an internal Trav-eller thing, and we sorted it, our way. But I wanted you to understand, and I wanted to be honest with you. And to thank you, like, for giving me something to say to Daddy about that night.'

I still say nothing, but I nod and climb into the passenger seat. I'm letting her drive.

CHAPTER 22

*H*alfway through Monday morning, it's no good – I have to go and see my mother. I know she went dancing with Teo on Sunday afternoon, and I have to know if things have moved on there. You may call it nosiness, but I call it human interest.

I grab three doughnuts and two cappuccinos from Teresa's and head on over to Mam's shop. I left the house in a hurry this morning and missed breakfast, so I'm starving, and I sneakily stuff one of the doughnuts into my mouth as I go. I'll be cursing the sugary thing when I'm lying on the bed trying to pull up the zip on my jeans, I know, but honestly, they're irresistible.

Joe waves to me from inside Dillon's as I pass but doesn't come out to speak to me for once; just as well, as my mouth is full. He's stretching up to arrange suits on a rail, and I note in passing that he's looking very trim. He's always well-dressed, of course, because he owns a menswear shop, but somehow he looks better turned out today, a touch slimmer maybe, with straighter shoulders. It's funny how even a slight change in posture can work wonders for a person.

Mam's shop is empty. When the tinkle of the shop door doesn't bring her out of the back, I bang the little brass bell on the counter.

Normally I would shout, but I'm still eating. More time passes. I swallow, brush the sugar off my mouth and shout, 'Mam!'

Immediately she appears, looking furtive. 'Goodness' sake, Mags, why didn't you say it was you in the first place?'

I'm confused. 'I thought the whole point of the bell was to let you know someone was here in the shop?'

'But I didn't know it was *you*, did I?'

'I... But...don't you usually come out if someone just rings the bell?'

She shrugs. 'Well, you know, people call out, like they call, "Marie?" or "Hello?", something like that, and then I know by their voice.'

An awful thought crosses my mind. 'You're not going deaf, are you?' I hate the idea of my lovely mam getting old in any way. 'Is the bell not loud enough for you?'

She glares at me indignantly. 'I certainly am not deaf. How would I hear the music for the dancing if I was deaf? Did you bring cake? It's the only way you'll get back in my good books. And I hope that's a cappuccino.'

'It is.' I pop the bag on the counter, lift out the cups and take out my second doughnut. I'm still puzzled about the bell, but I'm more curious about Teo. 'How did the dancing go yesterday?'

She sighs deeply, takes a huge gulp of cappuccino, shakes her head, and says, 'Don't ask.'

'Oh...really? Oh dear. Did something bad happen?'

'Yes. No. Sort of.' She looks at me in a hunted fashion. 'I don't know really. It's hard to tell. I don't know what I think. I've been sitting in the back all morning, trying to work it out. And yes, Mags, you're right. I am avoiding someone. Two people in fact.'

'Who?'

'Don't ask.'

'Mam...'

'OK. It's Joe. And...'

'And?'

'Teo.'

'*What?*'

'Mags, you won't believe what happened yesterday. It was...
extraordinary. Nothing like it has ever happened to me before. I don't
know what to think. Thank God Peggy wasn't there to spread it
around or the whole of the town would be in here "rubbernecking", as
Nora calls it these days after watching all that American television.
Did you hear that politician chap of hers is actually coming to Ballycarrick? I didn't think he even existed. Does he exist, Mags? Or has
Nora finally lost it?'

'He does exist, Mam, and I promise we'll talk about that later. But
tell me, please, please tell me, what happened at the dancing?'

She throws another glance at the door, then decides to scurry over
and turn the sign to CLOSED. 'Come and sit in the back so no one
can see us. I don't like shutting up so early, but if either of them comes
in, they'll hear us talking, and then there'll be no escaping them.'

Grabbing the doughnut bag and her coffee, she heads into the
back, and I follow her, mystified and agog. We sit on two big wooden
boxes of Irish dancing dresses; they're one of the most lucrative lines
my mother does, not as plentiful as school uniforms but far more
expensive.

'Right, tell me,' I say.

'Hang on...' She takes another gulp of cappuccino. 'OK. You're not
going to believe this. So as you know, myself and Teo went dancing
on Sunday afternoon in Salthill. They have a lovely hall out there, the
floor is perfect, and the man running the class is a pure dote – he's a
Spanish flamenco dancer called Enrico and he's Gearóid's boyfriend,
would you believe?'

I've got a mouthful of coffee and splutter a bit.

She claps her hand to her cheek. 'Maybe I shouldn't have told you
that? Does Kieran know? I only know because I saw Gearóid dropping Enrico off before the class, and they kissed each other properly,
if you know what I mean, so I stayed in the car until Enrico went in
and Gearóid had gone because I don't think they knew I was there.'

I swallow. 'It's OK about telling me, Mam, all his family knows.'

'They do? That's great everyone can be so open about it these days.
Even Nora, that's great.'

'Mam…the dancing?'

'Oh yes. Yes. Well, Teo was fooling around a bit and asked Enrico can he do the tango, and Enrico picked me out as the best dancer and demonstrated it with me, a rose between his teeth and everything – it was hilarious. And then the whole class wanted to try. And then, and this is the mad bit, Joe Dillon came in, marched up to me and, just like that, took over as my partner, and he was very good.'

'Joe took over doing the tango with you, from Enrico?' I'm stunned.

'Sorry, no, I missed a bit. By then I was waltzing with Teo. The older ones in the class found the tango a bit hard on the hips.'

The mad images in my head settle down slightly. But it is still an extraordinary story. 'I'm not really getting this, Mam. What was Joe doing there?'

'He told me later he's been doing private lessons with every dance teacher who will take him, early mornings with Deirdre Hickey and evenings with Enrico. And then Enrico told him he was good enough to come to the dance classes now without embarrassing himself, and there he was. Only he hung back when he saw we were trying out the tango, as he's not *that* good. Which is why I didn't know he was there.'

I'm finding it hard to wrap my head around this. 'So he just marches over…'

'That's right, and taps Teo on the shoulder, and he says, "Excuse me, do you mind if I have this dance?" And Teo is so surprised, and he's never even met Joe, and so Teo says to me, "Marie, do *you* mind?" And then both of them are looking at me, and it's just awful. It's like I'm choosing. But Joe is my friend, Mags, and I've known him nearly all my life. I can't just leave him standing there like a fool, even if he's been a "right weirdo", as Ellie says for the last few months. So I say, "No, I don't mind." And then to my total astonishment, Joe sweeps me off in his arms, and I think he's going to make a right show of us both, but he's good, very good in fact. And then he tells me how he's been taking lessons and that's what he should have done years ago, to prove the depth of his feelings for me.'

I'm melting. 'I can't believe how romantic this is. It's like a film.'

'It's not romantic, it's awful!' snaps my mother, glaring at me. 'There I was, perfectly happy with Teo and thinking I might as well get on with it and say yes, and then Joe Dillon comes along and completely upsets the apple cart. Now I don't know whether I'm coming or going, and Teo is all upset, and both of them keep ringing me... Look at this.' She shows me her phone, which has loads of missed calls. 'What am I going to do?'

'Why not set them twelve tasks, like the princess set her suitors in that fairy tale?'

'This isn't *funny*, Mags. I'm confused and upset. That's why I've been hiding all morning, in case one of them comes in. I think I might leave the shop closed now and sneak home the back way to avoid Joe's shop. Or I might not even go home. I might just leave Ballycarrick for good.'

'Ah now, Mam...'

To my horror she bursts into stormy tears, which is something she never does.

Horrified, I take her in my arms like she's one of my girls, her nose pressed to my shoulder and her whole body heaving. 'Mam, please don't cry. This isn't the end of the world. You've got two lovely men mad about you – you only have to decide who you like best.'

'But I don't *want* to decide,' she sobs against my Garda jacket. 'It's not fair, expecting me to choose between them. I don't *want* to hurt someone I really care about, and I care about them both. It's horrible. Why on earth didn't Joe say something before now? All these years, and I'd taught myself not to hope and just be glad he was my friend. And then a wonderful man comes along, and for the first time, I think I could be interested in someone other than Joe, and I *was* interested... And now Joe's ruined everything.'

'Oh, poor Mam.' My loving, clever mother has always helped and supported me in everything I do, whatever I decide. I wish I could help her in return; I just don't know how. Unable to think of anything more useful, I offer up her own advice, which she's always saying to me. 'You just have to follow your heart.'

'How can I follow my heart,' she wails, 'when my heart doesn't know where it wants to go?' She pulls a tissue out of her pocket and blows her nose, then wipes her eyes with the back of her hand. 'Maybe I should just toss a coin,' she says wryly.

There's a moment's silence, and then I say, 'Maybe you should. Why not? Let the fates decide.'

The thing is, I've just remembered that Sharon taught me a good trick back when we were thirteen and I was torn between two spotty boys, both wanting to take me to the chipper.

If you don't know what you want to do, Sharon told me, toss a coin. Then if you feel a bit disappointed with the result, you can decide to go again, do best out of three, just to be sure fate has it right. Or best out of five, or even seven. It sort of takes the responsibility off your shoulders because fate is helping you decide, but really it's you who decides when to stop tossing the coin.

I dig a two-euro coin out of my trouser pocket, wink at Mam and spin it up high in the air. 'Call. Heads or harp?'

She giggles weakly through her tears. 'Heads.'

The two-euro coin drops into my palm, and I slap my other hand over it. 'So who is heads and who is harp? You have to tell me before I show you.'

'I don't want to cheat. I want to let fate decide. I don't know... Harp, Teo, so heads, Joe.'

I lift my hand. Harp.

She sighs in disappointment. 'Oh, poor Joe, all those dancing lessons. How can I do that to him?'

'Best out of three?' I suggest gently. 'Just to be sure the fates have it right?'

She nods, with the flicker of a smile.

I spin again. This time it's heads. I look at her. 'Again?'

She nods, frowning.

This time it's harp. Teo wins. But I know she's not sure.

Best of five?

Our eyes meet. One more toss of the coin.

Heads.

'Last one,' I say. 'They have two each.'

'Ah this is stupid Mags…' Mam begins.

'We've come this far.' I reply with a grin. 'This one is the decider.'

I toss it and as it falls I slap my right hand on the back of my left, the coin, and my mother's future clamped between them.

She exhales. 'Right, check.'

I slide my hand off. It's heads.

'Oh, poor Teo,' she says sadly, although she still can't help looking happy. 'He's going to be so upset. But you know, if that's what the stars say, I suppose it's fate and I just have to go along with it.'

'I suppose you do.'

She casts around for excuses. 'I mean, Teo's such a lovely man, and so handsome and he's an oncologist, so he's not going to have any difficulty finding anyone else. Unlike poor Joe.'

'That's very charitable of you,' I say. Then I hug her, and we both start laughing. A huge wave of relief washes over me. Teo is the perfect man, an absolute star. I want Mam to be happy, of course I do, so whoever she had chosen would be all right with me. But I'd always thought it would be Joe, and now that it is, I feel that everything's somehow all right with the world.

'How about you go and see Joe now?' I ask.

She shakes her head. 'No. I have to talk to Teo first. Oh, Mags, this is going to be really hard.'

I hold her tight again. 'Love you, Mam.'

She hugs me back, shedding sad and happy tears onto my uniform. 'Love you too, my darling girl. I'd be lost only for you.'

CHAPTER 23

The first Tuesday of the month rolls around, and Kieran and I head for the town hall meeting. I'm in my normal clothes, jeans – the stretchiest ones I own; Teresa's cakes will have to go – and a light-blue jumper, because I'm there as a member of the public, not in my capacity as a guard.

When we arrive, the hall is filling up fast, and it takes us a while to find two seats together with a decent view of the stage, where four empty chairs are lined up behind a long table.

One of the chairs is for Derry, who will be running the meeting. Two of the others are for the chairperson of the Galway County Council, Ann-Marie Jenkins and Richard Moran, the chairperson of the school board.

Richard Moran refused to have anything to do with the meeting at first, according to Annette. He didn't want to talk about his plans in public, and it was only when she 'casually' mentioned that Jerome McGovern was going to address the audience that he threw up his hands. 'Well, if some knack…member of the Travelling community is going to get up there making excuses for the way they've been carrying on, then someone respectable has to tell it how it really is.'

Although Richard needn't have worried about Jerome speaking, because it looks like the fourth chair is going to remain empty.

* * *

DELIA CAME to me in my office two days ago.

'Dad's not going to make his speech. He thinks it's all pointless and humiliating.'

I dropped my pen and sat back in my chair. 'You have to change his mind. I really think he can sway people.'

'How would you like to stand up in front of the whole town and try to convince neighbours you thought were your friends, or at the very least not hostile to you, to let you keep your house and not move you to a dump?'

It was hard for me to imagine such a horrible scenario. 'He's wrong to give up without a fight, Delia. If the town hears what he has to say, they could refuse to fundraise for St Colm's to buy the site, and then it gets a lot harder for this backroom deal to be done.'

She shrugged, looking doubtful. 'I'll tell him what you said. But he's headstrong.'

'So are you, Delia. I'm relying on you to convince him.'

* * *

I SPOT DARREN AND MICHAEL, also out of uniform, and then I see Mam with Joe. I wave, and she waves back. I note she has finally decided to wear her diamond engagement ring in public. She's spent the last couple of weeks very embarrassed about being seen to change horses mid-race, but Joe has worn her down. He wants to show her off, and he's right; she's a lovely woman. But she's very self-conscious not to be a laughing-stock. I've assured her about a million times that she won't be, but she has maintained her dignity in this town for decades and it's important to her.

Poor Teo is back in Limerick nursing a broken heart, and we all feel really bad for him, but as Mam says, a man like him surely won't have a problem finding someone else once he's ready to try dating again.

Olive, Joanna and Nell McNamara are together at the front, looking like a confident coven. Nora is with them, but she keeps standing up to check the size of the crowd. She's very proud of herself because this was all her idea. Kieran and I nod to her, and she nods to us with a superior little smile. She's only delighted that she's got her own back about the congressman and the flags.

Annette and Martha are sitting near the high windows, Phillip between them. The owners of the hardware shop and the home and garden store, who benefit a lot from Traveller custom, are directly behind the two women, who are also great customers of theirs. I glance around, and there's representation from most of the businesses in town. Tatiana and the other publicans are clustered together. Tatiana is usually sympathetic to the underdog, but maybe as a publican she is prejudiced against Travellers. Lydia the Turkish Barber is sitting behind her, talking into her ear.

Deirdre Hickey is on the far side of the room. She has brought her own cushion, which is a great idea; these school chairs are hard on anyone's backside, as I know well from attending hours-long school plays for the girls. Oscar O'Leary is beside her and boring the ears off her, judging by her pained expression.

Bertie Mahony is on the other side of Oscar, in a canary-yellow cashmere jumper and cream trousers, next to his adoring wife. I'm surprised he hasn't the pope's gold medal still pinned to him.

Sharon and Trevor arrive and can only find one seat, so Trevor lets Sharon sit on his knee, much to the chagrin of Joanna and company. Sharon beams across at me and rolls her eyes at Bertie behind his back. And then she goes a bit pale because the horrendous Danny Boylan is only two rows in front of her, and Chloe from the chipper is making a big show of snuggling into him. I know Sharon doesn't love Danny any more, but it's still hard for her having the whole town see her ex-husband canoodling with someone young enough to be her daughter.

At five to seven the hall is standing room only, and I wish I could gauge how it will go. I want to believe that the people of this place are decent and fair, but prejudice is ugly and insidious and I'm just not sure. As Derry walks up onto the stage, the murmur of conversation stops and all eyes are on him. A woman I don't recognise joins him; she must be Councillor Ann-Marie Jenkins. Richard Moran takes the seat beside Ann-Marie, chatting away in an intimate fashion and looking smug, like he already has this in the bag. Which, if I'm honest about what I saw in the photo on Darren's phone, he probably has.

The other men from Darren's photo are also in the hall, I notice. Andy Maguire, the county councillor and estate agent who will benefit from the sale, is sitting discreetly in the audience, and there's James Delahunt, the halting site inspector.

Duckie is standing at the back, the slimy snake that he is. He won't nail his colours to the mast for fear it all goes wrong, but he's getting something out of the sale, I'm sure of it, so he has come to make sure he's on the right side.

The fifth man from the picture, the only one I couldn't put a name to, is also there. He's standing, leaning against the wall between two of the windows, having arrived too late to get a seat. What's noticeable is that all five are affecting not to know each other, which is very different from the champagne-popping, laughing group of men that Darren photographed in the snug.

In the same row as us, but on the other side of the aisle, is Matthew Hilser, the headmaster of St Colm's, his face unreadable. I doubt very much he's involved in the skulduggery; he's not long in the job. But the school board has far too much power. A few years ago, they managed to ensure a young teacher's contract wasn't renewed because he was a voice for the LGBTQ side in the marriage equality referendum. The last principal was an oily man and I couldn't warm to him, but Matthew Hilser seems to be a different kettle of fish.

The fourth chair on the stage is unoccupied, and I see Derry looking around the hall to see if Jerome McGovern has arrived. The wall clock goes from five past seven to ten past, and the woman from the council is checking her watch.

Derry meets my eyes, shrugs and takes the microphone. 'Good

evening, everyone, and thank you all for coming out in such numbers to discuss such an important issue. As you all know, Galway County Council are considering the sale of the Drumlish halting site. We in the neighbourhood watch committee felt that such a move should not happen without due consideration by the entire community, and I would like to thank Ann-Marie Jenkins, chair of the council, for coming here tonight to answer any questions that we, the people of Ballycarrick, have for her.

'I'd also like to welcome Mr Richard Moran, the chair of the board of St Colm's Academy, who are seeking to purchase the site should the council decide to sell. The school would use the land for additional sports facilities to supplement what is already there, including an open-air swimming pool, I'm told, which in return for fundraising by the town, will be open to the public in the summer holidays.'

There's a slight commotion at the back of the hall. The double doors open, and a number of the McGovern family enter. I'm delighted to see them, although Jerome is not among them. There's Delia, in a pink T-shirt and jeans, and her cousins Paddy and Niall, and Jerome's wife, Dora. Also, old Johnny B., who still proudly calls himself a tinker, and deaf Auntie Nonie, who has no problem lip-reading, along with several other cousins, aunts and uncles.

An uncomfortable ripple runs through parts of the hall, in the way it always does when a number of Travellers enter a space like a pub or hotel. But Sharon and Trevor get up to offer their one chair to Auntie Nonie, who takes it gratefully. The rest of the Travellers have to stand around the walls at the back of the hall because the seats are all taken. I think about offering my own chair to Johnny B., but I'm kind of trapped in the middle of a row, and then the man from the hardware store stands up and problem solved.

On the stage, Derry says cheerfully, 'So without further ado, I'll hand you over to Ann-Marie.'

The chairperson of the council takes the microphone and speaks clearly and with purpose, without getting to her feet. 'When the council was approached and it was raised that there were conflicting views in the local community regarding the potential change of purpose for the site at Drumlish, I thought coming here tonight to hear your concerns would be useful. The council is a democratically elected body, and so it is vital that we act at all times in the best interests of the people we represent. I'm not here to put my own viewpoint. I'm here to listen to yours, and I look forward to hearing your thoughts.'

There's a moderate level of applause, and she hands the mike back to Derry. Derry passes it on to Richard Moran, and he gets to his feet, comes around the table to the front of the stage, and he's off. He's a slippery one, I think, studying the way he carries himself. He's almost handsome, and almost symmetrically featured, and I know from past encounters that he smells a touch too strongly of aftershave. You know the type. He's like Jeremy Irons, but if you ordered him from one of those cheap Chinese websites. Almost right but not quite.

He drones on about the contribution of St Colm's to the life of the town, which is minimal actually. They tend to engage more with other private schools in the region. Then he is astute enough not to labour that point since nobody is buying it, so he goes down the road of extolling the aesthetics of neat green sports pitches over other, less suitable things. For this, read halting site. He then dangles the carrot of the open-air swimming pool, and says he hopes the community will get behind St Colm's fundraising efforts in return for the privilege of using it when the princes of the wealthy have gone home for the summer. Then he reads from the 'independent' inspector's report saying the road has been made dangerous around the site because of ponies tethered on the verge and the bins being put out once a fortnight, and that there are stoned and drunk young Traveller men partying at all hours and trashing first the cemetery and then the site, and how it would be safer for all concerned, including the McGoverns, to move them to somewhere more suitable, more off the beaten track. He references the chickens escaping across the sports fields and implies it will be rats next because of the filth.

He finishes, and the applause from Olive and company is enthusiastic, but the rest of the crowd seems a bit lukewarm, although that's maybe because the McGoverns are out in force and the audience feels intimidated. Which isn't good, because that will backfire on the Travellers. I glance behind me and see Jerome has joined his family. He looks impassive, his hands in his pockets.

Derry takes the microphone again. 'Now, ladies and gentlemen, I would like to introduce our next speaker this evening, after which we will move on to the questions-and-answers session. Please give a welcome to Mr Jerome McGovern.'

Delia's father hangs back until Delia gives him a discreet nudge with her elbow and jerks her head towards the stage. He makes his decision, takes his hands out of his pockets and walks slowly down the central aisle, chin up and eyes ahead. After his last-minute doubts, I hope he's decided to give it his all. He's such a handsome man, huge, with tattoos on his hands, and his dark hair and dark flashing gaze would draw anyone's eye. He's dressed in black trousers and a snow-white shirt, clearly brand new as the folds of the packaging are still in it, and he's clean-shaven with his dark hair oiled back. Travellers marry young, and Delia is one of his older children, so he's probably only mid to late forties, but life on the road can be hard and it shows on the faces. A gold sovereign ring glints on his huge hand, and a chain is nestled in the dark curly hair of his chest, visible at the open collar of the shirt. He looks like he'd flatten you as quick as look at you, and his former reputation as a bare-knuckle boxer precedes him. I hope fervently the audience will give him a chance. I think they will. Most people round here don't mind the McGoverns personally and can see they're a decent family. Or at least I hope so.

He steps up onto the stage. He has nothing with him, no notes, no pen. Derry hands him the mike, but he brushes it away as he sits down behind the table on Derry's right side.

'Thank you, Ms Jenkins and Mr Hartnett, for inviting me to talk to you this evening,' he says. He has a deep, strong voice which carries easily; it's the voice of a man who has sung all his life, although this evening, there's a slight tremor in it. He stops and takes a deep breath as if he doesn't know what to do next. Richard Moran smirks and shuffles his notes, and the councilwoman jots down something in her notebook.

The big man's eyes scan the audience and come to rest on me. He nods and does what you're supposed to do when addressing the crowd; that is, you find someone sitting in the middle of it and talk to them. 'My family,' he begins, his eyes fixed on mine, 'have been livin' around this part of Galway for at least six generations. There was a time, not all that long ago, when we were welcomed. We'd save hay or dig potatoes or whatever work was needed, and the country people were kind and happy to see us comin'. And we were happy to see them too. We'd friendships going back years and years. We'd set up our camp in a farmer's field, and his wife would give us food, and maybe some clothes for the childer.'

I smile at his use of the word. It's not Gammon. You wouldn't have a notion what they were saying when they speak their own language, which is precisely the point, I suppose. But they always call children 'childer'.

He carries on. 'I remember country people coming to our camp when I was a boy, singin' songs, playin' music. We liked and trusted each other. We were different, but we didn't hate each other.'

I wonder if the crowd know that when Jerome says 'country people', he means them.

'But somethin' changed. Our skills weren't needed any more, and the government wanted to get rid of us, make us live as country people do, but we never wanted that. They tried to justify this by tellin' you that we were descendent from the people who were evicted during the famine, and so we're only recently homeless, but that's not true at all. It suited them to say that, but 'tis a lie. We're not homeless. Our home is where we want it to be. We've been travelling this country for centuries.'

I hear fresh courage coming into his voice, and suddenly he gets up and comes around the table like Richard Moran did before him and addresses the crowd from the front of the stage.

'I was born in Cáit Kirby's lane, five miles from this town, under a canvas thrown over the shafts of a cart. My mother, Lord have mercy on her, bore twenty of us, sixteen lived, and we grew up happy and well. Some of you knew my mother, Dacie McGovern.'

There are a lot of smiles and nods in the audience. Dacie was liked by everyone. Olive glares over her shoulder, scanning the crowd for traitors.

'Dacie was proud to be a Traveller, and she taught us all the ways of our people. Our language, our stories, our songs. My father, God be good to him, taught us boys the skills of tinmanship, and woodwork, and how to survive. But as well as them things, they taught us to run if the cruelty man came – that was a man from the government that took children from Travellers on the grounds that the Traveller way of life was cruel to us, but I can tell you it wasn't. We hadn't much in the way of stuff, comforts and that, but we had each other, we loved living under the sky, and we had love. The only cruelty was ripping us from our families.'

You could hear a pin drop. *Good man, Jerome.* I silently will him on, feeling the strong presence of his mother in that room too. I know that might sound a bit daft, but honestly, I can sense her, tiny and wizened but steel to the core.

'I was taught to run from the guards too. We were campin' one time outside Limerick and we'd built a school ourselves, got a teacher in an' everythin', and we were all goin' in there and learning. They used to take us kids because we weren't goin' to school, so the families got together and set it up. It was lovely, a bright little room with books and a blackboard, and a grand country woman called Mrs Barry teaching us. My mother and all the other women would send us every day, and they were delighted to see us doing our books around the campfire in the evenings. But it didn't last, and one morning they came with bulldozers, the council and the guards, and my Auntie Bridie lost the use of her foot when a bulldozer rolled over her. She was trying to pull the children to safety out of the school. Poor Mrs Barry stood in front of the school, telling the bulldozer men to go, but they ignored her. Only my father got her away, they'd have injured her too. I'll never forget it. I was ten years old, and we were working on a project, my uncle was helping us, about the wagons and how they made them long ago. Weeks we were at it, in between the reading and writing and sums, and I cried when I saw the machine crush it.'

He swallows. 'I asked my mother why did they do it? I thought they wanted us in school. My mother said to me, "Jerome, don't be crying now. 'Tis the way of them. They don't want us at all, in school or any other way. They want us to disappear."'

He pauses then, choked with emotion, and I see several people around me wipe a tear away. Derry allows him time to recover but, after a few seconds, gives him an almost imperceptible nod. It's important that he doesn't lose the crowd. Jerome recovers himself and jokes, 'I don't feel that way about the guards now, by the way.' He nods at Delia, and there's a ripple of laughter, a kind of relief.

'I also want to take this moment to thank the master here, Derry Hartnett – well, he was the master of this school up to a few years ago. When we got put on the halting site in Ballycarrick, he took me into his school and made sure I could read and write. Derry didn't come hard on me, but he encouraged me to learn as much as possible, and it worked. And when the authorities tried to take me, saying I wasn't in school, he threatened them with all sorts and wouldn't allow it.'

I squeeze Kieran's hand. I remember my mother telling me how the Travellers used to cover their children when coming through the town for fear the authorities would see them and take the kids into care. The number of Traveller children physically removed from their parents and dumped into those awful industrial schools – now we know what they were, a haven for paedophiles – simply because they were from the Travelling community, will never be known.

The plan was always to eliminate the itinerant population of the country and assimilate them into the settled population. It would make you cry to learn about it. And Irish people can be hypocritical about it. They'll be up in arms about the Aboriginals in Australia, or the Native Americans in the US and Canada, banging the drum for First Nations everywhere. But when it's being done on their own doorstep, they don't say a word.

Jerome is talking about that now. 'It was Derry Hartnett who taught me about my own history, and how the government in 1983 set up a committee. They used the words "a final solution to the problem of itinerants in Ireland" – they used those words. A final solution.'

He stops and looks across the audience at his family, standing at the back, and then at the shocked and ashamed people of Ballycarrick.

'It's hard to imagine it, but if you can try,' he says, his deep voice gathering strength. 'Can you imagine havin' to tell your boys and girls at home that the land they were born in, that their ancestors know like the back of their hands, that the people of that place, their own place, don't want them? Little childer? They don't understand. I know I didn't. I still don't.

'I'm not saying there aren't problems. I know as well as you that some Travellers behave in a way that's not right. But all I can speak for is my family, just like you can only speak for yours. Nobody says, "Oh, your man there did something wrong. He's from Ballycarrick, so everyone from there must be bad." Of course not. But one Traveller does something and we're all tarred with the one brush.

'There's a dark history of my people on this island, a story of cruelty and doin' wrong, but this is a decent town, my mother always said it, and I'm asking you to support us in our efforts to keep our home. My people have endured racism all over Ireland for years and years. I think this place is better than that. Thank you.' He turns and goes to sit back down.

Trevor is the first one to start clapping, then Sharon beside him, then about two-thirds of the audience join in, including people like Tatiana and Lydia and Deirdre Hickey, and the applause is definitely warmer than the applause for Richard Moran. Jerome is right. The people of Ballycarrick *are* better than that.

Derry allows the clapping to go on for a while, then flaps his hands, palms down, to signal people to stop. 'That was a very moving speech, Mr McGovern, but I know there's many people who have serious matters to put to both you and Richard Moran, so I'm now going to take questions from the audience and ask the two of you to answer them if you can.'

Four or five people shoot their hands in the air. Derry points at Sharon. 'Is your question to Richard or Jerome, Sharon?'

'To Richard, please,' she says. 'Mr Moran, if the town wants a swimming pool, why would we not fundraise for one we can use all the year round? A swimming pool in summer would be lovely, but maybe we'd like the town children to have a swimming team, and then it's no good to just have access for two months in the year.'

There's a murmur of agreement, and Richard smiles his cut-rate version of Jeremy Irons's smile. 'We may well be able to arrange evenings as well. In fact, the board has discussed that. It all depends on how much the town is prepared to donate, Mrs Boylan.' Calling Sharon 'Mrs Boylan' is a nasty dig, because she's divorced from Danny. It throws her off, and she moves closer to Trevor and says nothing else.

One of the publicans puts up his hand. 'My question is for Jerome McGovern. Why do you lot want to stay where you are, when I've heard you in the pub complaining about the lack of facilities? Why not just make it a condition of moving, that the new site has all the facilities you want?'

Jerome looks at him seriously. 'My family's home is Drumlish, as yours is in Ballycarrick. It's old, it's not perfect, and we could use better facilities. A bathroom block would be nice, hot running water, a gas supply, things you might yourself take for granted. But my family can walk to Mass, to the shop or the post office. We've done a huge amount of work on the site over the years. We have a fully functioning vegetable plot, stables, a play area for the childer. We keep it clean, and you can ask Sergeant Munroe about that if you like.' The pride in his voice is clear for all to hear. 'We've had roots here for 100 years, and our children go to school in Ballycarrick. My daughter Delia is a guard in the station. We don't *want* to go anywhere else, and we've never given anyone in this town an ounce of trouble, so I don't think we should be made to.'

The next person to speak is Mairéad, one of the city girls Olive dragged along to the neighbourhood watch meeting. 'What I'm confused about is, I was told it wasn't Jerome's family in the graveyard smoking illegal substances, but Richard says it was. So who is right?'

'Who do you want to answer your question?' asks Derry kindly.

She shrugs. 'Both, I suppose.'

'Jerome, will you go first?'

Jerome nods. 'On the day the cemetery was vandalised, I know none of my family were involved because Sergeant Monroe and my daughter Delia were two of the four guards at the scene. My daughter would know everyone of our family. One of the Carmodys just went to jail for his part in it, if you care to check the court records. And as for the night Drumlish was vandalised and the inspector' – he points at James Delahunt – 'somehow turned up as soon as it was light and took photographs...' He pauses, letting this piece of information hang in the air, as James Delahunt looks uncomfortable. 'Well, I and almost all my family were away that night at a funeral, and Delia was work-ing, which left only my older sister Nonie and my nephews Paddy and Niall. They're good lads, so I don't know who did all that damage to our home, but it wasn't them.'

Derry waits a moment to be sure he's finished, then says, 'Richard? Do you want to add something?'

Richard stands up behind the table and beams at Mairéad. 'Jerome McGovern is making a great deal of the difference between his family and the Carmodys, but everyone knows that Travellers intermarry among themselves. In fact, I hear there would have been wedding bells between Natasha McGovern and Bernard Carmody a couple of years ago if he hadn't been executed by other criminals when out racing his sulky down a motorway of all places.'

Jerome clenches his fists on the table, and for an awful moment, I think he might punch Richard Moran. Natasha had kept the relation-ship between herself and Blades Carmody secret from Dacie because she knew it was forbidden. And poor Blades hadn't been racing his sulky; he'd been trying to get Natasha away from the men who later abducted her, and he'd succeeded at the cost of his own life.

'So,' says Richard, 'there isn't some wall between one Traveller family and another. They're all related. And as long as there are one set of Travellers in the town, the others will flock here too, for weddings and funerals, and each time the town has to be shut down and businesses lose money. Nora Munroe is doing a great thing for

Ballycarrick, bringing over her cousin who is a famous congressman in the States and who could be running for American president in a few years. What will it look like if there's a Traveller funeral or wedding going on then? We can't have a street party if that happens, and the town will suffer financially.'

It's horrible. I can feel all the goodwill generated by Jerome's speech draining away as the people around me decide maybe they should be practical about this rather than idealistic.

'And another thing,' says Richard, gaining confidence now that he feels he's winning. 'There's a lad here tonight called Phillip Turner, and we're all very fond of him. And we know what happened at the Drumlish site frightened him so much, he ran away for a whole day. And I ask you, do you really want the boys of St Colm's next door exposed to the same terrors? Or anybody's children? Jerome may be naïve enough to believe his nephews are "good lads", but we know there are drugs in the town, and we know there's a strong connection between the McGoverns and the Carmodys, with one family supplying the other with marijuana. Can I suggest it's no coincidence, Jerome, that Paddy and Niall waited for your back to be turned before they decided to have a big drug-fuelled party with their Carmody cousins and break up the site?'

Jerome suddenly shoves back his chair to stand up; he's nose to nose with Moran. My Garda instincts go to full alert, and I get to my feet.

Off to my right, an unmistakeable voice says loud and clear, 'It wasn't Paddy and Niall who scared me, it was him.'

I'm not exaggerating when I say everyone in the place, including Jerome and Richard, turns to look at Phillip, who has stood up and is calmly pointing at the fifth man, the white-blond, freckled fellow from the snug.

'I was in the chicken coop because I wanted to be sure the hens were happy when Jerome and Olivia were away. We're entering them for a competition because they are the happiest hens in Ireland. I was so warm in there, I fell asleep, and when I woke up, that man with white hair and a spotted face and piggy eyes was pulling down the wire with a big stick. He pushed me and shouted bad words at me, and the chickens flew at him. I ran away and hid, and I was very, very sad and scared.'

An amazed murmur runs through the audience, and everyone looks at the white-blond man, who shrugs and spreads his hands with a smile. 'I'm afraid this is a case of mistaken identity,' he says lightly. He doesn't seem at all fazed.

'What's your name?' snaps Martha, holding her son's hand.

'Can you tell us your name, sir?' asks Derry, more politely.

'And where were you the night Phillip ran away?' demands Annette angrily.

The man ignores the two women and addresses Derry. 'My name is Hugh Geraghty, and this is my first time in Ballycarrick. I'm a travelling salesman of medical supplies. I'm staying in the Samovar overnight, and when I saw the notice for the meeting, I came out of curiosity because nothing else is going on in the town.'

'He was wearing a black scarf round his face,' says Phillip loudly. 'But the hens pulled it off. And I wasn't sure at first, but I kept on looking and looking, and it is him.' And he sits down.

The man gives another helpless shrug and smile, and from the back, Duckie pipes up. 'Can we move on? With all due respect, we're not going to take the word of this...of a...er...this...er...young man, are we?'

There's a sprinkle of tutting around the hall, and I think Duckie just seriously blotted his copybook because everyone knows what he wanted to call Phillip, and it wasn't 'young man'.

'Well, you would want to cover for Geraghty, him being your friend,' says Delia loudly, from the back.

Instantly I look at Darren. He and Michael are both skewed around in their chairs to watch what's going on; they're enjoying the show. But when Darren catches me glaring at him, he turns white, then red, and shrinks down in his seat. There's only one way Delia could know Duckie is friendly with the white-haired man, and that's because she's seen the picture that I ordered Darren to delete on pain of suspension.

Meanwhile, Duckie is acting all shocked. 'What do you mean? I've never seen this man before in my life. I'm just saying –'

Geraghty also speaks up. 'Miss, I don't know who you are, but you're clearly from the halting site, and I think you want to be careful what you're implying about respectable citizens.'

Delia throws him a look of utter contempt, then turns her attention to the platform. 'And you, Mr Moran, have you never seen this Hugh Geraghty before either?' And then, 'Or you, Mr Maguire, or you, Mr Delahunt?'

All three men make a show of looking bewildered, although unlike Duckie and Geraghty, they've clearly realised something is going on so don't openly deny it.

'Well?' demands Delia.

There's no answer, just shifty looks. She says something in Gammon to Niall, who takes out his phone and starts doing something with it. There's a long pause, and the audience starts to fidget. It's all getting too complicated, and in a moment, people are going to file this interruption under 'don't know' or 'six of one and half a dozen of the other' and lose interest and move on.

Bertie the holy butcher takes advantage of this. He calls out assertively, 'This nonsense is neither here nor there. We need to be discussing the real issues. The fact is, the Travellers bring drugs into the town, probably from Dublin, and Jerome McGovern has no answer to what happened that night at the site.'

A murmur runs around the meeting, and voices are raised.

'Through the chair, please,' says Derry sharply. 'Put your hand up if you wish to speak, and I'll call you when it's your turn.'

Again, a forest of hands, but Martha shouts, 'Point of information!'

Derry shrugs and gives her the floor.

She gets to her feet. 'I've been keeping silent while everyone blames the Travellers for everything. But now I want to be brave and truthful like my son.'

'You always have to tell the truth, Mam,' says Phillip, and people laugh a little while wondering what's coming next.

'What are you talking about, Martha?' asks Annette, frowning up at her.

'Yes, what do you want to say, Martha?' prompts Derry.

After a slightly despairing glance at Annette, Martha turns to Derry and says, 'I want to say it wasn't any Travellers who brought the drugs to Ballycarrick, not even the Carmodys. It was me.'

There's stunned silence.

I put my head in my hands. I want to kick myself. Everything about Martha falls into place. Annette's miraculous recovery. My sister Dolores thinking Martha is the best thing since…well, vegan tofu and spending all her spare time up there helping her with the garden. The way Martha feels uncomfortable around me. I'm an absolute fool.

I lift my head again, to look at Annette. Did she know? She is staring up at Martha, as white as a sheet, in shock. Phillip is looking puzzled.

'Annette knew nothing about it,' says Martha loudly, still addressing Derry. 'Marijuana is legal in Canada and used for pain relief, but when I realised it was illegal in Ireland, I told Annette it was an herb called devil's claw.'

'Oh, Martha, *no*,' groans Annette.

'I also want to say, I didn't supply anybody. But the soil is so fertile here, you can grow anything, and so I had far too much, much more than was wanted. And then someone came and pulled most of the plants up overnight. I can guess who did it, but I need everyone at this meeting to know that it wasn't the McGoverns, who have been nothing but good to me and Annette, looking after Phillip and finding him when he was lost, and helping us with our vegetable business.'

'Quiet, please, let's have quiet!' shouts Derry as everyone starts talking at once, excited, scandalised. The Travellers at the back are whooping.

And then people's phones start to ping, including my own. I glance down at it and see there's an update to the Ballycarrick Facebook page.

It's Darren's photo of the five men in the snug.

There they all are. Duckie Cassidy. Andy Maguire. James Delahunt. Richard Moran. And Hugh Geraghty.

The photo keeps on arriving in my phone. It has been added to the school website and tagged to every WhatsApp group in the town, many of which I'm a member, including the neighbourhood watch, and the pinging is increasing at a rapid rate as everyone in the hall starts sharing and forwarding. Richard is looking at his phone with a fake fixed smile on his face, and now Derry has seen it, and now the woman from the council. Jerome has it now, and he sinks into his chair, staring at it.

As everyone pores over their social media, Hugh Geraghty starts to leave, sidling very quietly down the side of the room. I glance over my shoulder at Delia and then at Darren and Michael. They know what to do. As the two lads pass me on their way to help Delia detain Hugh Geraghty, Darren shoots me a questioning look. I frown and shake my head at him, but instead of cowering, he brightens up and grins, as if what I intended to come over as fierceness has come over as something else.

Pride in my flock maybe.

Annette also leaves the meeting in tears of shock, and Martha follows with Phillip. I let them go. I'll have to talk to Martha later, but for now, I leave it.

On the platform, the chairperson of the council is on her feet, stony-faced. She seizes the mike and speaks into it. 'I think I've heard all I need to hear on this subject tonight, thank you very much. This meeting is closed.' She hands the mike to Derry, picks her way down the steps to the floor and disappears through a side door.

Derry stands up to address the crowd once more, thanking everyone for coming and wishing them safe home. Fair play to him, he's managed to keep his head in very trying circumstances.

The crowd is abuzz as they make their way to the doors at the back of the hall, and I see Matthew Hilser approaching Jerome. The headmaster holds out his hand, and Jerome, after a moment's hesitation, takes it. Hilser leans in, smiling. I can't hear what's being said, but soon Jerome is smiling as well. The display of cordiality isn't lost on the people of the town, who notice everything; they're all craning to stare.

Sharon ducks away from Trevor and comes to stand beside me, murmuring, 'Trevor says Hilser is after buying the house, you know, the one by the bridge, the Verlings' old place?'

I did know that. Matthew Hilser and his wife have been renting in Tuam, and he is moving this summer now that the job in St Colm's is settling down. Foxy Clancy, the local estate agent, already told me the new head needed a place with stables; he's mad into horses, it seems. Maybe that's what the two men are talking about. There's nothing Jerome McGovern doesn't know about horses.

Sharon says, 'We're going for a drink. Will you and Kieran come?'

Kieran is deep in chat with some lads he went to school with. One of them is the father of the boy who was teasing Kate, and he seems to be saying something earnestly to Kieran. Kieran smiles and they shake hands, so I assume that's all dealt. To the left Tatiana and Deirdre Hickey are, amazingly, deep in chat with two of Jerome's brothers. I'm not saying this is some *Highway to Heaven* moment when we all become the best of buddies, but something happened here tonight, and I know Dacie McGovern is looking down and smiling.

'Take Kieran, and I'll try and catch up with you,' I say. 'There's something I have to do first.'

CHAPTER 24

I have to arrest Martha Turner for possession, and I'm not looking forward to it.

I go home from the meeting, change into my uniform, return to the station to collect the Garda car and take a drive up to Annette's cottage. Both Annette's and Martha's ancient cars are there. Phillip is sitting on the garden wall in the dusk, looking miserable, although he brightens up at the sight of the Garda vehicle.

'Can I go for a spin, Sergeant?' he asks.

'Not tonight, Phillip, but soon, I promise,' I say, passing him.

The front door of the cottage is slightly open, and when I arrive in the doorway, I can hear the two women arguing.

'I can't believe this, Martha.' There is such sadness and anger in Annette's voice. 'Why would you do this to me?'

'You were in pain –'

'You tricked me. You should have told me!'

'If I did, I was worried you wouldn't take it –'

'You don't even know that!'

'And it helped you, didn't it? It didn't do you any harm.'

'No harm? Driving with drugs in my system?'

'I made sure that didn't happen –'

'Falling outside SuperValu and lying there, laughing like a fool?'

Martha mutters, 'I'm sorry. I didn't know you'd find the biscuit tin and eat so many.'

'It was in the biscuits?'

'I'm so sorry.'

'You should have told me the truth! But you lied and lied and lied, not just about this but what happened in Canada.'

I stand still, listening.

'Annette, if I'd told you about Canada, you wouldn't have let me past your front door. And we'd never have got to know each other, and fall in love...'

Annette's voice drips fury. 'Are we in love, Martha? Really? How can I love someone I don't trust?'

Martha catches her breath tearfully. 'Please don't say that, please...'

I realise I'm eavesdropping shamelessly and thump on the door. The voices cut off. After a few moments, Martha throws the door wide open. She looks from me in my uniform to the Garda car behind me and pales.

'I'm sorry, Martha, but...' I glance behind me at Phillip, who has turned around to look. There's no need to make this traumatic for him. 'Actually, Martha, I'm here to give you that ride in the car, like I promised you. I might even let you operate the lights and the siren, like Phillip did.'

'I want to come too!' says Phillip excitedly, slipping down from the wall.

'No, Phillip, it's too near your bedtime,' says Martha, with grateful glance at me. 'It's my turn tonight.'

Annette has come to the door now and takes in the scene at a glance. 'Oh, Mags,' she says sadly.

Martha is putting on her coat. 'I know you don't know how you feel about me right now,' she says to Annette meekly, 'but if you wouldn't mind at least looking after Phillip while I go to the station...'

'Of course.' Annette's eyes are soft, and she no longer sounds angry. 'This is Phillip's home and I love him as if he were my own son, so there's nothing to worry about.'

'Thank you.' Martha smiles sadly at her. She walks over to the squad car and gets into the back, and I get into the front. We drive away, and when I glance in the rear-view mirror, the door to the cottage is still open and Phillip is waving, although Annette is just standing there.

I drive the long way round to the Garda station so as not to bring Martha up Main Street, not that there's likely to be many people around at this time. I read her her rights while I'm driving, and when we get to the station, I bring her into my own office. It's unorthodox, but I have an excuse – our one little interrogation room is still occupied by Hugh Geraghty, who I can hear being questioned by Delia. I'm sure he's regretting what he said to her in the school hall about her being a Traveller and being careful what she says about respectable citizens.

I show Martha to the chair by my desk, make us two cups of coffee and sit opposite her. 'Right,' I say, opening my notebook. 'Do you want to call a lawyer first? I have some numbers.'

Martha inhales. 'No, I just want to tell you my story, and then you can charge me. Is that OK?'

'OK.' I pick up my pen.

She looks at her lap, twisting her hands. 'My real name is Martha Cunningham. As I've told you, I left Ireland for Canada when I was still quite young. And I got married when I was there.'

'You were married?' This is news.

'He was called Bradley Jones, and he owned a marijuana farm, which wasn't legal then but the police turned a blind eye. I met him in a bar, and I fell in love with him and married him, and everything was good until Phillip was born. Bradley turned really nasty. He said Phillip was no son of his because he was a "mongol".'

I'm shocked. I haven't heard people with Down's syndrome called that word for years.

'He wanted to have Phillip adopted, and when I wouldn't sign the papers, he battered me. I tried to run away, but he dragged me back and made me work on the farm for nothing in return for keeping Phillip. And later, he decided to move into selling cocaine. You see, he'd started growing weed when it was still against the law and worth a lot of money. But then the government made it legal, and he had to pay taxes and have it inspected for quality, and he couldn't make the same amount of money he used to.

'I know I should have left him right away when he started selling cocaine. He made me drive around the country for him, and maybe I could have made a run for it. But I was scared he'd kill me if he found me again. He would have, I'm sure of it, and Phillip too...'

She swallows and I wait, twisting my pen between my fingers, saying nothing.

'The best thing that ever happened to me was getting arrested when Phillip was sixteen years old,' she continues in a low voice. 'I didn't dare implicate Bradley – he said he'd put Phillip into care if I did. So I stood trial for supplying cocaine and went to prison for a year. Phillip had to go into state care, it was awful. I was worried every minute of every day. When I was released, I didn't let Bradley know I was out. I used my prison connections to get myself and Phillip fake Irish passports under the name "Turner", and then I went to Phillip's school and collected him and went straight to the airport. Until the last moment, I thought Bradley would come after us. It was hard for Phillip to understand the change of name but he trusts me so he did it.'

She stops, shaking as she remembers.

'Go on,' I say, as gently as I can, taking notes.

'We flew to Shannon and took a bus to Galway. We stayed at a hostel for a few weeks as we couldn't find anywhere decent that was cheap enough to rent, and then I saw Annette's advert in the *Western People*, so I thought I'd apply. I did horticulture when I was in jail, so I knew a bit about growing things other than marijuana. And when I saw the cottage, I couldn't believe my luck. And then...'

I help her out. 'You fell for Annette?'

She fixes me with a raw, vulnerable stare, then decides there's no hostility in my tone and shrugs shyly. 'Bradley was always accusing me of being a lesbian, for not always being available to him, and as I got to know Annette, for the first time in my life, I thought in his wrong-headed way he might be right.'

'And because you loved her, you decided to "cure" her arthritis.'

'It was horrible to see her in so such pain and being so brave about it. I grew it among the tomatoes – the leaves look the same if you're not an expert. I don't know who robbed the plants, although I suppose it was the Carmodys.'

'How did they know about it, do you think?'

'I don't know. I keep going over that in my head. I worried at first maybe Paddy or Niall had seen it and told them, but I don't think so. They only delivered boxes we'd already packed. They never came into the tunnels.'

'And Annette didn't know.'

'No. I wanted to protect her. But it was stupid. I should have told her the truth. And now I've ruined everything. I just hope she'll look after Phillip for me while I'm in jail. Do you think she will, Mags?'

I pause in my note-taking. 'I think she will. And Phillip will be fine with her. But, Martha, maybe you won't go to jail. Tell the district judge the complete truth, as you've been telling it to me. It might not be as bad as you think.'

She looks at me and gives a sigh that says 'get real'. 'I've a drugs conviction behind me in Canada, and I've grown a controlled substance here. They'll throw away the key.'

'You don't know that. Wait and see. Now, I'm going to charge you and then drive you home.'

She looks startled. 'You're not going to keep me in overnight? Don't I have to go to court in the morning, and try to raise bail? Not that I have a hope of doing that…'

I shrug. 'Look, I know marijuana is illegal in Ireland, but like in Canada before it was legalised, there's a lot of discretion around it as well. The courts aren't obliged to send you down over small amounts for personal use, and I'm guessing since the Carmodys robbed your whole supply, that a small amount is all I'm going to find. You need to hand in your illegal passports, but you won't face deportation because you're an Irish citizen, and so is Phillip because he's your son. You'll be appointed a solicitor when you get a court date, and you'll get legal aid, I'd imagine. After that, it will be a case of wait and see. I can't promise you won't get jail time, but in the meantime, you're free to go home.'

Tears of relief and sorrow threaten. 'But what if Annette won't have me back?'

'Martha, what you did was wrong. You lied about your past, and you lied about what you were giving her. I don't know if she will forgive you, but you certainly owe her a very, very big apology whether she does or not. Now call her and tell her you're going back to the cottage. If she wants you to come in, well and good. If not, she can have your clothes packed ready and waiting for you.'

The tears flow freely. 'I love her so much, Mags. I just want her to be happy.'

'Don't tell me, tell Annette. Just wait here while I go and check on Hugh Geraghty.'

* * *

DELIA IS APPARENTLY TAKING a break from questioning because I can hear Darren's voice in the interrogation room. I find her in the meeting room, making tea.

'So what have you found out?' I ask, leaning in the doorway.

She looks up. 'Hugh Geraghty is his real name by some miracle, and he is booked in at the Samovar, but he's no "travelling salesman". He's just plain unemployed. He says he has an alibi for the night the site got vandalised, and he just laughed when we said Phillip would make a witness statement.'

I wince. The man is right, of course. The sad truth is that Phillip will never count as a credible witness even though he's the most honest young man ever.

'I showed him the picture Darren took,' she says. 'And he claimed he stepped into the snug to see was it empty and left straight away after, even though Darren knows that's not true. And then he tried to find out from me who took the photo. Sergeant, if it goes to court, will they be able to find out where Paddy got the picture?' She is clearly very anxious about my threat to suspend Darren if he made the photo public.

I sigh. I'm tempted to say yes to put the fear of God into her and therefore into Darren, but on the other hand, I can see why Darren did what he did, and it feels wrong to punish Delia for his bad behaviour.

'I don't think it will go to court,' I say. 'Neither the council nor the school would want that kind of terrible publicity. The private schools are facing an uphill battle as it is. They're trying to maintain funding from state coffers when taxpayers are saying let those who want to avail of private education pay for it and the state should have no role in that. They have a PR issue already, and this would be disastrous for them.'

She sighs with relief. 'Do you think so?'

'I do. And I've heard good things about the principal of St Colm's – I really think he'd run a mile from this sort of thing. I imagine he'll be pretty angry with Richard Moran, and that will strengthen his hand against the board.'

'He is nice. He had a long chat with Daddy after the meeting about horses. Daddy texted me about it.'

'Good. The point of the exercise is not so much to prosecute small fry like Geraghty, but to let the county council and St Colm's know there is a bad smell about this whole thing and encourage them to back off.'

'And will they, do you think?'

'I think they will. This is not the kind of thing councils like to see, accusation of collusion, old boys' network. Politicians are trying very hard to clean up their image, and this is the bad old days of how things were done.'

Judging by the activity on the Ballycarrick Facebook page and various WhatsApp groups, there should be a fair few letters and emails supporting the McGoverns going into the council. Of course, opinions can shift and change overnight and the council aren't meeting for a while, so it's not finished yet. Even so, I feel better about Delia's family's situation than I have in a long time.

* * *

I FIND Martha waiting for me in my office, her coat on and phone in her pocket.

'Ready to go?' I ask, picking up the keys to my own car.

She nods, dumbly.

I let her sit in the front.

All the way back to Annette's, she's on edge, repeatedly checking her phone and texting, and wiping away tears. When we turn into the driveway, I see the doorway is open, a rectangle of yellow in the inky night. No one is standing there waiting to greet us.

Martha climbs out and, without closing the car door, disappears into the house. I hear a brief muffled conversation, then Martha reappears with Annette. They are both carrying suitcases, and they put them into the boot of my car. Then Martha gets back in the front seat, and Annette comes round to my driver's window. 'Will you be so kind, Mags, as to run Martha down to Samovar? Tatiana has a spare room because she's kicked that low life Hugh Geraghty out of the place, and she's going to let Martha stay there for free for a while in return for the vegetables.'

My heart breaks for Martha, who is sitting in the passenger seat with her head bowed. But I keep my voice non-committal. 'Is Phillip coming?'

'He'll stay here with me – everything he has is here. And Martha will be back in the morning. We have a business to run. We're friends, Mags. Nothing has changed. It's just that we need a bit of a break from each other on the…personal front, I suppose you'd say.'

'Of course. You don't need to explain.' I put the car into gear, and Annette steps back from the window. As we drive off, she remains standing there, looking after us, but Martha doesn't see her because she still has her head down, the tears falling silently into her lap.

CHAPTER 25

$\mathcal{M}$am and Joe's wedding is a low-key affair, exactly as they want it to be. The ceremony is in a tiny church beside Lough Gara which is kind of synonymous with second weddings of older widows and widowers. Although there are fewer than thirty of us, we almost fill the place.

Dolores is back from Germany, and Jenny and Ahmed are over from Dubai. Sharon and Trevor are here as well, of course, since Sharon was virtually raised in our house, and Trevor's wedding band is providing the music at the reception. Peggy has got over her shock at Mam dumping Teo and now says she's pleased it's Joe, so she's there too. Then there's Kieran's parents, his brother, Gearóid, and sisters Orla and Aoife with their husbands Fergus and Leonard. It's the first time Nora has been within the same walls as Gearóid since he came out, and both of them keep shooting annoyed looks at each other when they think the other one isn't looking.

Joe's side of the family is represented by two decrepit maiden aunts from Dublin.

Ellie and Kate are flower girls scattering rose petals, and Jenny's boys, Mohammad, Achmed and Hassan, are pageboys in smart suits and ties. The boys seem very surprised by the inside of the church, staring at Christ nailed to his cross and the stained-glass windows showing the twelve stations. I suppose if you're used to mosques, where the decoration is all flowers and abstract patterns, Catholic iconography must come over as a bit bloodthirsty.

The service is short and sweet. Simple gold rings are exchanged, and the reception is at the local pub, an old stone building covered in ivy, where anyone who doesn't have a designated driver in their party has booked to stay overnight. There's a dance floor with a stage, and seeing my mam waltz to Trevor's wedding band with her new husband as we all cheer them on is honestly one of the happiest moments of my life, and for once I feel like dancing.

Kieran looks up as I approach him, and immediately he says, 'No!'

'Ah, come on.' I laugh. 'If Joe can learn at his age, how hard can it be?'

'Mags Munroe, I will do anything for you, you know that, but I'm not dancing, not now, not ever.'

I look around for another partner. Kate is having great fun with Sharon's Sean, but Jenny's boys are still being shy. Then Ellie comes over to us. She looks gorgeous, so grown up, in her navy dress. It's fitted to the waist and then flares out to just above her knee, '50s style. Gerry the hairdresser has given her a fabulous blow-dry, and her light make-up, just understated enough not to have her father lying in a darkened room from the stress of having a gorgeous daughter, really completes the look.

'Will you dance with me, Dad?' she asks. Clearly she's not heard his flat refusal of me, and I watch as my determined, stubborn man becomes putty in her hands.

'I'm terrible, I warn you. Will I go out to the van and get my steel-cap boots for you? Might be safer?'

She laughs and takes his hand, and all the teenage moments of the last year, when everything about us was 'mortifying', melt away. He's her daddy and she's his little girl again.

Trevor and his band are giving a very good account of themselves with 'Can't Take My Eyes Off You', and I see Sharon at the side of the stage gazing up at him, utterly besotted, holding a glass of champagne.

I won't be surprised if I'm pulling out the dreaded shapewear for her wedding soon too.

'Is he the marrying kind?' I ask, sidling up to her, holding my own glass.

'He might very well be.' She winks. 'I'd say he'll get the idea any day now.'

'Planted by you, of course.'

'Well, what man ever had a thought of his own? We come up with the ideas. The trick is to let them think they thought of it themselves, surely you know that.' She sips her champagne.

'Well, if anyone can snare him, it's you, no better woman.' I give her a one-armed hug. 'But I draw the line at peach taffeta.'

She guffaws. For some reason best known to myself, I went to our Debs dance in 1989 wearing peach taffeta, the same colour as my skin, and the result was photos of me looking naked. We were all permed to within an inch of our lives, and I even had that '80s mullet, tight at the sides and a perm up top, as bad as Trevor's before Sharon made him cut it off.

'Oh, if I get that hunk of destruction up the aisle, Mags Munroe, you'll be in taffeta head to toe, and me in ruffles and silk. Nothing surer than we'll have an '80s wedding.' She grins, and we clink our glasses of champagne.

It strikes me again, how much we are capable of doing for love. Joe with his dancing lessons. Sharon prepared to drop her obsession with current fashion for an '80s wedding.

'Talking of weddings,' says Sharon, 'did I dream it or did I see young Delia McGovern walking out of the Chinese last Saturday hand in hand with that guard of yours – what's his name, Darren?'

I chuckle. 'No, you didn't dream it. She and Darren are going out, and Jerome and Dora are all right with it. It's amazing really, but Darren was the one who gave Delia the photo of the five conspirators in the snug, so that and his guarding of the site got him in the good books. And sure, tradition or not, Delia has her father wrapped around her little finger. He'd take the moon out of the sky for her if she wanted it.'

'Like them all.' She smiles, nodding at my husband, who is dancing and joking around with Ellie while somehow not 'mortifying' her.

'Exactly,' I agree. 'And I'd say Delia and Darren will marry soon. Jerome might be stretching what's acceptable for a Traveller girl, but Darren won't be knocking round with her for years.'

'And Darren's own family, are they happy with the match?'

'I haven't a clue. Doubtful, I suppose, but more power to the young couple, I say. Things are changing, and we have to change with them.'

'Well, they'd be foolish people to reject her if she's their boy's choice. Family is very important to Travellers.'

'Era, once they get to know her, they'll realise she's great. She's tough. She'll be fine.'

Fair play to Trevor's band, they play the songs everyone knows, and the wedding party dances the night away. I eventually get my waltz with Joe. He's a great dancer now, I have to admit, and manages not to make it look like he is dragging a bag of spuds around the floor.

'Thanks for telling me to take lessons,' he whispers in my ear.

I grin. 'I didn't really. I just said it was a pity you hadn't before.'

'You showed me the way, and told me to fight for her.'

'And you fought the good fight and won, so congratulations to you, Joe Dillon.'

'I can't take all the credit. I had a helping hand from fate, I believe.'

I look at him, and he winks. 'She told me about the coin toss.'

I laugh. 'My mother is her own woman, Joe, so no matter what the fates said, she'd have done as she pleased. You *do* know we just kept tossing the coin until it came up with the right answer?'

He laughs with me, then grows serious again. 'And I have you to thank as well, and not just about the dance lessons. Your support for her decision was vital, I think. She loves all three of you girls, undoubtedly, but you're special, Mags. You're her best friend as well as her daughter, and your girls are the lights of her life. If I didn't pass muster with you, I'd have been given the high road, no doubt about it. So thank you.'

'Well, she deserves to be happy, you both do, and anyone can see you are mad about each other. So Kieran and I wish you all the love and luck in the world.'

'He's a good man.'

'I got lucky.'

'We both did,' he says.

The song comes to an end, and he hugs me and kisses my cheek. I don't remember my dad all that well – he was sick and in bed for most of my childhood and died when I was young – but I know because my Auntie Sheila told me that he adored Mam and felt that she got a very raw deal because of his illness. I feel him here now, just a fleeting thing, but I can feel him.

'My dad would be happy for you both too,' I say.

'Thank you for saying that. It means a lot. I feel that about my late wife.' He smiles, and there's a moment of deep sadness there. 'We were childhood sweethearts, and a part of me will always miss her, but she would want me to be with Marie and they are nothing alike.'

I have the next dance with Ahmed, who is pretty proficient himself due to having to go to parties with foreign clients in Dubai. I stand on his feet a couple of times – he's not as good at guiding me around as Joe was – but apart from that, it goes well. He's a bit astonished by the amount of alcohol being consumed, although he did have one glass of champagne himself out of politeness. I think as far as Ahmed is concerned, the Irish are awful heathens not long out of the caves.

When Trevor and his band complete their set, they set up a little disco with flashing lights and an '80s Spotify list, and soon my sisters, sisters-in-law and me are twirling around to 'I Will Survive' by Gloria Gaynor. It's great fun.

I'm so in love with everyone. I tell Dolores I forgive her for knowing all about what Martha was up to and never telling me. She looks a bit startled that I know she knew.

Talking of letting things go, I spot Nora and Gearóid at a table in the corner, deep in happy conversation and halfway through a bottle of champagne.

Weddings. You've got to love them.

CHAPTER 26

he day of Martha Turner's trial dawns grey and misty, and I
make my way to Galway to the district court to give
evidence. As I drive out of Ballycarrick, Delia calls and tells me that
Annette has asked for me to ring her. I do, on the hands-free set.

'Hi, Annette. All OK?'

'Thanks, Mags. I wasn't sure if I should ring your mobile since it's
kind of a personal favour?'

'Of course, any time,' I say, as I join the dual carriageway that leads
to Galway. I see the Carmodys have put up an enormous marble
monument to Blades on the side of the road where he died. No doubt
the council will have something to say about it, but I smile. What
harm is it doing?

'Have you left for the court yet?'

'I'm just on the way now. Can I help you with something?'

'Could you give me a lift? I want to go, to the trial I mean, and I
feel too stiff from the arthritis to drive.'

I'm a bit taken aback but pleased she wants to go. Martha has been
exiled to the Samovar for a good two months now. Phillip is still
living in Annette's cottage; he needs to be used to living there in case

his mother goes to jail. Kieran, from his elevated position on O'Grady's barn roofs, tells me that Martha is still working in the poly-tunnels during the day. The vegetable business is still going well, but the two women's relationship is clearly rocky.

'Of course. I'll swing up for you now. I'll be there in ten minutes.'

I make a U-turn and go back the way I came.

Annette is ready when I pull in outside her cottage, the weather is still mild so the last of the summer flowers and shrubs are growing all around. She's dressed today in purple wide-legged pants and a V-necked gold top with purple embroidery around the neckline. It's beautiful. Her silver hair is down and plaited, and in her ears, she is wearing beautiful silver and copper earrings. A gorgeous scent of rosewater fills the car as she settles in, wincing with arthritis pain.

'You look lovely,' I say.

'Thanks. I wanted to make a bit of an effort.'

We drive for a few minutes, then she says, 'You must be wondering why I'm going?'

'Well, the thought did cross my mind.' I smile over at her. 'But I'm glad.'

I join the dual carriageway again, passing Blades's monument once more.

'I've been very angry with Martha for all her lies. But I do know she was trying to help me. And she's right – if she'd told me the truth about her conviction in Canada, I would have sent her packing and we'd never have...well...'

'So now what?'

Annette shrugs. 'I don't know. I just know this – I don't want her standing in the court today all on her own, without a friendly face to rest her eyes on.'

I think carefully before speaking; I don't want to say the wrong thing. 'Annette, normally I'm very black and white. The law is the law, and that's all there is to it. If you break it, then you must pay the price. In this instance, I do think Martha made a bad mistake, for sure. But she strikes me as someone who never got a fair shake of the stick.

Terrible parents, a violent husband, a custodial sentence. I'm just not sure I blame her for wanting to hold onto what she had with you with both hands.'

Annette exhales but doesn't say anything.

* * *

THE COURT IS VERY busy as usual, and Martha's case is delayed by several bench warrants being fulfilled and the judge having to rule on barring orders and things of a more urgent nature.

It is almost 3 p.m. when Martha is brought before the court. She looks weary and depressed, but when she sees Annette, she straightens her shoulders and stands taller.

The case begins, and the prosecution talks about Martha's sentence for selling cocaine in Canada, and the illegal passports, and how she supplied drugs to the Travellers.

Martha's court-appointed solicitor calls me to the stand, and I speak of Martha's desire to help Annette with her pain, and how I believe she had no intention of 'supplying' whoever robbed her polytunnel.

The solicitor then calls another witness, and to my amazement, it's Lenny Carmody. He tells the court that he and his younger cousins are the ones who took Martha's plants. They never bought weed from Martha, and she wasn't supplying or anything; they just robbed her one night when the moon was full. I have no idea what background deal between the McGoverns and the Carmodys led to this, or what kind of pressure was put on Lenny to confess, and I'm not sure I want to know because he looks a bit shook.

The prosecuting barrister asks how in that case Lenny and his cousins knew the plants were there. If Martha didn't tell them, who did?

Well, apparently, Lenny and one of his cousins met an older woman in Ballycarrick park smoking a joint, and she was so high, she offered to share it with them. When Lenny wanted to know where she got the weed, she had a fit of giggles and said she borrowed it out of a polytunnel above on the hill but the owner didn't know, and not to tell.

'And who was this woman?' asks the barrister.

Lenny doesn't know, only that she wore a lot of beads and her hair was down to her waist in dreadlocks.

I mentally facepalm. Dolores. It's just as well for her she's back in the States, or I'd kill her.

Martha is next to take the stand, and she tells the district judge just what she told me about the cocaine and the passports, which she's now handed in, and the district judge nods and hides a yawn.

I glance at Annette, and she has tears running down her face.

The prosecution's summing up is lacklustre at best, the barrister clearly more interested in the juicy aggravated assault case next on the list, so he raises no significant objection to Martha's testimony. To everyone's indifference, she is given a suspended sentence and a thousand-euro fine, which she can pay down weekly. She is free to go.

I go to find Annette to see if she wants a lift home. I'm meeting Kieran for pizza in Luigi's, and I'm going to tell him that I've booked us a holiday in Greece in four weeks' time. Mam and Joe have agreed to mind the girls.

I find her in the lobby. Martha is by her side, looking vulnerable and exhausted again after the strain of the courtroom.

'Mags, are you off?' Annette asks.

'I am, Annette.' I smile. 'Congratulations, Martha.'

'Thanks, Sergeant. It was yours and Lenny's testimony that did it. I'm so grateful.'

I nod. 'I'm glad it worked out for you.' I turn to Annette. 'I'll be in the car. It's in the staff car park, just out the back door by the lifts.'

I walk away, leaving her to say goodbye to Martha, but she calls me back. 'Mags?'

I turn. 'Yes?'

'I think I'll go in Martha's car. We can stop off at the Samovar to pick up her things. Is that OK with you, Martha?'

Martha's face lights up with relief and love. 'It is, of course.'

'Well, then, will we go home?' Annette holds her hand out and the other woman takes it, and hand in hand they leave the courthouse.

EPILOGUE

*K*ieran and I get back from the best holiday ever to find things in Ballycarrick have moved on again. Delia gives me the low-down when I go into the station the next morning.

The Galway County Council have voted against selling the Drumlish site, and work is starting next week on a shower and toilet block with hot water and a laundry room too, so her family are delighted. The council are also going to make a proper lay-by for the bins at the side of the road, trim the surrounding trees and reinforce the fence between the site and the school so the chickens can't make a break for it again.

Phillip and Olivia have won the sustainability competition with what are being billed in this week's *Western People* as 'the happiest hens in Ireland', and urban blow-ins like Celine and Mairéad are already queuing up to buy Jerome's eggs, which has him – or rather, the hens – struggling to keep up with demand.

The last bit of news is that Lenny Carmody has been sent to a strict aunt and uncle in England, and his family are hoping he'll come back a changed man. Miracles do happen, I suppose.

Life in Ballycarrick trundles along. Mam and Joe are happy as Larry and the girls are fine.

Martha and Annette seem to have managed to overcome their problems and are a regular feature of life in the place now. I'm constantly astonished at how adaptable people are. If you'd have asked me how Ballycarrick would take to a lesbian couple in their twilight years I'd have said it would have caused nudging and winking at least, but nobody bats an eyelid. It's lovely.

The day flies by, Sharon calls to hear about the holiday, and tells me herself and Trevor are going to see Bon Jovi in Dublin next month. Who says the eighties are over?

On my way home from the station, I pop into Bertie's to get lamb chops for our tea and some of Annette and Martha's potatoes to make home-made chips. It's the last bag of potatoes.

'You're lucky, Mags.' Howya Phelan winks, while Bertie scuttles away into the back as usual. 'That's the end of Annette's spuds. All of the cabbage and broccoli is gone too, and I've only a few parsnips and turnips left.'

'She's flying, isn't she?' I say as I pay.

'Sure she's giving us twice what she used to, and no matter what she grows, we'll sell out. Those spuds are pure balls of flour. She's growing mushrooms now, and we can't keep them on the shelves. I don't know what she does to the plants, but they're delicious. You could never go back to the tasteless auld things from the supermarket after eating her stuff. That lady Martha was telling me they're growing sprouted greens now as well. Don't ask me what they are exactly, but there's a place in Galway, a juice bar, and they can't get enough of it from her.'

'Ah, that's great.' I smile as he gives me my change. Howya is an awful gossip. His real name is something nobody knows. Even his mother calls him Howya.

'And Annette's flying around the place again, after another bout with the auld arthritis. Although of course it's the devil's claw tea she's on now, like your own mother, after the other lady found out what's legal in Canada isn't legal here.' He winks theatrically, the story of the cannabis farm had been given arms and legs and Ballycarrick had talked of nothing else for weeks around the time of the trial.

'Really,' I say. Dolores is still sending Mam packets of devil's claw tea from the States, but I happen to know Mam just sticks it in the back of the cupboard these days because it's disgusting to drink and, despite what she says to Dolores about it being wonderful, it makes no difference. Mind you, what do I know? Maybe Annette has a different form of arthritis.

'The best thing is her tomatoes,' says Howya. 'Bertie sent me up there the other day when we ran out of them, and you wouldn't believe the number of plants she has. She says it's very fertile, the soil up there, she can't stop them. Not many of them had tomatoes on them, though. And the smell was fairly pungent now, but she says they're a late-fruiting variety.'

'Is that right?,' I say. I stand there in thought for a minute, then decide I haven't heard a word about any unusual plants and head home to spend a quiet, relaxing evening with my family and a glass of Rioja.

The End

*** * ***

I HOPE you enjoyed *Growing Wild in the Shade* as much as I enjoyed writing it. If you would like to explore another new series I'm working on right now, you might be interested in *The Kilteegan Bridge Story*. Here are the first 2 chapters to whet your appetite.

Chapter 1

KILTEEGAN BRIDGE, CO CORK, 1948

'Don't leave me, Paudie. Don't leave me. I'll die. I swear, I'll walk into the sea and I'll die.'

'Maria, why are you saying this?' Daddy's voice was strange – it was broken and sad. He was normally stronger sounding or something. 'Of course I'll never leave you.'

'I've seen the way Hannah Berger looks at you, Paudie. *Everyone* sees the way she looks at you, right there in the church in front of the whole parish, in front of her own husband. She wants you for herself. She's heart-set on having you.'

Lena kept very still in her special hiding place behind the carved and painted settle beside the fire. Her brother and sister were in bed, but she'd come down to fetch her doll. She was small for seven, and most days she liked it here behind this long wooden seat with the high back, which could fold down into a bed for visitors. You could hear things, and it was warm near the fire, and nobody gave you a job to do. But now she was listening to things she'd rather not hear, even if she didn't understand any of it. Mrs Berger couldn't have Daddy all to herself, even if she did find him useful around the estate. Daddy belonged to Mammy, and to her, and to Emily and Jack.

'This is all in your mind. I love you, Maria...'

'Then stop going to see her!'

'If we could afford for me to stop working up there, you know I would.'

A wild sob and a crash of crockery. Mammy had thrown something down from the dresser. Lena prayed it wasn't her favourite bowl, the one with the bluebells painted on it that Daddy had brought her from the fair in Bandon. He'd brought Emily a green velvet ribbon at the same time, to tie up her long blond hair. Emily was beautiful, tall like Mammy, and though she was only nine, people always thought she was much older. She could be bossy sometimes, but usually she was nice. Jack was small like Lena. He was only five. Daddy had brought him a small wooden donkey, just like Ned, their donkey that pulled the cart on the farm.

'Maria, Maria, stop now, love...' Daddy's voice was firmer. He was trying to calm Mammy, soothing her like he did with Mrs Berger's stallion up at Kilteegan House when it went wild in the spring. 'I can't stop going to the Bergers'. That's half our income, building stone walls, pruning the orchard, caring for the horses. Hannah Berger's not interested in me as a man. She just needs a strong pair of hands around the place. She's had nobody to do the heavy jobs since her father died.'

'Let her own husband do the work, now he's home from the war!'

'Ah, how can he do that, Maria, and him in a wheelchair?'

'There's that man of his, the Frenchman...'

'He's neither use nor ornament, that fella. All he does is wait on his master hand and foot, and he pays no attention whatsoever to anything that needs to be done around the grounds.'

'You're a fool. You can't see it – she's trying to seduce you, Paudie, with her red hair and her green eyes. I'm scared, Paudie, and if she gets you, then her husband will kill you. He's evil, Paudie. There's something terrifying about him.'

Lena felt a pain in her tummy when Mammy spoke like that, like she believed that evil spirits were in people. She was very superstitious. Sometimes it was fun when she told Lena and Emily and Jack about fairies and things like that, but mostly it was scary because it was a sign that things could be bad for days if Daddy didn't manage to coax her out of it. Lena wanted it not to be like that for Daddy, or for her and Jack and Emily, but when Mammy got into her imaginary world, she often stayed away a long time. It didn't happen often. She hadn't had a bad spell since last summer, when she'd screamed there was a demon on the stairs. Lena had wet her knickers, she got such a fright. Daddy had to tell Lena over and over that these things weren't true, that it was only in Mammy's mind, before she could get to sleep that night.

Daddy's voice was even firmer now, more like his normal self, like a big strong tree in a storm. 'Maria, my love, calm yourself. There's nothing to worry about, honestly. I go up there and do some work, and they pay me well. That's all. I love you.'

Mammy fell silent. She was still breathing harshly, but she let Daddy lead her over to the settle. Lena felt the wood creak as he sat beside her, and she heard the whisper of cloth on cloth as he put his arm around Mammy. He told her all about the wild flower meadow that would be growing between their farmhouse and the sea in the spring, in just a few weeks, and how they'd all take a picnic and go to the seaside. Lena knew that when he used that gentle, low and rumbling voice it usually calmed her down.

Lena often thought her tall, slim mother was like a selkie, one of those magical tricky mermaids who look like seals in the water but who come to live with human men until they can't stand to be on land any longer and go back to the ocean. There was a picture of a selkie in a book at school, and she had long white hair, same as Mammy's, and it looked a bit like ropes coming down. Mammy tied her hair up most of the time, but sometimes it was loose and reached all the way down her back. She had eyes the same colour as the selkie too, pale as the sea on a summer's day, and her eyelashes and eyebrows were so light that it looked like she didn't have any.

Emily and Jack both looked like Mammy, pale-skinned and fair-haired, but everyone said Lena looked just like her father – dark silky hair, brown eyes and skin that only had to see the sun for a day before it went copper.

In the quiet, the fire crackled in the range and the night wind threw drops of rain against the window. The radio that had been on all this time in the background began playing the popular new song by Al Jolson, 'When You Were Sweet Sixteen'.

Lena's father started singing it softly under his breath. 'I loved you as I've never loved before, since first I saw you on the village green. Come to me, ere my dream of love is o'er. I love you as I loved you, when you were sweet...when you were sweet sixteen...'

And slowly her mother's breathing softened and the pain in Lena's stomach went away. Daddy swept up the bits of broken crockery in silence.

'Dance with me, Maria,' murmured her father.

Mammy still didn't answer, but she let Daddy pull her to her feet. And when Lena peeped out from behind the settle, her parents were swaying together around the kitchen table, her father's big strong farmer's arms around her tall, slim mother, Maria's head on Paudie's shoulder and both of them with their eyes closed. The broken crockery was in a pile in the corner, and it wasn't her favourite bowl –

it was just that cracked yellow and green plate she'd never liked anyway.

Lena crept out of the kitchen, up the stairs of the two-story farmhouse and into the bedroom she shared with her sister. Emily was fast asleep, her long blond hair spread out across the pillow. Lena snuggled in beside her with her doll and lay on her back, gazing up at the sloped ceiling, the beams casting sharp black shadows in the moonlight. She was glad the storm had passed this time.

She hoped Mammy wouldn't spoil things between Daddy and the Bergers, because she liked going up to Kilteegan House with him. He let her bring up a basket of their farm eggs, and Mrs Berger always gave her an extra penny to keep for herself. Sometimes Daddy kept Lena busy, weeding the vegetable garden or picking up the branches he pruned from the trees in the orchard. But other times she played with Malachy, the little boy who was there when he wasn't away at boarding school. He had dark-red hair like his mother, and the same grass-green eyes. They would play hide-and-seek around the garden if it was fine, and if it rained, they'd hide in the tack house, where the saddles and bridles lived, and lay out a clean horse blanket on the stone flags and sit and play cards or draughts.

Chapter 2

KILTEEGAN BRIDGE, 1955

Lena sat in the front pew, staring at her black shoes. Her black calico dress was too tight across her chest, threatening to pop a button. Mammy had made it for her for Hannah Berger's funeral six months before, but she was fourteen then and still growing; now that she was fifteen, it was already too tight. The priest was murmuring in Latin, swinging incense around the coffin that lay before the altar. On her left, Jack looked so pale, she thought he might faint. Lena tried to take hold of his hand, but he pulled it away. He was the man of the house now, Mammy had told him, so he thought he wasn't allowed to cry or show emotion any more. On her other side, Emily sat stiffly next to Maria; they looked like sisters, they were so alike. Both of them were in tears. Lena wished she could cry as well, but everything felt so unreal, she couldn't believe any of it was really happening.

Only three days ago, Daddy had been on his way out the door to check on the lambs and saw that the crafty old fox had stolen another one. Daddy and the fox had what he called a 'mutually respectful relationship'. The fox had a job to do, but so did he.

Daddy had trapped lots of foxes in his life. He tried not to kill things if he didn't have to, but this fox must have been especially clever if Daddy decided he needed to shoot it.

She wished he'd just trapped it.

'We're not the owners of this land, Lena,' he would say. 'Nor are we the masters of the animals and plants that live here. We're just minding it. It was minded by my father and his father before him, and now it's for us to care for, and in due time, Jack will take over.'

Daddy loved his farm.

She would never hear his voice again. Never.

Now her father was in that wooden box, and the priest was telling everyone that Paudie O'Sullivan was happier now than he had ever been because he was at the right hand of the Lord. That was a load of rubbish. Daddy would never want to be anywhere except with his family.

It was Jack who had found him. Their father had been lying in his own blood in the top field with his shotgun, which he hadn't used for ages, beside him. Doc came from the village the minute he heard, but he hadn't been able to save his friend. It was a terrible accident, Doc told them. He must have fired at the fox, and his ancient shotgun had backfired, he was killed instantly. The doctor was nearly as broken by it as the rest of them. He had been Paudie O'Sullivan's best friend since they were children, and he was Lena's godfather, and he always came to see Maria when she was in one of her dangerously low moods.

The Mass was over now, and Doc, Jack and four other men from the village stepped forward to carry the coffin. Paudie O'Sullivan had been an only child, so there were no brothers to carry him, only his son and his best friend and his neighbours. Jack was barely tall enough for the task, but the undertaker put him in the middle and made sure the older men took most of the weight.

Lena's mother rose from the pew to follow the coffin, awkwardly, because she was very pregnant, her stomach huge under her loose black dress. Lena and Emily walked just behind her, holding hands. Emily squeezed Lena's fingers, and their eyes met briefly. Lena knew what her sister was thinking. Both of them had been dreading all morning that Maria would have one of her terrible breakdowns and scream the church down with fear, or else fall into one of her near-catatonic trances of melancholy. But so far, their mother had carried herself with great dignity. Maybe, like Lena, Maria didn't believe this was really happening.

The walk to the cemetery wasn't long, up a pale stony track fringed with wild monbretia under overhanging trees. The graveyard was on a hill overlooking the distant sea, and to Lena's surprise, the priest and coffin bearers headed towards the far corner, away from the O'Sullivan family plot where her father's parents and his two maiden aunts were buried. She touched her mother's arm. 'Is Daddy not going to be buried with Nana and Granda?' she whispered.

Maria said sharply, 'No. That grave is full.'

Lena fell instantly silent. There was an edge to her mother's voice that frightened her.

But then Maria softened and added, 'Anyway, girls, don't you think the plot I chose for him is much nicer?'

She was right. The plot over by the graveyard wall was lovely, shaded by a spreading chestnut tree and with a wide view of the distant bay. If it weren't for the stone weight of her grief, the beauty of the spot would have lifted Lena's heart.

After the graveside prayers and the sad, heavy rattle of earth and stones onto her father's coffin, Lena finally felt the tears come, and wanting to be alone in her grief, she walked a small distance away from the funeral crowd, muffling her sobs and wiping her nose with a scrap of hanky.

Blinded by grief, she nearly walked into Malachy Berger, who stood facing the Fitzgerald grave. She remembered him as the red-headed boy with bright-green eyes she used to play with as a little girl. She hadn't seen him in years except very briefly at his mother's funeral six months ago, and like her, he had grown since then – a couple of inches at least – and his hair was shorter.

The magnificent Fitzgerald family plot was right next to the more modest O'Sullivan family plot, where Lena's grandparents and grand-aunts were buried. Hannah's name and dates were the latest to be carved on the massive Fitzgerald headstone.

HANNAH BERGER née FITZGERALD

b.1919 – d.1955

Beloved wife and mother

Gone too soon

Only thirty-six when she died, five years younger than Lena's father.

Lena stopped. It felt rude to just walk on.

Malachy dug in his pocket and handed her a clean handkerchief. 'It's tough, losing a parent, isn't it?'

She nodded, wiping her tears with his handkerchief and handing it back.

'Keep it.' He said sincerely. 'I'm so sorry for your loss.'

Lena thought the words oddly stiff for people their age, but she'd never been in this position before. Maybe the whole wretched business had its own language, where young people spoke so formally.

'Thanks,' she managed.

'I remember him kicking a football around with me, back when I was only six or seven years old. My father had only just come back from the war, and he was in a wheelchair, and my mother was lovely but useless at football. Your dad was one of the people I missed most when I went to boarding school.'

Lena smiled through her tears. It was nice to hear this boy remembering her father so fondly. 'I remember your mam as well. She was always smiling and singing. She was full of life, and she always gave me an extra penny for the eggs to keep for my own pocket.'

He looked sad at the memory. 'That's exactly how she was, full of life. She liked you too. She missed you when you and your father stopped coming, but I suppose you were busy on the farm.'

Lena sighed and nodded. 'I missed her as well.'

Still, it had been easier not to go up to the Bergers' big house these past few years. Maria had taken against any of her family having anything to do with them, forbidding her to go, something to do with not liking or trusting Hannah or her husband. Maria took sets against people for slights or insults, a few real but mostly imagined.

For a while, her father had continued going by himself – they needed the extra money. But then Emily, Jack and Lena had all got old enough to help on the farm, and Daddy bought a few more cows, and soon the O'Sullivan homestead was bringing in enough income from milk, eggs and vegetables for Paudie to stop working odd jobs at the big house altogether.

There was a sharp jerk at her elbow, and Emily hissed in her ear, 'Mammy says come back to Daddy's grave.' And Lena stuffed Malachy's hanky in her sleeve and went with her sister without a backwards glance.

The crowd was beginning to thin. Doc had arranged for tea and sandwiches at the Kilteegan Arms, and everyone was moving towards the cemetery gate. Lena and Emily linked Maria on either side, relieved the funeral had passed without their mother making any kind of scene. As they approached the gate, people maintained a respectful distance. Clearly Mrs O'Sullivan was in no fit state to make conversation. Then, Lena saw him. Auguste Berger sat in a wheelchair right beside the gate, and he appeared to be waiting for them. As they walked past, he put his hand out.

He spoke in a French accent. 'My sincere condolences. I know how difficult it is to lose your spouse, the sense of loss, of abandonment.'

Maria stiffened and glared at him, and Lena mentally braced herself. This could be the catalyst for hysterics; that tendency of her mother's was never far below the surface. The risk was made greater because she could no longer take the tablets she used to stabilise her mood for fear of damage to the babies. 'My husband did not "abandon" me,' she said stiffly. 'It was an accident. An accident.'

'Of course.' Auguste Berger tutted sympathetically as he gazed at her hugely swollen belly. 'So sad Monsieur O'Sullivan didn't live to see this child. Or I believe it is *children*? You're expecting twins, *non*? Two new lives to replace the two lives that were lost…' His voice was barely audible.

'Yes, thank you,' Lena responded, not sure what else to say. There was something unsettling about him. Everyone knew Maria was expecting twins because she had to see the doctor in Cork for her pregnancy, whereas everyone else who was expecting just went to Doc.

'Come on, Mammy.' Emily took their trembling mother by the arm and led her gently to the car the undertakers had supplied that was waiting in the autumn sunshine.

Lena glanced over her shoulder at the man in the wheelchair, who raised his hand to her with a charming smile. Auguste Berger, Malachy's father, was now the owner of Kilteegan House. His wife, Hannah, had been found dead of a heart attack in the orchard last spring. The house was her family place, not his. She'd been the Fitzgeralds' only surviving child, one brother dying as an infant and another in a horse-riding accident years ago. So Berger, as her husband, got it all: the big old house, the extensive grounds and a fine farm.

Behind him, holding the handles of the wheelchair, was that strange stocky Frenchman with his oily slicked-back hair. He'd arrived with Berger the day he came back from the war and had not left his side since.

Lena helped her mother into the car, and she could feel the pair's eyes on her and her family as they left Paudie in his final resting place.

***

If you would like to continue reading you can buy the book here https://geni.us/TheTroublewSecretsAL

ABOUT THE AUTHOR

Jean Grainger is a USA Today bestselling Irish author. She writes historical and contemporary Irish fiction and her work has very flatteringly been compared to the late great Maeve Binchy.

She lives in a stone cottage in Cork with her husband Diarmuid and the youngest two of her four children. The older two come home for a break when adulting gets too exhausting. There are a variety of animals there too, all led by two cute but clueless micro-dogs called Scrappy and Scoobi.

f ⓘ

ALSO BY JEAN GRAINGER

To get a free novel and to join my readers club (100% free and always will be)

Go to www.jeangrainger.com

The Tour Series

The Tour

Safe at the Edge of the World

The Story of Grenville King

The Homecoming of Bubbles O'Leary

Finding Billie Romano

Kayla's Trick

The Carmel Sheehan Story

Letters of Freedom

The Future's Not Ours To See

What Will Be

The Robinswood Story

What Once Was True

Return To Robinswood

Trials and Tribulations

The Star and the Shamrock Series

The Star and the Shamrock

The Emerald Horizon

The Hard Way Home

The World Starts Anew

The Queenstown Series

Last Port of Call

The West's Awake

The Harp and the Rose

Roaring Liberty

Standalone Books

So Much Owed

Shadow of a Century

Under Heaven's Shining Stars

Catriona's War

Sisters of the Southern Cross

The Kilteegan Bridge Series

The Trouble with Secrets

What Divides Us

The Mags Munroe Story

The Existential Worries of Mags Munroe

Growing Wild in the Shade